DEADLY OBSESSION

Recent Titles by Betty Rowlands from Severn House

COPYCAT
DEATH AT DEARLY MANOR
DIRTY WORK
A HIVE OF BEES
AN INCONSIDERATE DEATH
TOUCH ME NOT

DEADLY OBSESSION

Betty Rowlands

This first world edition published in Great Britain 2004 by
SEVERN HOUSE PUBLISHERS LTD of
9–15 High Street, Sutton, Surrey SM1 1DF.
This first world edition published in the USA 2005 by
SEVERN HOUSE PUBLISHERS INC of
595 Madison Avenue, New York, N.Y. 10022.

British Library Cataloguing in Publication Data

Rowlands, Betty
    Deadly obsession
    1.   Reynolds, Sukey (Fictitious character) - Fiction
    2.   Women private investigators - Fiction
    3.   Detective and mystery stories
    I.   Title
    823.9'14 [F]

    ISBN 0-7278-6151-4

Typeset by Palimpsest Book Production Ltd,
Polmont, Stirlingshire, Scotland.
Printed and bound in Great Britain by
MPG Books Ltd., Bodmin, Cornwall.

One

'I wouldn't want to tackle that after a few drinks,' remarked the agent, indicating the wrought-iron staircase leading from the first-floor kitchen into the garden of the Victorian house in Rosemount Villas. 'Proper death trap, if you ask me.'

'As I never touch alcohol, I would not expect to find it a problem,' Arthur Soames replied frostily.

'Er, quite,' said the young man, only faintly abashed. 'No offence intended.' He went on to apologize for the state of the garden. 'The previous owner was an elderly woman,' he explained. 'Her garden was her pride and joy, so the neighbours tell me, but she became arthritic and couldn't cope with it any longer. Couldn't even get down those stairs, in fact. Then she had to go into a home and died shortly after. The heirs want a quick sale – that's reflected in the price, of course.'

Arthur did not reply. In fact, he was paying little attention to what the agent was saying. He was staring out of the kitchen window, utterly absorbed in contemplation of the neglected, overgrown plot. Already, in his mind's eye, the unkempt grass became as smooth and green and lush as Centre Court on the first day of Wimbledon. The old-fashioned roses threw off the tangle of nettles and bindweed. Apple and cherry trees, expertly pruned and sprayed and nourished, bore crops of ripening fruit. New borders sprang up, and a lily pond with a fountain. Arthur had few passions; his garden was one of them. Meeting the challenge that this one offered would go a long way to compensate for the move that circumstances had forced on him.

1

'Is there anything else you want to ask me?' said the agent, as his potential client remained silent. 'As you can see, the house itself has been well maintained . . . everything's in good order . . . carpets and curtains included in the price. Of course, they may not be exactly to your taste, but at least the place is ready to move into. And it's a nice neighbourhood, quiet, only local traffic. A bit different from London, you'll find.'

'Yes,' said Arthur, emerging with an effort from his reverie. He had already decided that the house would suit him very well and the garden had clinched it. 'Shall we go back to your office and discuss some details?'

Ten years later, the garden had been transformed. Every summer the borders were bright with yet more roses, hollyhocks and delphiniums, the promised fruit glowed rosy and luscious on the trees and water from the fountain played gentle music over the lily pads. All was lovingly and expertly tended – 'hardly a leaf out of place,' one of the judges in the annual garden competition remarked as, having beaten the previous year's winner, Arthur was for the first time awarded the trophy in the class for small gardens. 'A miniature Garden of Eden,' commented another. 'Congratulations, Mr Soames.'

One sunny July morning Arthur, as was his habit, was preparing to take his breakfast in the garden. He descended the wrought-iron steps leading down from the kitchen, brought out a small table and one chair from the shed and placed them on the lawn in the shade of the apple tree. Here, if he kept still, he could watch the birds drinking or bathing in the stone birdbath and taking seeds from the metal feeder that hung from the cherry tree a short distance away. As he went back indoors to fetch his breakfast tray, he reflected that soon he would have to buy a larger table and an extra chair – or possibly two or three. He and Elspeth would perhaps entertain friends from time to time, but he particularly looked forward to being alone with her, just the two of them, sitting together in the garden he had created with such love. Together they would enjoy the flowers, the birds and the lily pond.

2

A short time later, the garden was empty of birds. They had all taken fright at the high, thin scream of terror and the crash of broken crockery and glass that shattered the peace of the morning.

Two

'Mind how you go, Sukey,' warned the young uniformed constable who had shown her in. 'Those steps can be pretty tricky.'

Sukey Reynolds, Scenes of Crime Officer attached to the Gloucestershire Constabulary, went to the head of the decorative wrought-iron staircase leading from the kitchen into the garden and stared down at the man lying sprawled on his back on the concrete paving at the bottom. He was wearing a short-sleeved cotton shirt and shorts and his skinny arms and legs were splayed out in what appeared at first glance to be an attitude of complete relaxation. It crossed her mind that a casual observer might have thought at first that he was sunbathing, until the grotesque angle of his head on his scrawny neck told a different story. Around the body, in a mess of broken crockery and glass, was scattered the debris of an uneaten breakfast: an unpeeled banana, a pat of butter on a miraculously unbroken dish, a small pot of marmalade. A metal tray had fallen some distance away, having presumably been deflected before landing, possibly by striking the handrail.

'*He* obviously found them tricky,' she said in reply to the officer's warning. 'What do they want a SOCO for, I wonder, and what's the DI doing here?' she added, indicating Detective Inspector Jim Castle, who was standing a few feet away from the body, conferring with Dr Blake, the police surgeon. 'Sergeant Barnes didn't seem to know any details.'

The constable shrugged. 'I suppose they're treating it as suspicious, although it looks to me like the old boy missed his footing, went a purler and broke his neck. Dr Blake must

4

have his doubts, though; he wouldn't give us permission to move the body till CID had had a look at it.'

'Is that the dead man's wife in there?' Sukey cocked her head in the direction of the sound of weeping coming from the next room.

'Fiancée, I understand. She and a neighbour found him.'

'It doesn't look as if they were planning to have breakfast together. There's only one chair been put out.'

'I understand she doesn't live here. She called round about ten thirty to pick him up for a shopping trip. Got no answer to her knock, guessed he was in the garden and out of earshot and went next door to ask the neighbour to call to him over the fence. He looked across, saw him lying there and climbed over. They sent for an ambulance; the paramedics realized he was dead and called us.'

'It must have been a nasty shock for the poor woman,' Sukey remarked. 'Who's with her?'

'DS Chen.'

'I see. Well, I'd better go and get my orders,' she added as, with a farewell gesture to DI Castle, Dr Blake picked up his bag and began climbing the staircase.

The officer nodded. 'It looks as if they've finished their chat. I'll go back to front-door duty.'

'Morning, Sukey,' said Blake. 'I take it you're bursting to view the exhibit?' he added breezily as he walked past her through the kitchen and opened the door leading into the hall. 'Feel free – he's all yours now.'

'Thank you, Doctor, I thought you'd never ask,' she replied. The touch of grim humour came as a welcome, if momentary, relief from the tragedy of the situation, but the sound of weeping had subsided and she hoped that the stricken woman had not overheard and been distressed by the exchange. She shifted her bag into her left hand and grasped the handrail with her right while cautiously descending the steps.

Castle looked up from his contemplation of the body and nodded. 'Morning, Sukey. Not the best start for his day, was it?'

'Morning, Guv. You could say that again.' Although they were for the moment alone at the scene, they both instinctively kept to their self-imposed rule of not betraying by word or glance while on duty that they were lovers. Sukey glanced round for a suitable place to put down her bag before opening it to take out her camera. 'Where do you want me to start?'

'The usual shots of the body from all angles first. Then I suggest a general shot of the garden, followed by close-ups of the various bits of debris so that we have an exact record of where they were found. And some shots of the staircase as well – look out for anything that might have caused him to miss his footing.'

'He was having a pretty Spartan breakfast by the looks of it,' she commented. 'Just a glass of juice and a banana, and presumably he was planning to make some toast as there's butter and marmalade.'

'There are some bits of toast over there. As you can see, there's no hope of knowing exactly where they originally landed.' The DI pointed to a spot the other side of the lawn where a couple of blackbirds, more concerned with rivalry than the presence of humans, were squabbling over something on one of the flowerbeds.

'Can I have a word, Guv?' DS Chen had descended the stairs silently in her rubber-soled shoes and was standing just behind them.

'What is it, Dalia?'

'I think Ms Maddox, the gentleman's fiancée, is feeling calm enough to answer a few questions. She's still very distressed, but I've put the kettle on for a cup of tea and she says she'd rather get it over with now than come to the station later.'

'Right, I'll be with you in a moment.' Castle turned back to Sukey. 'OK, I'll leave you to get on with it, but I'd like another word before we arrange to have the body removed.'

In a small sitting room next to the kitchen, a woman was sitting in an armchair with her back to the window. Her shoulders were slumped, her head bowed and her hands lay loosely on her lap, palms upward. Castle was accustomed to reading body language and the position of the hands struck him as particularly significant. In his experience, the freshly bereaved were more likely to use them to cover their eyes, move them restlessly to indicate shock and disbelief, or clench them in anger and resentment at their loss. In Elspeth Maddox's attitude he read a kind of helpless acceptance.

'Ms Maddox?' he said gently. She raised her head and nodded. She appeared younger than he expected and although her features were blotchy and her eyes red with weeping, he realized immediately that she was an exceptionally attractive woman. She was simply but stylishly dressed and her short mid-brown hair was expertly cut.

'I understand you are Mr Soames' fiancée?' he continued.

'Was,' she said. 'Always felt it was too good to last.' There was a note of resignation in her voice that matched the position of the hands.

'I'm Detective Inspector Castle,' he went on. 'Please accept my sincere condolences in your sad loss.' She acknowledged the conventional expression of sympathy with another nod and a twitch of the lips that was not quite a smile. 'I apologize for having to cause you further distress, but we need to clear up one or two points. My sergeant is making you some tea; would you like me to wait till she brings it before answering any questions?'

'No, please carry on. I'd like to get this over.' Without waiting for him to speak, she added, 'I told him he should see his doctor, but he said there was no need.'

'He was ill?'

'He had a dizzy spell the other day and I wanted him to go for a check-up, but he said it was nothing, just that he hadn't had much to eat and was feeling empty.'

'Do you think he might have had another dizzy spell that made him lose his balance and fall down the steps?'

'It's pretty obvious, isn't it?'

'We have to consider all possibilities.' There was a pause;

for a moment he thought she was going to speak, but when she remained silent he said, 'You said just now that you thought it was "too good to last". What did you mean by that?'

'Only that when two people are as happy as we were, even when everything seemed against us . . .' Her voice disintegrated on the final words and a gush of fresh tears rolled down her cheeks. She reached out and took a handful of paper tissues from a box that someone – probably Dalia Chen – had left on a small table beside her. At that moment there was a gentle knock at the door and in response to Castle's summons the young sergeant entered with a mug of tea, which she placed on the table before sitting down beside Castle. After a moment, Elspeth dried her eyes and picked up the tea. Castle waited without speaking while she drank it, which she did slowly but steadily. When she had finished, she put the empty mug back on the table with a murmured word of thanks to Dalia. It crossed his mind that a lot of people tended to cling on to theirs, as if deriving comfort from the residual warmth.

'Well, Ms Maddox,' he said, 'you've been very helpful. I've only got one or two more questions at the moment. First, do you happen to know the name of Mr Soames' GP?'

'He goes to the same doctor as me. Dr Gardner.'

'Thank you. There may have to be a post-mortem, but I'll make sure you're kept informed. And I'll need details of his next of kin, if you know who they are.'

'Oh, I know all right.' A new note crept into Elspeth's voice that up to now had been quiet and resigned. A hard, almost sarcastic note. 'He's got a daughter somewhere. Her name's Sabrina. She doesn't bother with him, but I suppose she'll have to be told.'

'Do you have her address?'

She shrugged. 'It's probably in the book by the telephone. I think she lives near Cheltenham – if she hasn't moved without telling him, that is. It wouldn't surprise me.'

'Is she married or is her name still Soames?'

'How would I know? I don't think Arthur knew either.'

'I see. Well, I won't keep you any longer, Ms Maddox. Do

you live near here? Would you like one of my officers to drive you home?'

'No thank you, it's only a few streets away. I walked here and I'll walk back. Don't worry, I'll be quite all right on my own,' she added, as if anticipating his next question. She stood up and retrieved her handbag from where she had dropped it by her feet. 'I'll just go and freshen up before I leave, if there's no objection. It's OK, I know my way around this house; it was going to be my home, remember?'

He stood aside and held the door open as, with her head erect and her back straight, she walked out of the room and up a carpeted staircase to the next floor while he and Dalia returned to the kitchen.

'Right,' he said. 'Let's check those phone numbers.'

'There's a Dr Gardner in here,' she said after a brief search in the leather-bound address book, 'and just two entries under "S" – supermarket and Sabrina.'

'It seems the old boy might have had some medical condition that caused him to lose his balance. Before you came in she mentioned a recent dizzy spell, but he'd refused to see his doctor.'

'That could explain why he appeared to have fallen backwards.'

'Exactly. He could have been starting on his way down the stairs with the tray, felt dizzy, turned round to come back indoors until he felt better . . .'

'But didn't quite make it,' she finished as he broke off.

'It seems a fairly obvious explanation, but we'll have to do the usual checks with the GP. Will you have a word with him? Ask him particularly if Soames had a history of any condition that might have caused the dizziness.'

'Right, sir.'

'And then go and break the news to the daughter. There's not much love lost there, by the look of things.'

'Sabrina's an unusual name – I've never heard of it.'

'That's because you're not a native of these parts. Sabrina is the ancient goddess of the River Severn. According to legend,

9

she was the illegitimate daughter of an ancient Welsh king. When the Queen found out about the baby she had it drowned in the river.'

Dalia pulled a face. 'They were cruel times, weren't they? They have legends like that where my family came from. My mother often told them to me when I was a child; many are connected with water. I wonder why her parents chose it?'

'It's quite an attractive name; I don't suppose there's any particular significance to it. I understand from the neighbour that Soames originally came from London.'

'There's no address for Sabrina here, only a mobile number. Shall I ring that and ask her where she lives?'

'That's probably the quickest way to find out, but be diplomatic. I have a hunch there might have been some rancour over the engagement. Right, that's all for the moment. I'll just go and have another word with our SOCO.' He went down the steps into the garden, where he found Sukey repacking her bag.

'I've taken all the shots you asked for, Guv,' she said. 'The birds have eaten quite a lot from the bits of toast they carried off, so they've obviously been lying around for a while.'

'You're suggesting they might help establish the time of death?'

She shrugged. 'Probably not, but I thought it worth mentioning. I couldn't find anything wrong with the steps, but there are traces of hair on the second from the bottom. The steps have rounded edges, so there wouldn't necessarily be a cut – you can't see the back of his head because of the way he's lying – but there's likely to be bruising. I've taken samples of the hair to compare with the victim's; they look like a match, but I'll send them to the lab for confirmation.'

'Do that. On the face of it, he just went crashing down backwards, bashed his head on the edge of the iron step and somersaulted over, breaking his neck in the process. He might have had a dizzy spell; according to the fiancée, he's had at least one recently.'

'So why call in CID?'

'Dr Blake wouldn't have known about that; he was just being super-cautious as usual. As I see it, it's a simple case of accidental death, and I'm pretty sure the coroner will agree.'

Three

'Is that Ms Sabrina Soames, the daughter of Mr Arthur Soames?'

'Yes.' The voice sounded wary. 'Who wants to know?'

'This is Detective Sergeant Chen of Gloucestershire Police.'

'Police? What's the old bugger been up to?'

It was hardly the response Dalia expected, but she kept her tone even as she replied. 'Something rather serious has happened. It concerns your father. May I come and see you, please?'

'Why can't you tell me over the phone?'

'I should prefer to come and see you, if it's convenient.'

'It's not convenient. I'm just going out.' Before Dalia had time to decide how to respond, Sabrina continued impatiently, 'Oh, for goodness' sake, tell me now and get it over with.'

'Very well, if you insist. I'm sorry to have to tell you there's been an accident.'

'What sort of accident?' Irritation changed to concern.

'Ms Soames, we prefer to break this kind of news in person but . . . I'm afraid your father is dead. His body was found in his garden. He appeared to have fallen down a steep iron staircase.'

'Who found him?' The tone became sharp, with an edge of suspicion.

'A Ms Elspeth Maddox. I understand she is your father's fiancée.'

'That bitch!' The tone became positively venomous. 'I wouldn't be surprised if she pushed him.'

'Ms Soames, I assure you we have found no evidence to

indicate that your father's death was anything but a tragic accident.'

'Then I suggest you try looking for some.'

'Do I understand you have reason to suspect foul play?'

'Since she got her claws into him, nothing would surprise me.'

'I'll make a note of your comments and pass them to my superior officer,' said Dalia. 'In the meantime, my information is that you are his next of kin. Is that correct?'

'I suppose so. Does that mean you want me to come and identify the body?'

'We're hoping you'll be prepared to do so.'

'If I say no, I suppose you'll ask the Maddox woman.'

'We always ask the next of kin first, but we realize that it can be a very distressing task. If you are unwilling to undertake it, perhaps you can give us the name of another relative? Otherwise—'

'No!' Sabrina cut in. 'I'm the only one. I'll do it. Tell me where to go.'

After directions were given and a time agreed, Dalia put down the phone and went to DI Castle's office to report the conversation.

'Well, it's obvious there's no love lost either way,' he said. 'You've spoken to both women, Dalia – what do you make of it?' He sat back with his hands spread, palms downwards, on his desk and gave her an encouraging smile. She thought how attractive he was, with his greenish eyes, aquiline features and long, slender fingers. She had been in the department only a short time, but had already heard hints that he and Sukey Reynolds were an item and wondered if there was any truth in them. She conjured up a mental picture of the Scenes of Crime Officer; she must be well into her thirties to have a teenaged son, but with her short, dark curly hair and pert elfin features she could pass for several years younger. So far, Dalia had noticed nothing significant in her dealings with DI Castle, but you never could tell.

'Sabrina certainly didn't volunteer any specific reason for

her suspicion,' she said cautiously. 'My guess is that it's a case of jealousy on her part and resentment on Elspeth's towards someone she sees as a neglectful daughter.'

'If what the fiancée implied is correct, father and daughter certainly weren't particularly close,' he agreed. 'Sabrina's initial reaction seemed to confirm that, so why should she be jealous?'

'Money?' suggested Dalia. 'Maybe she can see her inheritance slipping away.'

'That's more than likely.' Castle gave a wry grin. 'In which case, she'd be the one with a motive for murder, with the fiancée the obvious victim.'

'Wouldn't killing her have been almost too obvious, sir?' Dalia ventured.

Castle raised his eyebrows. 'What are you suggesting?'

'Once he remarried, it's plain the wife would automatically inherit. But if he were to die before the wedding, leaving a will and possibly life assurance in the daughter's favour—'

'The daughter would inherit it all,' Castle continued. 'That would seem a classic motive for her to have killed her father – but in that case, why try to plant the notion the death was suspicious?'

'It does seem illogical,' she agreed.

'It was probably nothing more than an emotional outburst on Sabrina's part,' he said. He picked up a pen and jotted a few words on a pad. 'I'll mention it in my report, but as there's nothing at the scene to suggest foul play, I doubt if DCI Lord will consider it worth bringing to the Super's attention at this stage.'

'Yes, that's my father.'

Sabrina Soames stepped back from the trolley on which Arthur Soames' body was lying and turned away. At a sign from DS Chen, the mortuary attendant pulled the sheet over the face.

'What was the exact cause of death?' asked Sabrina. Her

voice shook a little and she wiped her mouth with a hand-kerchief.

'Let's go next door and have a chat.' Dalia put a hand on her arm and led her to a small anteroom. 'Sit down,' she said gently, pointing to a chair. 'Would you like a cup of tea?'

'No thanks, just tell me—'

'Detective Inspector Castle has the result of the post-mortem and he'll be able to answer your questions. He'd like a word with you anyway; when you're feeling up to it I'll take you to see him.'

'Thanks. Just give me a couple of minutes.'

'Of course. Would you like me to wait outside?'

'No, please, stay here. I . . . don't want to be alone, not just yet.'

'All right. Take as long as you like.'

Dalia sat down beside her and waited. Sabrina sat twisting the handkerchief between ringless fingers, gnawing restlessly at her lower lip and staring blankly at the opposite wall. She had large, china-blue eyes set in a round, freckled face beneath a mop of short, fair curls, which gave her an air of almost childlike innocence that Dalia found hard to reconcile with her vitriolic outburst on the telephone. She remained silent for several minutes without shifting her gaze. Then, without warning, she burst into tears.

'He never loved me because my mother died when I was born,' she said, the words at first barely distinguishable. 'He said I killed her . . . he never forgave me. D'you know why I was called Sabrina? He told my Aunt Pru – his sister, she moved in with him and brought me up – to drown me as if I was a . . . an unwanted kitten. He left it to her to give me a name and she chose Sabrina. She was a great believer in myths and legends, and because of what my father had said she had this notion that calling me after a river goddess would somehow protect me from death by water.'

'But that was an appalling thing for your father to say!' Dalia exclaimed.

'It was just his first reaction after losing my mother.' From sounding bitter and angry, Sabrina's tone became almost defensive.

'Is your aunt still alive?'

Sabrina shook her head. 'She died when I was fifteen. I think I was hoping Dad and I would become closer, maybe comfort each other a bit, but he simply packed me off to boarding school. He was always cold and distant . . . and I did so want him to love me . . .' Her voice had been growing steadily weaker as she told her sad history; now it failed altogether, washed away by a tide of grief.

Dalia put an arm round her shaking shoulders and stroked her head, murmuring, 'It's all right, it's all right,' in a soft voice as if she were soothing a child.

'I did try,' Sabrina went on when she was able to speak again. 'Truly I did . . . just lately we seemed to be getting a bit closer . . . and then he met *her* and . . .' The faltering voice changed to steel and the reddened eyes became hard as flint beneath the film of tears. '*She* should have been the one to fall and break her neck, not him. For two pins I'd have shoved her down those stairs myself, given half a chance.'

'Shh. Don't say things like that.'

'It's the way I feel. She didn't love him, she was just after his money.'

Unwilling to be drawn into a discussion of Elspeth Maddox's possible motive for marriage to an older man, Dalia remained silent for a few moments. Then she said quietly, 'I expect you'd like to freshen up before we go back to the station to see the DI?'

'I suppose I'd better.' The tone was steady again, but resigned and submissive, as if all emotion had died.

While her charge was in the toilet, Dalia called CID on her mobile and asked for DI Castle. 'I think you should know there's a very sad family history behind Sabrina's wild accusations, Guv,' she said in a low voice. 'She's in a highly emotional state.'

'Thanks for the warning,' he said. 'When you get back to

the station, make an excuse to leave her for a minute or two and come and fill me in before I see her.'

'Oh Sook, it's been one hell of a day!' Jim Castle stepped inside the hall of Sukey's semi-detached home in Brockworth, hung his jacket on the newel post at the foot of the stairs and pulled her into his arms. They stayed locked together for several seconds while a warm tide of desire flowed through her body in response to the pressure of his. With his lips still against hers he murmured, 'I've got the whole weekend free! How about you?'

'I'm not sure. I don't know yet what plans Gus has. He's out in the garden; go through and we'll have a drink before dinner.'

As Jim stepped out on to the patio, Sukey's son, Fergus, looked up from his task of trimming the edges of the patch of newly mown lawn in Sukey's little back garden and called a greeting. He was naked to the waist, the lean young torso lightly tanned, smooth skin glistening under the late afternoon sun, fair hair straggling untidily round his shoulders. He had still been at his comprehensive school when they'd first met; now he was a young man on the threshold of a university career.

'You're making a good job of that,' Jim remarked. 'I hope she pays you the going rate!'

'We've come to a sort of arrangement.' Fergus snipped the last corner and stowed the shears, together with the mower, in the little shed that Jim had erected the previous summer by the back door. 'I keep my room tidy and put my dirty washing in the machine instead of leaving it lying on the floor, and she pays me the minimum wage for keeping the lawn in trim.'

'Sounds fair enough.'

'It's blackmail, if you ask me.'

Jim chuckled. 'It's good training for when you're at uni. Does she still nag you to get your hair cut?'

'Not since yesterday.'

'Anyway, I'm sure she appreciates your help, even if she

does drive a hard bargain. She's going to miss you when you go.'

'I guess that's when I hand over to you,' said Fergus with a grin. 'You'll have to fix your own terms, of course,' he added. His tone was flippant and casual, giving no sign that any veiled reference to the relationship with his mother was intended, yet for a moment Jim felt a twinge of embarrassment. Then he reminded himself that the lad had guessed at an early stage how things were between them and accepted the situation as perfectly natural. Today's youngsters seemed to know it all before they were even potty-trained.

His thoughts were diverted by Sukey's appearance with a tray of drinks. She set them on the patio table, drew up the chairs and sat down. 'Terms for doing what?' she asked as the others joined her and reached for their glasses.

'For taking over my gardening duties when I'm away,' said Fergus. He poured beer from a can with a practised hand. 'If I were you, Jim, I'd refuse to do anything until she replaces that clapped-out old mower.'

'There's nothing wrong with that mower that a drop of oil won't cure,' said Sukey.

'There was nothing in my contract about maintenance of the equipment,' her son retorted.

'Remind me to include it when it comes up for renewal.'

The conversation continued in the same light-hearted, inconsequential mood until Sukey announced that the food was ready and they went back indoors. As they settled down to eat she remarked, 'Jim, I got the impression when you arrived that the rest of today's been a bit trying.'

He paused with a piece of fish halfway to his mouth. 'You can say that again. I've had to deal with two emotional females who would cheerfully slaughter one another given half a chance.'

'Meaning who?'

'The late Arthur Soames' daughter and fiancée.'

'I didn't know he had a daughter.'

'It came out while I was talking to the fiancée. It's pretty evident there's no love lost between them either, as Dalia Chen quickly found out. That girl's a real asset to the department,' he added with an appreciative nod.

'Oh? In what way?'

As soon as the words were uttered, Sukey was conscious that her voice had a sharper edge than usual. She was aware, too, from the slightly startled look that flickered over Jim's features, that he had noticed it as well, but all he said was, 'I was impressed by the way she handled the situation. She elicited a lot of surprising information about the family history.' He repeated Dalia's account of her interview with Sabrina, ending with the comment, 'I suppose it's her sympathetic manner that encourages people to talk.'

'I'm sure you're right.' Sukey stood up and went to the oven. 'More chips, anyone?'

'Jim, do you suppose there's anything in what this Sabrina woman said?' asked Fergus. 'About Elspeth having pushed the old boy down the stairs, I mean.'

Jim chuckled. 'You'd just love it to turn into a juicy murder for your mother to solve, wouldn't you?' he said. 'We all know you're a detective *manqué*, love,' he added, turning to Sukey. He grabbed her hand as she walked past him with the plate of chips and gave it a squeeze. She returned the pressure and gave him a smile, but at the same time felt a pang of irritation. It was true that she had often expressed a desire to rejoin the police and eventually the CID; moreover she had several times incurred his displeasure by becoming actively involved in his cases.

'I *have* been known to point you in the right direction,' she said, 'but I suppose, now that—' She broke off, aware that she had been about to say something caustic, such as, 'now that you've got the lovely Dalia to help you out you won't be needing me,' but checked herself in time.

'Now that what?' he asked.

'Now that you've more or less decided Soames' death was an accident, there won't be anything for me to do,' she improvised hastily.

19

'That's up to the coroner,' he said, 'but as I told you earlier, I honestly can't see him coming to any other conclusion.' To her relief, the subject was dropped.

When they had finished their meal, Fergus went out to meet some friends, saying that he might be back late and his mother was not to wait up for him. It was not long before Sukey found herself forgetting the stab of jealousy that Jim's reference to DS Chen's valuable contribution to the department had aroused.

Four

'Oh Sook, what the hell am I going to do about Sabrina Soames?' Jim Castle sank on to the couch in Sukey's sitting room and clapped his hands to his temples in mock despair. 'The bloody woman's obsessed with the notion that Elspeth Maddox murdered her father. She's been at the station every day since the inquest, demanding to see me and insisting that we reopen the case.'

'On what grounds?' asked Sukey.

'On the grounds that we didn't take her allegations seriously and didn't look for evidence of foul play. You know her father made a new will shortly before he died, leaving half his fortune to Elspeth and half to her, don't you?'

'Yes, you told me. What about it?'

'Sabrina sees that as sufficient motive for Elspeth to murder him because then she'd inherit without actually having to marry him. There was a thirty-year age gap, remember.'

'I thought you said Soames had given instructions that neither woman was to know about the change until after he and Elspeth were married.'

'That's right, he did. He'd told his solicitor that he'd do it "in his own good time", and the solicitor was emphatic that there had been no breach of confidence. Sabrina claims that Elspeth must have had a contact in the solicitor's office and found out about it that way.'

'Has she any proof of that?'

'If she has, she hasn't revealed it to us.'

'But it is theoretically possible.'

'I suppose so, but the solicitor insisted it couldn't have happened.'

'Has anyone thought to enquire among the staff at his office?'

'Oh, for God's sake, don't you start!' Jim exclaimed in a sudden burst of exasperation. 'The case is closed, finished, *kaput*! End of story. Let poor old Arthur rest in peace.'

'All right, calm down, I get the message,' she said, putting a hand on his arm. 'Anyway, it's Friday, so you're safe for the weekend. What would you like to drink?'

'A beer would be heaven.'

'Coming up. I think I'll have a G and T.'

'Do you want me to get them?'

'No, you stay there and put on some soothing music. I have to check on the food anyway.'

When they were settled with their drinks and a dish of nibbles, with a CD of 'Music To Unwind To' playing softly in the background, Sukey remarked, 'Family disputes often break out when there's a lot of money involved, don't they? The old boy was pretty well-heeled by the sound of it.'

'It's par for the course,' he agreed, helping himself to crisps. 'I've no idea how much he was worth, but Sabrina claims it goes into seven figures.'

'Wow! That's serious money!' Sukey exclaimed.

'A big chunk will go in inheritance tax, of course, but there'll still be a tidy sum left for each of the women. You'd think she'd be satisfied with that, wouldn't you? It isn't as if she and her father were very close.'

'I wonder why he made that stipulation about not revealing what he'd done?'

Jim shrugged. 'Who can tell what goes on in people's minds?'

'Do you suppose that deep down he was afraid Elspeth might have second thoughts about marrying him if she knew she was only going to get half his fortune?'

'That's something we'll never know.'

'When did Sabrina first make her allegation?'

'She said something to that effect when Dalia phoned to tell her about her father's death, and she repeated it to me when she came to identify the body. I did my best to reassure her that we had examined the scene with a fine-tooth comb without finding any suspicious circumstances, but it was obvious she wasn't satisfied.'

'Did she say anything about a new will?'

'Not a word, so presumably she didn't know about it then. It was only later that she came out with this preposterous claim that Elspeth knew about it and killed him before the wedding so no one would suspect she'd done it for his money. I tell you, the bloody woman's obsessed.' Jim drained his glass and held it out to Sukey. 'Any chance of a refill?'

'Sure.' She fetched another can from the kitchen and sat down again. 'Dinner in five minutes.'

'Great.' He poured the second beer, frowning in concentration as he carefully tilted the glass to avoid foaming. Then, as if there had been no break in the conversation, he said, 'The medical evidence supported the verdict of accidental death; his GP testified the man had hypertension, which could have caused the odd fit of dizziness. We found a prescription in the kitchen that he'd never had made up, so obviously he didn't take the medication he'd been prescribed. What else does she expect us to do?'

'Now who's getting obsessed?'

He gave a rueful grin. 'Sorry, love. I promise not to say another word about Sabrina for the whole weekend. What sort of a week have you had, by the way? I've hardly seen you since the inquest.'

'Pretty routine; the usual crop of break-ins, stuff stolen from cars and a couple of RTAs – but no fatalities, thank goodness.'

'What's Gus doing this weekend?'

'What's that got to do with you?'

He took her empty glass from her hand, put it down beside his, slid an arm round her shoulders and drew her close, his other hand cupping her breast. 'I think you know the answer to that one,' he whispered.

When at last he allowed her to speak, she said, 'He's staying at Anita's tonight and tomorrow.'

'Brilliant!'

His embrace became increasingly ardent, but after a few moments she pushed him away. 'We have to eat dinner now or it will spoil,' she said.

'The hell with dinner.'

'Not after I've spent the best part of an hour preparing it,' she said firmly. 'You've got two days and nights to have your evil way with me.'

'And I intend to make the most of them.'

'I'm delighted to hear it.'

While she was serving the food, he said, 'So when did Anita get back from France?'

'At the beginning of the week. Cath and Adrian are taking her and Gus to Le Vieux Manoir for dinner tomorrow evening, by way of a welcome home celebration.'

'That'll set Adrian back a bob or two. The Masterses must be rolling.'

'I'm sure they are, but there's no snobbery about them at all. They want their daughter to do well at university and have a good career and all that, but most of all they want her to be happy. And they really like Gus; they invited him over for meals quite a few times while Anita was doing her *au pair* thing in France. Oh, I forgot to tell you, I sort of promised to go and watch them play tennis tomorrow afternoon, and they're coming here for Sunday lunch.'

'I take it I'll be welcome at the tennis as well?'

'Of course. More chips?'

Some hours later, Jim remarked sleepily, 'Those kids have been an item for quite a while now, haven't they?'

'Since they were at their comprehensive school – over three years. Gosh,' Sukey went on reflectively, 'it was quite a shock when I found out my little boy was having an affair.'

'He knows about us, of course.'

'I'm sure he does, but he's never said so outright. A very tactful lad is my son, and surprisingly perceptive for his age.'

'You have every reason to be proud of him.' He propped himself up on one elbow and kissed her gently on the mouth. 'Good night, love,' he whispered. 'Sleep well.'

'Morning Josie,' said Sukey to the receptionist as she signed in for her shift on Monday. 'Is that the woman who's been pestering the life out of DI Castle about the death of Arthur Soames?' she added in a low voice, with a slight backward movement of her head towards the woman sitting on a chair opposite the desk.

Josie nodded and leaned across the counter. 'His daughter,' she whispered back. 'She's here every day from nine to five; the only time she leaves that chair is to buy coffee from the machine or go to the loo. She even brings sandwiches. Every day I tell her the DI won't see her, but she won't take no for an answer.'

'Has anyone else had a word with her?'

'DS Chen spent a few minutes with her on Friday, trying to persuade her that she should give up and accept the situation. She did leave early that day and we thought maybe Dalia had got through to her, but this morning she was back again, saying if she didn't get some satisfaction she'd make a formal complaint or go to the press, or both.'

'Do you think she means it?'

'I shouldn't be surprised.' Josie turned away to greet a man who had just approached the desk and Sukey was about to key in the security code on the door leading to the main part of the building when, on impulse, she turned back and sat down in the seat beside the patiently waiting woman.

'Excuse me, are you Ms Sabrina Soames?' she said. The woman, whose gaze appeared to have been fixed on some point in the distance, started as if she had been unaware of being approached, and then gave a slight nod. 'You won't know me,' Sukey went on, 'but I'm a . . .' She was on the point of saying, 'Scenes of Crime Officer', but, fearing mention

of the word 'crime' might give a false impression, changed it
to 'police photographer.' When the information did not arouse
an immediate response, she added, 'I think I might be able to
help you.'

'The only person who can help me is Detective Inspector
Castle, and I intend to see him if I have to come here every
day for the rest of my life.'

'At least listen to what I have to say.' Sukey glanced at her
watch. 'I'm early for my shift so I have ten minutes to spare.
Why don't we go somewhere private?'

Sabrina hesitated for a moment, gave another nod and then
stood up. 'All right. Where do we go?'

'In here.' Sukey led the way to a small interview room,
signalling on the way to Josie, who gave a covert thumbs up
in response, relieved no doubt at the prospect of being spared
a few minutes of Sabrina's doleful countenance facing her
every time she looked up.

When they were settled on either side of a table, Sukey
said, 'Whenever there's an unexpected death, I or one of my
colleagues is called in to make a detailed record of the scene.
It so happens that I was on duty the day of your father's accident.'

The effect of the final word was electrical. Sabrina reached
across the table, grabbed Sukey by the arm and said fiercely,
'How many times do I have to tell you people? My father's
death was no accident; he was murdered.' The blue eyes that
had made such an impression on Dalia Chen blazed with an
almost fanatical intensity.

'My colleagues in CID have told me of your allegation,'
said Sukey, 'and I assure you that even before you were
informed of your father's death that possibility was considered.'

'So your people suspected it, but as no evidence jumped
up and hit them in the face they didn't look any further,' said
Sabrina bitterly.

'I assure you that isn't true.'

'Then why—?'

'It's standard practice in the case of an unexpected death. Occasionally it's found to be suspicious, but more often than not it's due either to natural causes or a tragic accident.'

'Which my father's death wasn't.' There was a note of steel in Sabrina's voice that contrasted oddly with her somewhat childlike features.

'Could I make a suggestion?' Sukey said.

'What's that?'

'First of all, accept the fact that the case will not be reopened unless and until new evidence is produced.'

Sabrina's face crumpled and her eyes filled. 'I can't do that. I simply must find out the truth,' she said piteously.

'I understand that, and since the police aren't going to look for evidence to support your allegation, I suggest you do a bit of digging around yourself.'

Sabrina's jaw dropped. 'I wouldn't know where to begin,' she said helplessly.

'I'm told you suspect Elspeth Maddox of causing your father's death. You must have some reason for your suspicions.'

'I've told DI Castle over and over again, she wanted his money.'

'But as his wife she'd have inherited it anyway.'

'Which would have been seen as a motive for killing him. Under the new will, she gets half without having to marry him.'

'Are you saying that she didn't care for him, that she was simply a gold-digger?'

Sabrina made wild, despairing gestures with her hands that seemed to indicate that she hardly knew what she was saying. 'All I'm sure of is, she killed him,' she insisted. 'You said you'd help me and now you're telling me to go and play detectives myself. How on earth do I do that?'

'You could try talking to some of the people in the solicitor's office. They might be able to reassure you there was no way Elspeth could have known about the will if your father gave instructions for it to be kept from both of you.'

'I can't do that. I wouldn't know what to say. And what will they think of me? They'll think I'm trying to prove the will's invalid or something, that I wanted all the money.' To Sukey's consternation, Sabrina broke down completely. 'I didn't want his money, I just wanted him to love me a little,' she sobbed.

Sukey got up, went round the table and put an arm round her shoulders. She waited until the storm had subsided and then said, 'Look, I have to go now and start work. Why don't you think over what I've said and make a few enquiries of your own? If you discover anything at all that supports your theory, come back and tell us about it.'

For a moment, Sukey thought she had got her message across. Then Sabrina grasped her hand and said urgently, 'I can't do it, not by myself. You must help me.'

Five

'Excuse me, Sarge, can I have a word?'

DS Dalia Chen, seated alone in the staff canteen, looked up from her cup of coffee and said, 'Sure, Sukey, have a chair. What is it?'

Sukey put her own coffee on the table and sat down. 'You interviewed Elspeth Maddox, didn't you?' she said.

Dalia thought for a moment. 'You mean the woman who was engaged to the chap who fell down his garden stairs and broke his neck – what was his name now?'

'Arthur Soames.'

'That's right. I remember her, of course – a very attractive woman. I was surprised at how much younger she was than her fiancé. DI Castle interviewed her, but I had the job of comforting her after she found Soames' body. What about her?'

'Do you happen to know where she lives?'

'Not off-hand. It'll be in the case file. Why do you ask?'

'She's been on my conscience.'

'Why?'

'It's just that I was waiting in the kitchen to go into the garden and photograph the scene when Doc Blake came in and made some wisecrack about me being in a hurry to view the exhibit, and I said, "I thought you'd never ask."'

Dalia smiled, showing a row of perfect, pearl-white teeth. 'Yes, I know, I heard you,' she said. 'It's the sort of thing one does say in those circumstances. It doesn't imply any disrespect; surely you know that.' She finished her coffee and put the mug down on the table.

Sukey found herself reluctantly admiring her pretty, oriental features and her small, dainty hands, and recalling the praise that Jim had lavished on her. With an effort she put the thought to one side and said, 'Of course it doesn't, but the fact is that if you heard it, Elspeth Maddox probably heard it too. It worried me at the time that it might have upset her, but there was nothing I could do; the words were out.'

'I don't suppose for a moment she heard you, or if she did she didn't take it in. She had calmed down a bit by then, but she was still pretty upset. She certainly didn't comment.'

'Just the same, I feel badly about it. She could have heard it without thinking about it at the time, but it might have occurred to her later that it was a pretty callous thing to say. She must be feeling desolate at the moment and I'd like a chance to see her and tell her there was nothing personal in it.'

'Are you asking me to give you her address?'

'If you would.'

Dalia reached for her handbag and stood up. 'I'm sorry, Sukey, I don't think I can do that without authority. I suggest you have a word with DI Castle.'

It seemed to Sukey that the young sergeant's eyes met hers in a slightly meaningful way when she mentioned Castle's name. It had been on the tip of her tongue to say that Jim Castle was the last person she wanted to know about her request and would she please be kind enough not to mention it to him. Instead she said casually, 'Maybe I'll do that if an opportunity arises. Thanks anyway, Dalia.'

When she was halfway to the door, Dalia turned back and said quietly, 'I do know that she lives quite close to Arthur Soames' house, because she declined a lift home on the grounds that her home was within walking distance.'

'Thanks, Sarge, you're a pal.'

'I don't think Jim would approve of this,' Fergus remarked that evening after his mother put him in the picture regarding Sabrina Soames' disturbing request and the preliminary – and unsuccessful – start she had made on her inquiry.

'Too right, he wouldn't,' she agreed, gloomily sipping her late-night glass of milk. 'I'm beginning to wish I hadn't mentioned it to Dalia; it was a pretty flimsy excuse anyway, but I couldn't think of any other way of finding Elspeth's address. All I hope is she doesn't say anything to him.'

'Even if she doesn't, I don't see what you were hoping to achieve by tackling Sabrina in the first place,' said Fergus, frowning.

Sukey ran a hand through her short curly hair and sighed. 'I suppose I thought, seeing as I was one of the first on the scene and went over everything with a fine-tooth comb, I might be able to convince her there was nothing to be gained by any further investigation. I might as well have saved my breath.'

'And now you've landed yourself in a bit of a hole. What on earth possessed you to agree to help her?'

'I felt desperately sorry for her. Her father's treatment of her over the years has left terrible scars. Plus it seemed the only way of persuading her to go home and stop pestering Jim. Gus, what the hell do I do now?'

'Well, you got one useful bit of information,' he pointed out.

'It's not much use, is it? I can hardly go round knocking on every door within a mile radius of Arthur Soames' house and saying, "Excuse me, does Elspeth Maddox live here", can I?'

'Mum, you're slipping.'

Sukey rinsed out her empty glass, put it on the draining board and sat down again. 'How d'you make that out?'

'If she's been in the district for any length of time she'll be on the register of electors. You know roughly whereabouts she lives so—'

'Gus, you're a genius! Why didn't I think of that?'

'It's old age,' he taunted her. 'The little grey cells aren't what they used to be.'

'I'll give you old age!' she retorted, giving him a friendly punch on the arm. 'It's more likely sheer mental exhaustion. I've had a hard day and it's past my bedtime.'

'Any interesting cases?'

'Not really. Just having to deal with victims of petty crime who spend ages bending my ear about slow police reaction is a chore in itself. I've lost count of the number of times I've had to listen to someone banging on about how we need more bobbies on the beat and how much safer the streets were when they were young. They have a point, of course, but what do they expect a mere SOCO to do about it?'

'Getting back to Elspeth Maddox,' said Fergus, 'do I take it you're going to press ahead with looking for her?'

'What else can I do? I promised Sabrina, and if she doesn't hear from me she'll only start coming back to haunt Jim.'

'And supposing you find Elspeth, what then?'

'Have a chat with her, try and assess what kind of woman she is and – hopefully – be able to go back to Sabrina and convince her that she has absolutely no grounds for her suspicion.' Sukey stifled a yawn and got up from her chair. 'I need my head examined,' she groaned. 'All I was trying to do was get Sabrina off Jim's back and now I find myself involved in this mad wild-goose chase.'

'You don't think there's anything in her allegations, then?'

'Not for a moment.' Sukey picked up her handbag and headed for the door. 'I'm off to bed. Will you see to the locking up, Gus?'

'Ms Elspeth Maddox?' Sukey held out one of her business cards. 'I hope you won't think I'm intruding,' she went on, 'and I want to make it clear that this is not an official visit, but I wonder if I could have a word with you?'

Elspeth Maddox hesitated on the doorstep of the semi-detached Victorian villa – of similar vintage but of far more modest proportions than that of her late fiancé – while she studied the card. After a few moments she said, 'Can you give me some idea what it's about?'

'It is rather confidential,' Sukey began. 'I've recently had a conversation with Mr Soames' daughter and—'

'That woman sent you?'

Elspeth's voice took on a harsh note and her mouth set in a hard line. She handed the card back to Sukey with a gesture that plainly indicated refusal, but at that moment the front door of the adjoining house opened and a plump, grey-haired woman emerged, carrying a shopping basket. She beamed across the low privet hedge dividing the two small front gardens and said, 'Good morning, Miss Maddox. What a lovely morning!' Her smile included Sukey as she added, 'It's nice to see you with a visitor; you've been hiding yourself indoors far too much since the tragedy.' She cocked her head on one side with an enquiring expression on her round face: plainly she was hoping for an introduction.

Elspeth returned her greeting, but without an answering smile. In a sudden change of attitude she stood aside and, without a word, beckoned Sukey into the house.

'I don't want you to think this means I'm agreeing to your request,' she said stiffly as she closed the door behind them. 'It was either invite you in or have that old witch standing there with her ears flapping, hoping to pick up something worth repeating at one of her old fogies' clubs.'

'Nosey neighbours can be a pain, can't they?' Sukey agreed. 'I often see the lace curtains quivering when I attend a crime scene.'

'I can imagine. Other people's misfortunes are always good for a bit of *Schadenfreude*. Well, since you're here, I suppose you might as well tell me what this is all about. This way.'

Sukey followed her into a sitting room decorated in shades of green and cream, with an open French door giving on to a patio with a small garden beyond. She had evidently been relaxing in the sun when interrupted by Sukey's knock, as a book, sunglasses and a glass containing a sparkling drink were on a small table beside a cushioned lounger. She stepped outside, picked up the glass, came back indoors and sat down in an armchair, indicating with a flick of a finger that Sukey should sit in the one opposite. 'I hope this won't take long,' she said curtly. 'I'm going out very soon.'

She crossed her legs and sat making restless, circular movements with one sandalled foot while taking sips from her drink, which she held in her right hand; her left, on which she still wore her engagement ring, rested on the arm of her chair. She was simply dressed in jeans and a T-shirt that flattered her well-rounded breasts and slender thighs. Sukey judged her to be in her mid to late thirties and found herself mentally comparing her with Arthur Soames' ageing body as it lay sprawled on the ground. Whether or not there was any justification for Sabrina's suspicions, questions must surely have been asked and eyebrows raised when the engagement was announced.

In stark contrast to Sabrina, she showed no outward sign of distress, nor did she give the impression of being particularly vulnerable. *Nothing significant in that; we all have our own way of handling grief*, was the thought that ran through Sukey's head. She opened her mouth to speak, but before she could utter a word Elspeth said, 'I suppose she's feeling sore at having been done out of half Arthur's money. Well, if she wants to contest the will, let her try. She can't claim I influenced him when I didn't even know about it until after he was dead.'

'I assure you, it isn't that,' Sukey replied. 'She's adamant that she doesn't care about the money.'

'Then what's her problem? And why couldn't she approach me directly instead of sending you?'

'She's very, very distressed . . . distraught would perhaps be a better word.'

'Or guilty?' said Elspeth contemptuously. 'She wasn't exactly the perfect daughter, was she?'

Sukey decided to let that pass for the moment. 'She wants the police to reopen the inquiry into her father's death,' she said, 'because – I'm sorry, there's no way of putting this diplomatically – she's convinced that it wasn't an accident.'

Sukey had prepared herself for some expression of scorn, or possibly outrage, at the suggestion. Instead, Elspeth inhaled sharply and put a hand over her mouth. 'Oh, my God! Maybe it wasn't such a crazy idea after all!' she whispered.

34

Sukey stared at her in amazement. 'Are you saying the same thing occurred to you?' she asked. Elspeth nodded. 'Why didn't you say so at the time?'

'It was a . . . a kind of gut reaction. When I saw him lying there I found myself thinking . . .' Her voice wavered and for the first time her eyes betrayed a hint of grief. She took one or two deep breaths and then continued, 'I found myself thinking: The poisonous bitch, I knew she'd find a way to stop him marrying me.'

'Who do you mean by "she"?' Sukey asked, although she had no doubt of the reply.

'Sabrina, of course, that harpy who passes for a daughter.' Elspeth fairly ground out the words through clenched teeth. 'Poor Arthur, it hurt him so much that she never gave him any affection. He tried so hard, but . . .' Her control failed altogether; she fumbled blindly in the pocket of her jeans and began silently weeping. After a minute or two she took a few mouthfuls from the drink that was still clutched in her right hand and said brokenly, 'You must think I'm completely bonkers.'

'Of course I don't,' Sukey said gently. 'I'm really sorry to have upset you like this, but Sabrina has been pestering the officer who was called to the scene when your fiancé's body was found. She's trying to persuade him that he was murdered, and—'

'She thinks I did it!' Elspeth interrupted with a mirthless laugh. 'That's one hell of a joke – because the same thought occurred to me, only I thought she'd done it!'

Six

Sukey stared at Elspeth in bewilderment. 'I don't understand,' she exclaimed. 'If you thought there was something suspicious about Mr Soames' death, why didn't you say so at the time instead of saying it was probably caused by a dizzy spell?'

Elspeth gnawed her lip and shook her head. She finished her drink, put the empty glass on a small occasional table and covered her eyes with both hands. 'I . . . this probably sounds crazy, but meeting Arthur . . . it was a revelation . . . he was so kind and considerate . . . for the first time in my life I felt loved instead of just desired. You'll probably think I'm talking a load of romantic rubbish –' at this point she dropped her hands and looked directly into Sukey's eyes – 'but it was like a fairy story. We seemed so right for one another and the age difference didn't matter at all.'

A faint smile drifted across her features as she recalled happier times and Sukey found herself smiling in sympathy. 'How did you come to meet him?' she asked.

'In church, would you believe? I hadn't been in years, but I was feeling pretty low at the time and I thought maybe it would do something for me. Arthur was giving out the hymnbooks and when he gave me mine he said something like, "Welcome to St Bartholomew's." Then he came and spoke to me afterwards and said how nice it was to see a new face and he hoped I'd come again. Of course I did, and a couple of Sundays later he invited me to his house for a coffee after the service. It started from there.'

'So he was a churchwarden? I hadn't realized.'

'Why should you?' Elspeth's expression hardened. 'As far as you were concerned, he was just another body – or perhaps I should say, exhibit.'

Sukey winced. So she had overheard and been hurt by the exchange between Dr Blake and herself. 'I'm truly sorry for that remark,' she said humbly. 'It didn't mean we weren't affected by the tragedy; dealing with sudden death is never easy, even in our job. It gets to us like anyone else and sometimes a bit of black humour helps us carry on with doing what we have to do.'

Elspeth shrugged. 'If you say so.'

There was an awkward silence; then Sukey said, 'Tell me, when did Arthur first tell you about Sabrina?'

'Quite early on. He said it was the great sorrow of his life, after losing his wife, that his only child had no love for him. My own father died when I was a child, but I was always very close to my mother, so I could only imagine how he felt.'

'Is your mother still alive?'

Elspeth blinked and swallowed hard before saying in a husky whisper, 'She died a few months before I met Arthur.'

'I'm so sorry.' Sukey picked up her shoulder bag that she had let drop to the floor. 'I'm upsetting you; I think perhaps I'd better go.'

'No, you may as well hear the rest of it.' Elspeth straightened her back and lifted her chin. 'I've done nothing to be ashamed of, no matter what that woman says.'

'That she thinks you killed your father, you mean?'

'No, I mean the lies she spread about me when he told her he'd been seeing me. As soon as he mentioned the difference in our ages, he said she flew into a rage and said I was nothing but a gold-digger who'd take him for every penny he had and then ditch him.'

'Do I take it she's never actually met you?'

'Oh no,' Elspeth sneered, 'she wouldn't lower herself to be in the same room as the likes of me. She was at the inquest of course, and so was I, but she didn't deign to look in my direction. Arthur was terribly hurt by her attitude; I thought he was going to cry when he told me. If I could have got my hands on her at that moment I think I'd have killed her. And that's why, when I saw him lying there, I thought to myself: Well, she's got her way, I wonder how she did it. As if she was a bad fairy who'd cast a spell on us. It was a gut reaction, of course, completely irrational. And then I remembered the dizzy spell and how I'd begged Arthur to have a checkup and that seemed the obvious explanation.' She gave a long, shuddering sigh before continuing. 'He always boasted that he was in pretty good shape for his age, so I guess that's why he wouldn't admit there was anything wrong with him. I never knew he'd seen Dr Gardner, or been prescribed medication. I remember saying at the time to that young Chinese detective – what was her name now? – that I'd felt all along it was too good to be true.'

'Detective Sergeant Chen? Yes, she did mention you'd said something like that.' There was a pause, during which Elspeth seemed to be deep in thought. After a moment Sukey said, 'So I take it that apart from that initial shock reaction, you've never seriously considered that Arthur Soames' death was anything but a dreadful accident?'

'Of course I haven't. And now Lady Sabrina is going round accusing *me* of having murdered him.' Elspeth gave a short, bitter laugh. 'That's rich, coming from her.'

'Before we go any further,' said Sukey, 'there's one point that needs clearing up. According to what your late fiancé told you, he loved his daughter and was hurt by her hostility towards him.'

'Haven't I just said so?'

'So it may surprise you to know that, according to her, he rejected her at birth because he blamed her for the death of her mother, and that throughout her life she has tried repeatedly to overcome the barrier he erected between them. She claims he never showed her the slightest affection.'

'That's a load of rubbish!' Elspeth retorted. 'He told me over and over again how many times he'd pleaded with her to show *him* just a little affection. Anyway, what's her game in sending you to talk to me? Hasn't she got the courage to face me herself?'

'She didn't send me; she doesn't even know I'm here,' said Sukey.

'So why are you here? What's in it for you?'

'It seemed the only way to stop her pestering the police to start a murder inquiry. It's become an obsession with her. I had a long talk with her and explained that she'd have to find some evidence of skulduggery for that to happen and she said she wouldn't know how to begin. I felt so sorry for her that before I knew what was happening I'd agreed to help by tracking you down, and if possible having a talk with you.'

Elspeth's scornful expression changed to one of alarm. 'You haven't told her where I live, I hope?' she said sharply.

'No, of course not, but in view of what you've been saying, it might be an idea for you to either meet her or speak to her on the phone.'

'What for? I've nothing to say to her. In fact, you can go back and tell her that if she persists in repeating her allegations I'll get my solicitor to take out a writ for slander, or libel, or whatever.'

'As she and her father have given totally conflicting accounts of their relationship, don't you think it would be better to find out who was telling the truth?'

'I've no doubt whatever who was telling the truth. Arthur was a decent man through and through. He would never have lied to me.' Elspeth's voice shook; once again, she was close to tears.

'I'm sorry, I don't mean to upset you, but please believe me when I say that Sabrina is every bit as unhappy as you are.'

'It's no more than she deserves after all the misery she caused him.'

There was obviously no point in prolonging the interview. Sukey got to her feet and said, 'I'll go now. Don't get up, I'll see myself out.' There was no response. She was almost at the door when a thought struck her. 'You said just now that

Sabrina wouldn't have anything to do with someone like you. What did you mean by that?'

Elspeth gave a wry smile. 'You don't know about my showbiz career?'

'No. Do tell me.'

'It's nothing very spectacular. I tried to break into the film business but all I managed was a bit of modelling and a few walk-on parts in some seriously unmemorable movies. In her book that's only one step away from being a tart.'

'How did she know all this?'

A look of surprise crossed Elspeth's face. 'I . . . well, I sort of assumed Arthur must have told her. As I said, he was an honest, open sort of person and I suppose he thought it was the right thing to do. He said he couldn't believe anyone could be so prejudiced.'

'Perhaps her aunt had rather puritanical ideas and dinned them into her when she was a child,' was all Sukey could think of saying.

'Her aunt?' Elspeth looked puzzled.

'Her father's sister, the one who brought her up. Her mother died giving birth to her, remember.'

'Oh, yes.' Elspeth's brow puckered as if vaguely disturbed by the reminder.

After a moment, Sukey said, 'You have my card; if you feel like talking again, or if on reflection you think you'd like to talk to Sabrina, just give me a call and I'll pass the message along.'

'D'you reckon you got anywhere?' asked Fergus when Sukey returned home that evening and told him of her encounter with Elspeth.

'I think I gave her something to think about, but whether she'll follow it up remains to be seen. Cheers, love,' she added, picking up the mug of tea he had just put on the kitchen table in front of her before sitting down opposite.

'It sounds as if her Arthur wasn't quite as honest about his relationship with his daughter as she makes out,' he said between mouthfuls of tea.

'That was my impression,' she agreed. 'Elspeth poured scorn on Sabrina's version and insisted he would never have lied to her, but I think she was just a little taken aback when I referred to the aunt who brought Sabrina up. I have a feeling she didn't know about her.'

'You reckon the old boy never told her? I wonder why?'

Sukey shrugged. 'Who knows? Anyway, I've done what I can.'

'D'you think you'll hear from her again?'

'Maybe, when she's had time to think things over. In spite of what she said, I have a feeling she'll be curious to know more about Sabrina's side of the story.'

'Are you going to tell Sabrina that Elspeth thought for a moment that *she* might have killed her father?'

'I think so; it might help convince her she's completely off message with her own murder theory. I'll also say I'm sure Elspeth's grief is absolutely genuine. I suppose Arthur made up the story about Sabrina having nothing to do with him to cover up the real reason for the rift,' she added, frowning.

'It doesn't tie in with the picture Elspeth painted of him,' Fergus agreed. 'What do you know about him, by the way?'

'Nothing really. I don't know if anything about his background came out at the inquest, but there's no reason why it should have. Basically, if there are no suspicious circumstances, all the coroner needs is evidence of identity and to be satisfied as to the cause of death. If there are suspicious circumstances then of course further enquiries have to be made, but this was a perfectly straightforward case.'

'Just the same, it would be interesting to find out a bit more about him.' There was a gleam in her son's eye that Sukey immediately recognized. She reached across the table and patted his hand.

'There you are, a project to fill your spare time between now and going up to uni,' she said with a chuckle. '"Thoughts on the phenomenon of dual identity" – how does that sound as a theme for a dissertation?'

'You can laugh,' he retorted, 'but I have a hunch there's more to Arthur than meets the eye.'

'What are you suggesting?'

'Doesn't it strike you as curious that the same thought occurred to both the women in his life – that he was murdered?'

'Not really, considering the circumstances. As far as Elspeth's concerned, it was just an emotional, knee-jerk reaction anyway. She admitted it was irrational.'

'She could have experienced some vague doubt, instantly suppressed, about whether he'd been telling her the truth about Sabrina. I mean, if his daughter was so indifferent to him, why should she kill him to stop him marrying his girlfriend?'

At the sight of her son's earnest expression, Sukey burst out laughing. 'Oh Gus, why didn't I talk you out of doing A-level psychology?' she exclaimed in mock despair. 'I'm sure you're on the wrong track; she was adamant that he wouldn't lie to her.'

'How long had she known him?'

'I've no idea – except that it seems to have been something of a whirlwind romance. A fairytale, she called it.'

'There you are, then. He could have told her any amount of porkies and if she was as starry-eyed about him as you say, she'd have swallowed them whole and come back for more.'

Sukey stared reflectively into her empty mug. 'I suppose you could be right,' she admitted, 'but I don't see what we can do about it. Anyway, it's Sabrina's problem, not ours.'

'You said you've got to let her know you've talked to Elspeth; why don't you see what you can find out about his past?'

'I'd have to tread carefully. I have a hunch she'd be quick to resent any hint of a slur on her father, in spite of his rejection of her. I do know he wasn't a local chap because there was a brief obit in the *Gazette* after the inquest that said he'd retired down here around ten years ago.'

'We can start there,' said Fergus eagerly. 'There may be more information in the obit that would give us a lead. I'll go to the *Gazette* office first thing tomorrow and have a look through the back numbers.'

'Yes, you do that.' Sukey deliberately made her tone indulgent, as if she was humouring him in some harmless but pointless exercise, but she could not entirely suppress the feeling that there might be something in his suspicions.

Seven

It was going to take a great deal of diplomacy on Sukey's part to persuade the two women in Arthur Soames' life to meet. She was hopeful that Elspeth would, on reflection, agree; the next step was to raise the subject with Sabrina.

'I thought you'd be interested to know that I've been to see Elspeth Maddox,' she began when Sabrina answered the telephone. 'I told her you had some doubts about your father's death and—'

'Don't tell me!' Sabrina interrupted. 'She thinks I'm after the money.'

'She did think that to start with,' Sukey agreed. 'I told her you were adamant that wasn't the case; I'm not sure she was entirely convinced, but the interesting thing was . . .' Reading from the notes she had made immediately after her conversation with Elspeth, Sukey explained that she too had had suspicions – more or less immediately dismissed – about the cause of Arthur's death.

There was silence for several seconds at the other end of the line. Eventually, Sabrina muttered, 'Extraordinary,' but after another pause went on to say, 'the cheeky bitch probably made that up on the spur of the moment to throw you off the scent. It doesn't alter my opinion.'

'Which is?'

'That she killed him, of course. I've a good mind to go and sort her out face to face. Where does she live?'

'I'm not giving you her address without her permission,' said Sukey. 'And in any case, I'm sure you're wrong. I had quite a long chat with her, and I'm convinced she's genuinely heartbroken by your father's death. She's aware of your hostility towards her of course, which she puts down to her age and her background—'

'What background? I don't know anything about her.'

'What she calls her showbiz career . . . she said you more or less called her a tart because—'

'I haven't a clue what you're talking about – what showbiz career?'

'Your father didn't tell you she'd had some bit parts in a few what she called "seriously unmemorable movies", and also done some modelling?'

'He didn't tell me anything except that he was getting married, that his wife to be was what he called "a bit younger than him" . . . and then he had the gall to invite me to the wedding, "if I cared to come", knowing jolly well I wouldn't want anything to—' Sabrina's voice broke before she could finish.

Sukey waited a moment before continuing. 'Look, there are one or two things that need straightening out and I'd rather do it face to face than over the phone. Where can we meet?'

'I could come to the police station again if you like.'

'No, not there. All this is off the record, and before we go any further you must promise not to say anything to the police without asking me first.'

'OK. What about your house, then?'

'Not here either,' said Sukey hastily. The suggestion called up a vision of Jim dropping in unexpectedly on some pretext – unlikely in the normal state of events, but not impossible – and discovering that she was once again exceeding her professional remit. 'Could I perhaps come to your place?'

'I suppose so.' She gave Sukey an address in Bishop's Cleeve and they agreed to meet the following morning.

'Excuse me, madam, I wonder if you could help me?'

'Certainly, if I can.' The middle-aged woman who was re-arranging the books and postcards set out on a table at the back of St Bartholomew's Church looked up from her task and gave Fergus a friendly smile. 'What would you like to know? If it's about the services for the month you'll find a list on the noticeboard over there.'

'No, it isn't that. I'm interested in the work of churchwardens and I'm wondering if a new one has been appointed yet.'

The woman's eyes widened. 'A new one? Has Dr Gardner resigned? I haven't been told.'

'Oh.' Fergus was momentarily nonplussed. 'I thought Mr Arthur Soames – the late Mr Soames that is – was the churchwarden here.'

'No, Mr Soames was a sidesman.' A sorrowful expression crossed the woman's pleasant features. 'He was also a member of the PCC. He played a very active part in the life of the church and we all miss him very much.'

'I'm sure you do – especially the lady he was going to marry,' Fergus ventured.

'Ah yes, Miss Maddox – or Miz, as she insisted on being called.' Her lips twitched in a half-smile that held a hint of condescension. 'It seemed a very surprising engagement, considering the difference in their ages . . . but I shouldn't be passing comments like that. I take it this is a project you're doing for school? I'm sure Dr Gardner would be happy to help you. Would you like me to give you his telephone number?'

'Thank you.' Fergus jotted down the information in the notebook he had brought along to support his role as a researcher into parish administration. 'I understand this is a very old church,' he added. 'The windows are beautiful – are they medieval, do you know?'

The woman shook her head. 'I believe most of them are Victorian,' she said. 'Arthur Soames would have been the person to ask about that,' she added with a sigh. 'It's sad to think his history of St Bartholomew's will never be completed. Last time I spoke to him about it he said there was still quite a lot to do before it was finished.'

'Yes, I remember it was referred to in his obituary in the *Gazette*. Did you know him well?'

She appeared to consider for a moment. 'I'd known him for some time through the church, but I wouldn't say I knew him well. He was what people call a private person – very pleasant to everyone, but so far as I know he had no close friends – until he met Miss Maddox, of course.'

'It said in the *Gazette* that he was a retired schoolteacher, but it didn't say where he taught.'

'It wasn't anywhere local. He came here from London when he retired.'

Fergus felt a twinge of excitement at the thought that he might have stumbled on a clue to Arthur Soames' life before Gloucestershire. 'Do you happen to know what school he was at?' he asked – a little too eagerly, as he realized the moment he had spoken.

'I'm afraid I've no idea.' She gave Fergus a curious look. 'I thought it was the role of a churchwarden you were interested in.'

He felt himself turning scarlet. 'Er, yes, of course it is,' he said hastily. 'I . . . it was talking about church history that made me . . . I'm quite interested in that as well. Anyway, thank you so much for your help. Goodbye.' Clutching his notebook, he turned and fled.

The moment Sukey walked into the house that evening, Fergus pounced on her.

'Mum, have you spoken to Sabrina again?' he demanded.

'Why do you ask?'

'I'll tell you in a minute. Well, have you?' he persisted as his mother dumped her bag on the kitchen floor and went to the sink to fill the kettle.

'As it happens, I called her before I started my shift. When I told her how Elspeth had the idea she'd killed her father to stop the wedding she was pretty taken aback and then claimed it was probably to divert suspicion from herself and demanded her address so that she could "sort her out", as she put it.'

'You didn't give it to her?'

'Of course not – what do you take me for? If she'd kicked

up a fuss I'd have told her to calm down and talk rationally, otherwise I'd have nothing more to do with her, and if she went back to pestering DI Castle she could end up being charged with wasting police time.'

'Is that true?'

'I doubt it, but she's not to know that. Anyway, it didn't come to that; she started talking more sensibly and in the end she agreed to meet me again so that we could get a few things straightened out.'

'Where are you going to meet?'

'At her house, tomorrow.'

'Wow!' Fergus's face glowed with admiration. 'Well done, Mum!'

'Thank you. Now tell me about your day. You've been up to something; you've got that look in your eye.'

'I've had a *very* interesting day,' he said smugly. 'I've been enquiring into Arthur Soames' past history.'

'And?'

'According to the obit in the *Gazette* he was a retired teacher, but it didn't say what school he taught at before he came to Gloucester and nobody round here seems to know.' He repeated the gist of his conversation with the woman in the church. 'Doesn't that strike you as strange?'

Sukey shrugged. 'Not necessarily. Maybe he was just a very private person.'

'That's what this lady said – but there could have been another reason. Mum,' he went on, seeing Sukey's indulgent smile, 'when you see Sabrina tomorrow, why don't you ask her what school he taught at?'

'I suppose I could,' she said doubtfully, 'but like I said, I'm not sure how she'd react to being questioned about him. She's in a very fragile emotional state.'

'Well, maybe Elspeth knows,' he went on eagerly. 'If you could find out, I could do more research. There might be something in his past that even his daughter doesn't know about ... something that made him enemies who've been on his trail for years and—'

Sukey burst out laughing. 'Now why didn't I think of that?' she exclaimed. 'At last the ring of drug dealers he's conned out of thousands have caught up with him and pushed him down the stairs to his death by way of revenge. "This has all the hallmarks of a classic gangland killing," say the local police. Well done, Gus!'

Despite himself, Fergus had to join in her laughter. 'Just the same, Mum,' he said, 'do see what you can find out. Please.'

'Oh, all right,' she said resignedly. 'Anything for a quiet life.'

'And in the meantime,' he went on, 'I'll have a word with Dr Gardner.'

Sukey looked at him in astonishment. 'You can't do that!' she exclaimed.

'Why ever not? They must have chatted together from time to time over their church duties.'

'Their . . . just a minute. What church duties?'

'Arthur was a sidesman and a member of the PCC, and Dr Gardner is a churchwarden at St Bartholomew's. The lady I spoke to said she was sure he'd be willing to help me with my research; I could ask him what qualifications are needed to become a churchwarden – he might let drop something useful that way.'

'Dr Gardner was also Arthur's GP – he gave evidence at the inquest.'

'Even better. He's more likely than some of the others to know a bit more about his earlier history.'

'Gus, I think you'd better stay out of it. You can't go questioning a doctor about a patient, even a deceased one.'

'But, Mum—'

'No buts,' said Sukey firmly. 'I do agree with you that it would be interesting to know, but Elspeth's the person to ask. You'd better leave that one with me. Now let's drop the subject,' she added firmly as he opened his mouth to argue further. 'In the hope that Sabrina will stop tilting at windmills, I'll do what I can to get her and Elspeth to talk to each other and then I can just bow out before Jim gets wind of what we've been doing.'

Fergus grinned. 'I'd love to be a fly on the wall if those two ever get together. It'll be the mother of all cat fights!'

Sabrina lived in a detached house on a modern development on the edge of the village. It had a neat front garden with a bed of roses in the centre surrounded by a low box hedge, and an elaborately paved forecourt. Sukey parked her ageing Astra behind a sleek new Citroën that stood on the drive and walked up to the front door, reflecting as she waited for an answer to her ring that, to outward appearances at least, Sabrina had achieved a fairly comfortable lifestyle without her father's support. It occurred to her that her knowledge of the woman's background or professional standing was virtually nil; suddenly, the sheer foolhardiness of what she was doing struck her so forcibly that she was almost on the point of chickening out when the door opened and Sabrina was beckoning her into the house.

She responded with an unsmiling nod to Sukey's greeting, merely saying, 'Come into my study; I've made some coffee.' She showed her visitor into a room at the back of the house that the architect had evidently intended as a dining room, since it had a hatchway to the kitchen, but was instead furnished as an office with filing cabinets, a bookcase, a desk and a computer. She motioned Sukey to a chair by the window in front of a low table while she poured coffee from a cafetière into delicate porcelain mugs before pulling the swivel chair away from the desk and sitting down herself.

Until now, Sukey had not paid a great deal of attention to Sabrina's overall appearance, being principally conscious of the unexpectedly youthful features and strikingly large blue eyes that had, in the midst of her distress, hardened so dramatically when speaking of the woman who had laid claim to her father's affections. Watching her as she poured the coffee and offered milk, sugar and biscuits, she was surprised as much by her fashionable linen suit and impeccable grooming as by her air of confidence. Altogether, she presented a very different image to the one she had shown at their previous meeting; on that occasion she wore no make-up and was casually, almost shabbily dressed.

Sukey's surprise must have shown in her expression; as she sat down, Sabrina gave a half-smile and said, 'I didn't want you to think I spend all my time looking as scruffy as I did when I was lobbying your boss. To tell the truth, I couldn't have cared less then about the way I looked, but since you've given me your support I've tried to pull myself together.' She jerked her head towards the desk behind her and added, 'Working from home, you don't see many people and it's all too easy to let yourself go.'

'What work do you do?' Sukey asked.

Sabrina shrugged. 'Nothing very spectacular. I did a degree in modern languages after I left school, but I didn't need to find a job right away because Aunt Pru left all her money – quite a lot of it – to me. So I did a bit of travelling and got interested in photography. I wrote a few articles that got published, and then a publisher of travel books asked me to do some copy-editing for them. I'm currently writing a book of my own about the early Greek churches. I'd actually managed to get Dad interested in that – he was a historian himself – and we'd had several quite amicable meetings . . . and then he had to go and meet *her*.' Once again, the tone became venomous and the blue eyes turned to ice.

'I think I . . . that is, I'm trying to understand why you feel so bitter towards Elspeth,' said Sukey, 'but the fact is that your father hasn't been entirely honest with her – with either of you.'

'Meaning?'

'She says he told her that the one great sorrow of his life after losing his wife was the fact that his only child had never shown him any affection.'

Sabrina's jaw dropped and the hand with which she had been about to put her empty coffee mug back on the table froze in midair. 'She said that? The lying bitch!' she exclaimed.

51

'I don't think she was lying,' said Sukey. 'In fact, I'm sure of it. When I told her your version of the story, she rejected it completely and insisted that your father would never have lied to her. I'm convinced she truly loved him, and trusted him completely.'

'I simply don't understand. Why would he tell her a story like that?' Sabrina put down the mug and gazed at Sukey with the piteous expression of a child that has been unjustly punished.

'Perhaps he felt if she knew the true situation she'd think twice about marrying him,' Sukey suggested.

'Or perhaps . . .' Sabrina broke off and sat for a long time, apparently deep in thought. Sukey waited patiently for her to speak; when she did so, it was obvious that her mind was far away. 'I've often wondered . . .' she muttered, half to herself.

'Wondered what?'

'It doesn't matter. I'll have to think it over. Maybe you're right, maybe I should have a talk with her. Will you give me her phone number?'

'Not without her permission. And I'm not sure yet whether she'll be prepared to meet you.'

'I think she should. Will you have a word with her and tell her what I've said? It might be important.'

'Can't you tell me any more? You haven't really told me anything I didn't know already.'

'No. What I have to say, I can only say to her.'

Eight

When Sukey arrived home that evening she found a message from Elspeth. It was short and to the point.

'I've thought about what you said and I agree to meet Arthur's daughter. Will you arrange it, please?'

'Well, it seems I've achieved something,' she remarked to Fergus as she put the phone down and relayed the message.

'Cool!' he exclaimed. 'Now all you have to do is get them together – assuming Sabrina agrees, of course. How did it go this morning? Did you find out any more about Arthur's background?'

'Not really. She confirmed he was a historian, but we knew that already. I think I convinced her that he'd been a bit devious, to say the least – and she's not only agreed to meet Elspeth, she insists that it's important. She gave me the impression that she'd remembered something significant, but she wouldn't say what it was.'

'Great stuff! I just knew there was something fishy about him,' said Fergus jubilantly. 'How are you going to set it up, Mum? Will you invite them here?'

'Are you kidding? It's up to them to arrange when and where they meet. It'll be a relief to bow out; I haven't felt all that comfortable about getting involved.'

Her son's face fell. 'You said you wanted to be present,' he protested.

'I didn't say I wanted to, I thought it might be diplomatic in case the claws came out. Now I've spoken to both of them I think that's unlikely. Anyway, it's their show, so let them sort it out. I'll give Elspeth a call in the morning – it's a bit late now.'

'But how are you going to know what's behind it all if you aren't there?' he protested.

'Gus, I don't *need* to know. It's a family matter, not a murder inquiry in spite of the wild accusations that have been flying about. I think both of them accept that now. I'm a SOCO, in case you've forgotten, not an agony aunt.'

'We don't know for sure it wasn't—' he began, but Sukey had had enough for one day of Arthur Soames, his daughter and his fiancée. Despite his protests she flatly refused to discuss the matter any further.

In response to Sukey's call the following day, Elspeth had no hesitation in agreeing to Sabrina being given her telephone number.

'I hardly slept last night thinking about what you told me,' she said, and there was a note of weary resignation in her voice as she went on, 'I think it's important for both of us – Sabrina and me, that is – to understand what lies behind all this. If what she told you is true, then it looks as if there was some reason why Arthur didn't want us to meet.'

'You could be right,' Sukey agreed, 'and talking to Sabrina is the only way to find out what it was. You've both suffered a loss and it would be nice to think you could bring one another some comfort.'

'I'm not sure about comfort,' said Elspeth. Her voice sank to a shaky whisper. 'Last night, while I was lying awake, I changed my mind a dozen times – should I go ahead and hear what Sabrina has to say, or just cling to my happy memories of Arthur and put all this out of my head? In the end I realized I'd have no peace until I'd found out the truth.'

'I'm sure you're doing the right thing,' said Sukey. 'I'll call Sabrina and tell her what you've said. I really do hope you can sort it out between you.'

'I hope so too.' Sukey was about to say goodbye and put the phone down when Elspeth added, 'Thank you very much for your help. I'll let you know how we get on.'

'Yes, please do that,' said Sukey, and meant it. Despite her refusal to discuss the matter with Fergus, she could not help being curious.

'Thank goodness we're on early shift next week,' she commented to her colleague, Mandy Parfitt, as they studied their assignments over mugs of vending machine tea at the start of their afternoon shift. 'Late nights don't agree with me.'

'Interfere with your love life, do they?' said Mandy slyly.

'Interfere with my sleep, more like,' Sukey retorted. 'It's not easy to get a lie-in when you have a teenage son who has to get up early and couldn't do it quietly to save his life.' Although she had a closer relationship with Mandy than with any other member of the department, she had never admitted, either by word or implication, that her relationship with DI Castle was anything other than professional.

'You should make him get his own breakfast,' said Mandy.

'He does that anyway, but more often than not he manages to wake me up with the clattering around that goes on while he's doing it. Still,' she added, a little wistfully, 'I'll miss him when he goes to uni. The house'll be like a morgue.'

'It'll give you time for other activities.' Mandy was still gently probing. When Sukey again refused to take the bait, she continued, 'Any plans for the weekend?'

'Not really. Fergus is going off camping with some of his friends, so I'll have a chance to catch up with some house-work and gardening.' The prospect was unappealing, but as Jim was on duty all weekend there was little alternative. 'How about you?' she added.

'There's a film on at the Odeon that I'd like to see. I might go tomorrow if I can get someone to keep Mum company.'

Mandy's mother was an invalid who spent much of her time either in a day centre or being looked after by carers while her daughter was at work. At other times, the whole responsibility lay on Mandy's shoulders and it had often struck

Sukey how restricted a life her colleague led compared to her own. On an impulse, she said, 'I could stay with her if you like.'

Mandy's freckled face lit up. 'Bless you, that would be lovely. Better still, if Mrs Cranham down the road could do it, you and I could go to the movie together. How about that?'

'Great. Give me a ring in the morning.'

'Will do.'

'When you two have quite finished organizing your social diaries . . .' Sergeant George Barnes, the officer in charge of the section, interrupted.

'On our way, Sarge,' said Sukey and the two hastily finished their tea, gathered up their equipment and departed.

Sukey was on the point of leaving the house on Saturday evening when Jim rang.

'How are things?' he asked.

'Fine. I'm just off to the movies with Mandy. How about you?'

'Not much action at the moment, so I'm catching up on paperwork. I'm on duty till eight tomorrow – OK if I pop round for an hour or so then? It seems ages since we had any time together.'

'That would be lovely,' she said. Her pulse quickened at the prospect, but his next words brought her back to the present with a bump.

'By the way,' he went on, 'I understand you were instrumental in persuading Sabrina Soames to stop pestering me. Is that right?'

'In a way. I suppose Josie told you?'

'She said you'd had a word with Sabrina, and then –' there was a slight but unmistakable hesitation before he went on, 'Dalia Chen happened to mention you'd asked for Elspeth Maddox's address. I assume there was a connection?'

'Dalia just *happened* to mention it?' Sukey said – a little too quickly, as she realized the moment the words were out.

'There's no need to be so touchy. She was only checking that she was correct in referring you to me for information from the case file. Why didn't you come to me in the first place – and why did you want to talk to Elspeth anyway?'

Damn you, Dalia Chen! Sukey found herself thinking waspishly. *Why did you have to go running to the boss about such a trivial matter?* Deliberately ignoring the first part of the question, she said, 'There seemed to be some quite serious misunderstandings between Sabrina and Elspeth and I thought it might help if they could be persuaded to talk to each other, that's all. I understand they're going to meet.'

'Well, it's got Sabrina off my back, so many thanks. How did you manage to arrange it?'

'Haven't got time to tell you now.'

'All right, you can tell me tomorrow evening. Enjoy the film.'

At about the same time as Sukey and Mandy were settling into their seats to watch *Cold Mountain*, Sabrina Soames was standing on Elspeth's doorstep with her finger on the bell push. Even now, she found herself hesitating while the fears, frustrations and doubts of many years churned around in her head. *What am I trying to achieve? He's dead; why not leave him in peace?* she asked herself for the umpteenth time. But back came the reply, *Ah, but will he leave you in peace if you don't find out the truth?* Squaring her shoulders and lifting her head, she pressed the bell and waited.

When the door opened she tried to speak, but her vocal cords seemed to freeze and it was left to Elspeth to say, 'You must be Sabrina. Won't you come in?'

'Thank you.' Her voice was somewhere between a whisper and a croak. She stepped through the door, aware that she was being appraised by a slim, elegant woman whose appearance was far from what she had expected. She felt suddenly at a disadvantage, eyeing her hostess's simple but beautifully cut trouser suit and wishing she had put on something a little smarter.

Her surprise must have shown because Elspeth said with a hint of a smile, 'I imagine you thought I'd be a brassy blonde in tight jeans and wearing too much make-up.'

'No . . . no, really, I . . .' Sabrina stammered, knowing the remark was uncomfortably close to the truth.

'No need to feel embarrassed; I pictured you as a hard-faced sourpuss. You're much younger than I thought.'

'I'm thirty-five. I know I don't look it.'

'And I'm thirty-four. If Arthur hadn't died you'd have had a stepmother younger than yourself. Life plays odd tricks, doesn't it? Come this way.' Elspeth showed her into the sitting room and indicated the chair that Sukey had occupied earlier in the week. 'On a fine evening like this I'd suggest sitting on the patio, but my next-door neighbour has ears like a cat and curiosity to match,' she explained. 'What will you have to drink? I've got quite a nice Chardonnay in the fridge.'

'That would be lovely.'

Elspeth disappeared and returned a few minutes later with two misted glasses of white wine on a tray. She gave one to Sabrina, sat down opposite, lifted the other and said, 'Cheers!'

'Cheers!' Sabrina drank deeply before putting the glass down on the small table beside her chair. 'This is bizarre, isn't it?'

'On the contrary, it seems to me to be entirely normal,' said Elspeth. 'Newly engaged woman meets daughter of fiancé. Only unusual feature is . . . meeting might never have taken place if fiancé was still alive.' Without warning, her voice wavered and her face crumpled. 'Oh God, we were so happy,' she whispered. 'Why did it have to happen?'

'That's what I've been asking myself,' said Sabrina. Her hostess had poured generous measures of wine, she had drunk deeply and already her nerves were becoming steadier. 'Still,' she went on after another mouthful, 'if it hadn't happened, you and I would still be hating each other.'

'That's not true,' Elspeth said quickly. 'I never hated you. I just felt a strong resentment towards you for being so horrid to him.'

'And now you know I'm not the unnatural daughter he made me out to be and that in fact he'd been telling us both a load of porkies, do you still love him?'

Elspeth made a despairing gesture. 'I don't know, I don't know! Do you?'

'Yes, God help me, I do. That's why I'm here.'

'But if what you say is true,' said Elspeth, 'and my reason tells me it is, I can't deny he was being less than honest with us. Have you any idea why?'

'Yes, I think I have, but you aren't going to like it . . . any more than I do.'

Elspeth uttered a faint, humourless laugh. 'You know something? I always had a feeling it was too good to last. I said as much to that policewoman who came to the house the day he . . .' The final words were lost in a drawn out, shuddering sigh. She fished a handkerchief from the pocket of her pale-green trousers and held it to her eyes. It was a minute or two before she regained control, took another mouthful from her glass and said, 'So there's something you think I should know. What is it?'

It was the moment Sabrina had been dreading. She sat biting her lips and twirling the stem of her glass between her fingers while a long-case clock in the far corner of the room ticked away the seconds. All her previous doubts came racing to the surface. *Suppose I'm wrong, suppose I'm doing him a terrible injustice? If I tell her, I'm going to poison her memories of him for ever. I was so wrong about her; I can see now that she truly loved him, so how can I do this to her?* But it was too late to back out now; in Elspeth's steady, unwavering gaze she read nothing but a determination to know the truth, whatever the emotional cost.

At last she began, and her voice seemed to echo in her head like the voice of a stranger. 'When I heard he was dead, I was sure someone had killed him and my first thought was that it was probably you. I had this distorted picture of the kind of woman you are, as you know . . . but after Sukey had been to see you she convinced me that I was completely on the wrong track. Then it dawned on me that the fact of the matter was that I had *wanted* it to be you. If it should turn out you'd killed him to get your hands on the money without having to marry him, my darkest fears could have been buried along with the father I'd convinced myself had never loved me. Any other explanation would have meant that something I'd suspected for a long time, but couldn't bear to face . . . but I have to face it now . . . I have to know the truth and I want you to help me uncover it.'

Elspeth shook her head in bewilderment. 'Sabrina, you're talking in riddles. Are you saying you still believe Arthur . . . your father . . . was murdered?'

'Yes, I do, and I want his killer caught, because in spite of everything I loved him and if what I suspect is true it's the reason why he kept me at a distance all these years.'

'I don't understand,' Elspeth said with a sob. 'He was a kind, loving, God-fearing man who was good to me. Why would anyone want to kill him?'

Sabrina tossed back the rest of her wine and said in a low, almost conspiratorial whisper, 'This may sound fantastic, but the more I think about it, the more I'm beginning to wonder if my father had some kind of connection with the police.'

Nine

When her doorbell rang at seven o'clock on Sunday evening, Sukey had just stepped out of the shower. She hastily wrapped her head in the towel she had been using to dry her hair and pulled on her dressing gown. A somewhat alarming thought struck her as she hurried downstairs: supposing either Sabrina or Elspeth had managed to track her down? If so, and Jim should happen to turn up early, it would surely lead to complications. As it was, he had made it clear that he expected to be told how and why she had arranged for the two women to meet. She was already beginning to regret her involvement; if after the meeting Sabrina was still clinging to her conviction that her father had been murdered, it was almost certain that she would expect advice and possibly practical help from Sukey herself.

Such negative thoughts were swept away as she opened the door and saw Jim standing there with his briefcase in one hand and a bunch of freesias in the other.

'How lovely, you're early!' She buried her nose in the flowers and sniffed in appreciation. 'Thank you, darling, they smell heavenly.'

'Not half as heavenly as you do.' He dropped his briefcase, hung his jacket over the newel post and drew her close. 'Mm, delicious,' he murmured, nuzzling her neck.

'Careful, you'll squash them,' she said happily, wriggling out of his embrace. 'I'll go and put them in water and then I'll get dressed. I haven't started to get supper yet. Do you mind eating cold – or were you thinking of going out?'

'No hurry about getting dressed; just deal with the flowers

and then I'll tell you what I'm thinking of,' he said softly. Her body responded to the innuendo with a surge of desire that made her knees tremble and her hands fumble with the vase that she was holding under the tap so that half the water spilled into the sink. She reached for scissors to cut away the wrapping, but he took the flowers from her and dropped them as they were into the water. 'You can arrange them later,' he said and the surge became a tidal wave.

When the telephone rang half an hour later it never occurred to either of them to answer it and it was only when at last they went downstairs and began to think about food that Jim spotted the light flashing on the answering machine.

'Whoever called earlier has left a message,' he said. 'Do you want to play it back? It might be Fergus.'

'I doubt it. He phoned not long before you arrived to say they were staying on at the camp until tomorrow. I'll check it later.'

'You never know, it might be important,' he said and without waiting for her to respond he pressed the button to start the message. To her dismay, it was from Sabrina.

'Just thought I'd let you know I had a long chat with Elspeth and we find we've got quite a lot in common,' she said. 'We've worked out a plan and we'd like to discuss it with you. We think we might need your help. Would you ring me when you've got a moment?'

The message ended and Jim reset the machine. The silence that ensued lasted several seconds. Sukey took salad ingredients from the refrigerator and began washing them at the sink, trying to think of something to say that would not sound lame and apologetic. It was Jim who spoke first.

'You were going to explain how you managed to bring those two together,' he said.

'It wasn't all that difficult,' she replied, busy with the salad spinner and avoiding his eye. 'Sabrina claimed her father kept her at arm's length and denied her any affection, while Arthur had been bleating to Elspeth that his only child refused to have anything to do with him. Once they realized he'd been less than honest with both of them, they naturally wanted to know why – hence their willingness to meet and get it sorted. It sounds as if they've managed it.'

'So what's all this about a plan, and needing your help?'

'How should I know? You heard the call.'

'You must have some idea.'

'What is this – some kind of inquisition?' She spoke lightly to conceal her irritation at the unwelcome turn of events. She tipped the prepared salad into a bowl and began dressing it with oil and vinegar. 'I've got Sabrina off your back, so I don't see why you should be concerned.'

'I'm concerned about you. It sounds very much as if she's not only still trying to prove her father was murdered, but also that now she's got the fiancée on her side the pair of them are trying to get you involved.'

She put the salad aside and brought out packs of cold meats and cheese. 'Will you unwrap those while I warm up some soup?' she said.

'You haven't answered my question.'

'Which was?'

'Why do you have to be so evasive? You know very well what I'm getting at, but I'll spell it out if you insist. What do you suppose they're planning and what kind of advice and help do they expect from you?'

'I'm not being evasive. I've told you, I don't know until I've spoken to them. And for the record, I'd like to remind you that I'm not a suspect, you aren't on duty and you've no right to cross-examine me like this.' To her chagrin, Sukey felt her throat tighten and her eyes start to prickle. Only a short while ago, she and Jim had shared an hour of sheer ecstasy. Hearing Sabrina's message had changed him from an ardent lover to an interrogator. She compressed her lips and turned away from him.

He must have sensed that he had pushed her too far. He put down the pack of ham that he had been about to open, took her by the shoulders and turned her to face him. 'Darling, I didn't mean to upset you,' he said in a more gentle tone. 'It's just that you have a habit of getting caught up in situations that lead you into danger.'

'Aren't you being just a little paranoid? What possible danger is there in getting Sabrina and Elspeth to talk to each other?'

'On the face of it, none, but you never know what it might lead to.'

'Just the same, it doesn't mean you have a right to know about everything that happens when I'm off duty.'

'All right, I'm sorry. I didn't mean to sound bossy, but will you promise me something?'

'What?'

'That if what these two women are plotting strikes you as being fishy, you'll let me know. Not as a policeman, just as someone who cares about you. Please?'

His face was very close to hers and she felt her resentment melting away. 'All right, I promise.'

'That's my girl.'

'Right, let's get on with the food,' she said. 'Shall I do a couple of jacket potatoes in the microwave?'

'Aren't you going to make that phone call first?'

Sukey felt her hackles rising again. 'I wasn't thinking of calling back this evening,' she said.

'Why not?'

'Because I want my supper, and anyway I'd rather leave it until—'

'Until I'm not around to hear what you say, I suppose.'

'If you must know, yes. I don't want you breathing down my neck while I'm talking to Sabrina.'

'You mean you don't want me to know what arrangement you come to with her? I thought we'd agreed—'

They were back to square one and it was time to get things straight. 'Jim,' she said quietly, 'I've promised I'll let you know if there's anything fishy going on, as you put it. That doesn't mean I'm giving you carte blanche to monitor everything I say and do.' She met his eyes without flinching; this time, he was the one to back down.

'OK,' he said. 'Jacket potatoes will be great.'

*   *   *

When Sukey reached home at the end of her shift the following afternoon, Fergus had returned from his camping trip and was busy stuffing the contents of his kitbag into the washing machine.

'Did you have a good time?' she asked.

'Great, thanks. How was your weekend?'

'OK. I went to the pictures with Mandy on Saturday. Jim was on duty most of the weekend, but he popped round for a couple of hours yesterday.'

'There's a message from Sabrina, by the way. She wants to know why you didn't reply to her earlier message. Has something happened while I've been away?'

'She's had a meeting with Elspeth and wants to tell me about it. Not only that, she's talking about a plan, and they want my advice.'

Her son's eyes lit up. 'That's great! I was afraid we wouldn't hear any more about it. Why didn't you return her call?'

'Because Jim was here and wanted to know what was going on. It got a bit edgy and I had to tell him to back off.'

'That was bad luck,' said Fergus. 'But you are going to speak to her, aren't you?'

'Of course. I'll do it now, while you're making us a cup of tea.'

'Oh, right.' Fergus reached for the kettle and Sukey picked up the phone.

It rang several times before Sabrina answered. 'What took you so long?' she demanded.

'I couldn't call while I was at work,' said Sukey, trying not to sound impatient. 'What's all this about a plan, and what do you want me to do?'

'It's . . . well, the fact is that after we – Elspeth and I that is – had talked for a while, we both realized that neither of us knew very much about my father. I'd had so little contact with him, and she'd known him for only a few months. It was obvious he hadn't levelled with her about me, or with me about her either. We think there may have been a reason why . . . anyway, we want to find out more about him and we're

65

wondering if you can help us. To find out whether . . .' at this point Sabrina's voice became hoarse with what sounded like embarrassment as she went on, 'whether perhaps he was . . . known to the police.'

'The police? Why on earth—'

'The fact is,' Sabrina interrupted, 'I haven't been entirely honest with you.'

'In what way?'

'I think I told you my father's sister – my Aunt Pru – came to live with us after I was born, to look after me.'

'Well?'

'That was only partly true. When I was about five – just before I was ready to start school in fact – we moved back to Aunt Pru's house and I lived there with her until she died. When I asked my aunt why we didn't live with Dad any more I never got a straight answer.'

'I'm sorry, I don't understand,' said Sukey. 'Why are you telling me this? Do you think it was because your father was in trouble with the police and they were trying to protect you?'

'I didn't say he was in trouble with the police exactly, only that he might have been known to them.'

'For what reason?'

'I . . . I'd rather not tell you . . . at least, not at the moment, not until I know for certain.'

'Are you saying that this has got something to do with your belief that someone murdered him? Because if you've got any evidence—'

'That's just the point, I haven't, not yet. Look, Sukey, if I tell you where he was living and what his job was, can you find out for me? You've got contacts with the police and—'

'I'm sorry, but no,' Sukey interrupted. 'I work for the police but I'm not a member of the CID and even if I were I couldn't start that kind of investigation without authority.'

'But I have to find out.' There was a note of pleading, almost of desperation, in Sabrina's voice. 'Elspeth wants to know as well. It was your idea that we started asking around.'

'I never said anything about taking an active part in your enquiries,' Sukey pointed out.

'Are you saying you won't help us?'

'I can't possibly do what you asked.'

'So what can we do? Haven't you any ideas?' Sabrina was plainly on the verge of tears; despite her anxiety to detach herself from the situation, Sukey could not help feeling sorry for her.

'I suppose you could try going through the local papers at around the time you think this may have happened,' she suggested, speaking more gently. 'Or you might be able to track down one of their reporters who might remember something. You'd have to give them a lot more information than you've given me,' she added pointedly, but Sabrina failed to take the bait.

'And if that doesn't work, what else can I do?' she asked.

'If it's that important to you, I suppose you could engage a private detective. That can be pretty expensive, though.'

'I told you once before, the money isn't important. I have to know. I'm sorry to have bothered you.'

There was a click and the line went dead. 'Well, what do you know!' Sukey exclaimed as she replaced the receiver.

'So what was that all about?' Fergus wanted to know. When she told him, his eyes sparkled with excitement. 'I just knew there was something fishy about that old boy!' he exclaimed. 'What a pity she never gave you any gen about where he lived or what his job was.'

'What difference would that have made? It would be interesting to know, of course, but—'

'It would mean we could do a little nosing round on our own without having to tell her.'

'Gus, don't you dare even think about it,' Sukey said sternly. 'Jim would go ballistic if he got to hear about it. Anyway, what about that tea you were supposed to be making?'

'Oh, right. Coming up.'

The pair of them sat musing in silence over their tea for several minutes. After a while, Sukey said, 'I wonder if

Sabrina's hoping to find out something that would show he was trying to protect her.'

'What from?'

'I don't know. All I know for certain is that it's desperately important for her to be able to believe that he did have some feeling for her.'

'Some guilty secret from his past, perhaps?'

'I suppose it's possible.'

'I seem to remember suggesting something like that and being shot down in flames,' Fergus reminded her slyly.

'So you did. Well, I suppose you could be right.' Sukey finished her tea, took her mug to the sink and rinsed it under the tap. 'Poor Sabrina, I feel really sorry for her – and for Elspeth – but I doubt if we'll ever know the full story.'

Ten

D espite having forbidden Fergus to do any private 'nosing around' as he put it, and her own assertion that they were unlikely to hear anything further about the early life of Arthur Soames, Sukey found herself hoping every time the phone rang during the next couple of days that it would be Sabrina calling to tell her that she and Elspeth between them had unearthed some significant piece of information.

The same thought had evidently been running through Fergus's mind, as over their meal on Wednesday evening he said casually, 'Why don't you give Sabrina a call to see how they're getting on?'

'To be honest, I've been tempted once or twice,' she admitted, 'but I'm afraid that if I show too much interest she'll have another go at getting me involved – especially if they haven't made any progress.'

'I've been thinking,' he went on. 'The lady I spoke to at St Bartholomew's the other day said Arthur was writing a book about the church. We know he was a teacher; maybe he wrote history textbooks.'

'So?'

'So maybe they're still in print.'

'What if they are? They're hardly likely to be autobiographical.'

Fergus gave a sigh of mock exasperation. 'Mum, you're not being very bright. Most books, especially academic ones, contain some information about the writers – you know the sort of thing, what degrees they hold, what their background is and so on.'

'Of course they do! And in Arthur's case, maybe what schools he taught at. Gus, take a Brownie point!'

'Thank you. Why don't we look him up on the Internet?'

As soon as they had finished their meal they went to the computer. Fergus logged on and entered the name of Arthur Soames. Within seconds the search engine came up with a list of half a dozen history textbooks under the imprint of a well-known scholastic publishing house.

'Bingo!' he exclaimed in triumph. 'Why don't you pop into a bookshop in Gloucester and order a copy of one of them?'

'At those prices? You've got to be joking.' Sukey had been studying the details under each title. 'Besides, they're all pretty old. The most recent was published nearly fifteen years ago. They're probably out of print by now.'

'It's worth a try. Tell you what, I'll go to the library tomorrow and look them up on their catalogue.'

'Aren't you going to work?' While waiting to start his degree course in October, Fergus had found a temporary job at a local supermarket.

'Yes, but I finish at four and the library's open till five. Gosh, Mum!' His face shone with enthusiasm. 'Wouldn't it be great if we could crack the mystery before Sabrina and Elspeth?'

'Now who's being dim?' she said with an indulgent smile. 'Aren't you forgetting something?'

'What's that?'

'They have a head start on us. Sabrina must surely know what school her father taught at.'

His face fell. 'Yes, I suppose so,' he admitted.

'And for all our speculation,' she pointed out, 'there may not be a mystery at all.'

'So why should Sabrina drop those hints about the police? By the way,' Fergus gave his mother a searching glance, 'talking of the police, Jim hasn't been round once this week. You haven't fallen out with him, have you?'

Sukey shook her head. 'I've hardly seen him since Sunday. I know a couple of his people are on sick leave so he's been pretty busy.'

'You must surely see him around.'

'Only when other people are there. You know what he's like; discretion is his middle name.'

'So things are still all right between you?'

'Oh, sure.' She tried to sound confident, but privately she had begun to wonder why he hadn't been in touch.

Her first assignment the following morning was to examine the scene of a fire in a basement flat close to the city centre, which the police suspected had been started deliberately. She arrived just as the fire engines were driving away, leaving behind a sight typical of many that she had seen before yet never failed to find depressing: someone's home reduced to a soaking, smoke-blackened wreck. The charred remains of a teddy bear lying face down in sooty water gave this one an added poignancy.

'Was anyone hurt?' she asked one of the officers attending the scene.

'No, thank God, they all got out in time. A young mum and a couple of kids; the neighbours are looking after them.'

'You reckon someone had it in for them?'

'Can't be sure, but it looks suspicious.'

Sukey put on her protective clothing and set to work. By the time she got back to the office to write her report and send her samples to the laboratory for examination it was almost two o'clock. Absorbed in her task, she had forgotten about lunch. Rather than go to the canteen, she went to a sandwich bar a short distance from the station. As she returned with a cheese roll and a carton of fruit juice she all but bumped into DI Castle in the corridor. He gave a quick glance round, saw there was no one else about and took her by the arm.

'Sukey, I've been looking for you,' he said in a low voice. 'Come into my office for a moment.'

'If it's about the fire in Penfold Street, it was definitely arson,' she said. 'There were traces of accelerant all over the place.'

'Never mind the fire,' he said, closing the door behind them. 'It's us I wanted to talk about.'

'What about us?'

'We've hardly exchanged two words since the weekend.'

'I had noticed.'

'Are you still mad at me?'

'I thought it was the other way round.'

'I seem to remember being told to back off.'

'Only because you started laying down the law.'

'So I'm not permanently out of favour?'

'Don't be silly.' She lifted her face with the intention of giving him a quick kiss by way of reassurance, but he took a hasty step backwards.

'Not here,' he said, and she almost burst out laughing at his horrified expression.

'Sorry,' she said in an exaggerated whisper. 'Are you free this evening?'

'As it happens, yes.'

'Then come to supper.'

'Love to. Shall I pick up a takeaway?'

'Fine. Make it Indian for three.'

Things were back to normal. Sukey went back to the SOCOs' office with a spring in her step.

When she arrived home that afternoon she found Fergus in the kitchen. He was poring over a somewhat dog-eared, battered-looking book, which he held up as she entered with the air of a sportsman brandishing a trophy. '*A Brief History of the Tudors* by Arthur Soames MA,' he exclaimed. 'It was the only one in the local branch and they had to dig it out of their archives. It's the most recent of the titles they used to stock; the woman who found it for me said the earlier ones had fallen to pieces and been thrown out. It's been borrowed quite a few times, but not for ages,' he went on, showing her the record inside the front cover. 'I've been reading bits of it – it's quite jolly. Old Arthur had a sense of humour. Henry the Eighth was a real goer, wasn't he?'

'I thought we knew that already.' Sukey dumped her bag in the corner and took the book from him. 'Does it tell us anything useful about the author?'

'At the time this was published – about fifteen years ago – he was teaching at Priory Park School in Bracknell.'

Sukey thought for a moment. 'I wonder if he was still there when he retired. Gus, can you remember how long he'd lived in Gloucester?'

'The obituary said ten years.'

'And he was sixty-eight when he died, so he must have retired at least that long ago, maybe earlier.'

'So?'

'So he took early retirement. I wonder why. And another thing,' she went on, 'it's generally thought he came here from London. Bracknell's hardly London, is it?'

'What are you getting at, Mum?'

'Only that he doesn't seem to have been telling the entire truth about himself.'

'He could have moved to London when he left Bracknell, before he decided to come to Gloucester.'

'Which would mean he retired even earlier.' At that moment the doorbell sounded. 'That'll be Jim; I invited him to supper. Better put that book away, Gus, or he'll start asking questions.'

It felt good having Jim there again, sharing a drink and a meal, chatting with Fergus about his university course and answering his questions about crimes currently under investigation by the CID. For the most part Sukey was happy to sit back and let them do the talking; she realized as the evening wore on that it was the first time for several days that she had felt completely relaxed.

The telephone rang just as Jim and Fergus finished the washing-up and were putting the dishes away while Sukey made coffee. Fergus was the nearest; he picked it up, said 'Hello' and after a moment passed it to his mother. 'It's for you,' he said. 'Why don't you take it in the sitting room? I'll make the coffee.'

'Who is it?' she said, but he affected not to hear and she had an immediate premonition that she was about to receive unwelcome news.

Elspeth was on the line and she sounded agitated. 'Sukey, have you heard from Sabrina?' she asked.

'I spoke to her on Monday, after she left a message for me.'

'Not since then?'

'No. Why do you ask?'

'I'm worried about her. She rang me that evening to say she'd asked you to make some enquiries for her, and you'd said you wouldn't.' There was a note of reproach mingled with the anxiety in Elspeth's voice.

'I couldn't,' said Sukey, having first made sure the door was closed behind her. 'I explained I don't have access to police files, which is what she was after.'

'Yes, she told me that.' Elspeth's tone suggested that, in her opinion, Sukey could have stretched a point if she'd had a mind to. 'Anyway,' she continued, 'she then said she was going to make some enquiries of her own and she'd be in touch.'

'And?'

'I haven't heard from her since, and I'm worried.'

'It's only Thursday,' Sukey pointed out. 'Maybe it's taking longer than she expected.'

'I thought I'd at least get a progress report.'

'Did she give you any idea of where she was going to make her enquiries?'

'She said she was going to see someone in Bracknell. That's in Berkshire, isn't it? I wonder why—?'

'*Where* did you say?' Sukey broke in. Elspeth repeated the name and Sukey said, 'How extraordinary! Did she give you any details?' She was conscious of a movement behind her; glancing over her shoulder, she saw Jim standing in the doorway.

'Sabrina?' he mouthed. She shook her head and turned away from him, but he took a step forward and stood beside her. 'Who then?'

She made an impatient gesture at him and spoke hurriedly into the phone. 'Sorry, what was that?'

'I said, you sounded as if Bracknell meant something to you.'

'I . . . I'm sorry, I can't talk now. I'm sure she'll be in touch soon. I'll call you tomorrow.' She switched off the instrument and said angrily, 'Really, Jim, aren't I allowed to have a private telephone conversation in my own house?'

'It's obvious it's something you don't want me to know about or you wouldn't have gone off to take that call in secret. Fergus said he didn't know who was calling, but I'm not sure I believe him.'

'I don't care whether you believe him or not. What right have you to poke your nose in anyway?'

'I thought we agreed you'd tell me if you were getting involved in something dodgy. In case you hadn't noticed, I happen to have your well-being at heart.'

'And in case you've forgotten, I promised to tell you if there was something I thought you should know. So far, there hasn't been, so please get off my back.'

For several seconds they stood glowering at one another. Then he said, 'Sook, I'm sorry. I didn't mean to sound officious, but I worry about you. You mean more to me than anything in the world,' he added, almost humbly.

Her anger melted away and she put her arms round him. 'All right, I forgive you,' she whispered. 'So long as you bear in mind that you can boss me around all you like at work, but not when we're off duty,' she added after a short, enjoyable interlude.

'I'll bear it in mind,' he promised, 'but I reserve the right to renege if you get out of hand.'

Eleven

That evening, as they were locking up for the night, Fergus said, 'Doesn't Jim trust me any more?'

Sukey looked at him in surprise. 'What do you mean?'

'He all but accused me of lying when I said I didn't know who was phoning you earlier.'

'And were you?'

'Sort of. I mean, she didn't give a name, but I guessed it was either Sabrina or Elspeth. Anyway, I thought it was up to you to tell him if you wanted him to know.'

'He thought at first it was Sabrina. Actually, it was Elspeth, but I didn't say who it was. In fact, I more or less said it was none of his business.'

'Good for you, Mum. I don't like to think of him bossing you around.'

Sukey gave him a quick hug. 'I know, love, but it's only because he cares.'

'I suppose so.' Fergus appeared only partly convinced. 'He doesn't usually keep a check on your phone calls, does he?' he said. 'I wonder why he's so edgy.'

Sukey frowned and shook her head. 'That's what I've been asking myself. It's almost as if he shares Sabrina's suspicions about the death of her father, but won't admit it because there's no evidence.'

'If that's the case, you'd think he'd tell you.'

'And give me an excuse to play detectives? That's the last thing he'd do. Just the same,' she went on musingly, 'there's obviously something bugging him. Ever since I persuaded Sabrina to give up haunting him at the station, he's never missed an opportunity of questioning me about her. Which is odd, considering he seemed only too glad to have her off his back.'

'What did Elspeth want, by the way?'

'She's worried because she hasn't heard from Sabrina since Monday.' Sukey repeated the conversation up to the point when Jim interrupted her.

'But that's amazing!' Fergus exclaimed. 'What's the betting she's trying to track down some of Arthur's former colleagues?'

'I'd say it was a racing certainty, but it doesn't explain the silence. I played it down, but it does seem surprising that she hasn't been in touch and I could tell Elspeth's seriously worried. I said I'd call her tomorrow; let's hope she's heard by then.'

'It looks as if Sabrina thinks someone from his past had something to do with his death,' said Fergus.

'It does, doesn't it?'

'I seem to remember suggesting it a while back and being laughed out of court,' he said slyly.

Sukey grinned back at him. 'Touché,' she admitted. 'Well, Gus, you could just be right. It'll be interesting to hear what she has to say when she comes back.'

'She might not feel like telling you,' he pointed out. 'Your saying you couldn't help her wouldn't have made you flavour of the month.'

'True, but I'm pretty sure we'll hear, one way or the other.'

Had Sukey realized how prophetic her words would turn out to be, or had the slightest inkling of the terrifying events that lay ahead, she would have slept less easily that night.

'Any news of that misper you were telling me about last week?' DCI Lord, known throughout the department as Charlie on account of his short stature and small black moustache, looked up from the toffee he was unwrapping and cast an enquiring glance at DI Castle. 'The one your girlfriend was getting so exercised about? Want a sweetie?' he added, offering the bag.

Jim shook his head. 'Not for me, thanks. You mean Sabrina Soames?'

'That's the one.'

'No, not a word. The last we heard, she said she was going to visit a school in Bracknell. We've established that her father taught there many years ago and we assume she was hoping to pick up something that would confirm her insistence that he was murdered. I got DS Chen to have a word with the headmaster. He confirmed she called on him on Tuesday of last week, but he had no idea what she was talking about. It seems she got quite worked up and he had some difficulty in persuading her to leave. He put her down as a hysterical woman with an obsession. Which has been my impression all along,' Jim added. 'I've told Sukey to keep out of it.'

Lord raised a sardonic eyebrow. 'You reckon she'll take any notice of you?'

Jim shook his head. 'Hanged if I know. She's being a bit cagey about things in general just lately.'

'Anyway, who reported the Soames woman missing?'

'The woman who was engaged to marry her late father.'

'I thought you said those two weren't on speaking terms.'

'They seem to have joined forces to track down Arthur Soames' killer.'

Lord groaned and put a hand over his eyes. 'Oh no, not another nutcase! Why can't they accept the coroner's verdict? His death was an accident.'

'They don't believe it.'

'And now the daughter's gone AWOL. Any idea where she might be?'

'None at all – unless, having drawn a total blank, she's crawled off somewhere to be alone with her grief. From what I saw of her, she seemed to be in a very precarious mental state. Let's hope she hasn't done anything foolish.'

'Who's her next of kin?'

'I don't think she has any. If she hadn't been prepared to identify her father's body, we'd have had to ask the fiancée and she wasn't having that.'

'What about her GP?'

'I've no idea who she was registered with. Do you want me to find out?'

'It wouldn't do any harm. People are always saying we don't take their concerns seriously enough. Get your little oriental tottie to check it out. The one who's sweet on you,' he added, his black eyes twinkling.

'What?' Jim's jaw dropped in astonishment.

'Oh, come on, man, you can't be that lacking in perception. Everyone else has noticed, including Sukey, no doubt. You'd better watch your back, my lad!' He began unwrapping another toffee. 'Talking of missing persons, I take it there have been no sightings of Janice Burlidge.'

'Not a glimpse since her husband took a plane for Barcelona,' Jim agreed. 'We've asked the Spanish police to look out for him, but no luck as yet. His stepdaughter is still convinced he topped her mother before skipping the country, but we've no leads at the moment.'

'Oh well, keep trying.' Lord threw his screwed up toffee paper into the bin and closed the file that lay open on his desk. 'OK, Jim, I think that's all for the time being.'

As Castle stood up to go, Lord's telephone rang. He picked it up, listened, let out a muttered, 'Good heavens!' listened some more and then said, 'Right, I'm on my way.' He put the phone down and got to his feet. 'Just as I was beginning to think I was in for a quiet Monday.'

'What is it?'

'A group of ramblers have discovered a female torso in a ditch near Westington. Naked with her head missing.'

Jim whistled. 'Perhaps they've found Janice for us.'

'Could be. Uniformed are at the scene and George Barnes has scrambled a couple of SOCOs.'

'My God, I hope he hasn't sent the women!' said Jim. The prospect of Sukey being confronted with such a grisly sight filled him with horror.

Lord gave a malicious chuckle. 'Scared your ladylove will have nightmares? That's all right, you can be her comforter when she wakes up screaming in the small hours!' He grabbed his jacket and headed for the door. 'Come on, let's go. You drive.'

The spot where the walkers had made their gruesome discovery was in woodland bordering a lay-by on the A38, which was already occupied by several police cars. Castle pulled in behind them and he and Lord got out and hurried over to where half a dozen or so women in walking gear were clustered around one of their number who was half-sitting, half-lying on the ground. Her face was streaked with mud and her trousers were soaked to the knees. She was shivering violently and repeating over and over again, 'A body . . . no head . . . oh, dear God, someone cut off her head!' A woman officer was squatting beside her, holding her hand and trying to soothe her, while a second, whom Castle recognized as Sukey's friend Trudy Marshall, was urging her dazed and shocked companions to stand back and give her some air.

'The lady lying down is the one who found the corpse, sir,' said a uniformed sergeant who was waiting by a stile with a sign indicating a public footpath. 'As you can see, she's in severe shock, so we've called an ambulance. Doc Hillbourne has been to look at the body and made some notes, but he said there's nothing more he can do till he gets it back to the morgue.'

'Well, we know our pathologist is a genius, but we can hardly expect him to stick the head back on, even if he could find it,' said Lord drily. 'Here come the first-aiders,' he added as an ambulance, blue lights flashing, pulled up alongside the other vehicles. A couple of paramedics jumped out and ran over to the shuddering, weeping woman on the ground. Lord beckoned to the policewoman who had been comforting her. 'What's your name?'

'PC Jean Forbes, sir.'

'Right, Jean, tell me what you know about this.'

'Well sir, it's not been easy to find out exactly what happened because, as you can see, she's pretty incoherent. We gather from the others that she was a bit ahead of them; the path is slippery and muddy after all the rain we've had lately and they were watching their step. Next thing they heard a yell and they looked up in time to see her fall into the ditch. They ran to help, but before they got to her she started screaming like a banshee and pointing at something in the water that turned out to be the nude body of a woman. That was bad enough, but when they realized the head was missing . . . you can imagine the shock they had. One of them called us on her mobile while the rest brought her back here. They're all pretty upset, but she's the worst affected. I gather she found the body by grabbing hold of the leg as she fell.'

'Nasty,' said Lord laconically. While they were speaking, the paramedics had produced a blanket in which they wrapped their patient before escorting her to the ambulance. 'No hope of a statement from her just yet,' he went on. 'Find out where they're taking her and then go and help Trudy get statements from the others.'

'Right, sir.'

Lord turned back to Castle. 'Come on, Jim, let's have a look at the goner.'

As they clambered over the stile, Castle glanced over his shoulder and saw Sukey's van pulling in behind the police cars. He would have given anything to hang back so that he could at least give her an encouraging word or two, but Lord was forging ahead, cursing volubly at the tangle of brambles and weeds lying across the narrow track.

'Someone should chase the council about this jungle,' he complained.

'It'd be even worse if the ladies hadn't trampled some of the brambles,' said Castle, pausing to detach a thorny stem from his trouser leg.

'Not only the ladies.' Lord pulled up short and looked about him. 'The killer must have used this path – there isn't any other.'

'He could have approached from the opposite direction.'

'Good point. It might help us if he did; assuming this happened after the rain, there'd be more chance of finding his prints in the mud. Not much hope of finding anything this side after all the comings and goings. I wonder how far this path goes until it comes to another road.'

'Uniformed will find out while they're securing the scene,' said Castle, pointing to a group of shirt-sleeved figures who were looping yards of blue and white tape round the trees at the far edge of the wood.

They moved forward again, keeping as close as possible to the side of the path, partly to preserve possible evidence and partly to avoid losing their footing on the treacherous surface. Some way ahead, two more uniformed officers were waiting for them. As they approached, one took a step forward and pointed. 'There she is, sir. Not a pretty sight, is she?'

Lord grunted. He and Castle moved gingerly towards the edge of the ditch and peered down at the corpse. It was lying on its back, barely submerged in the brownish, stagnant water. It was evident that the ditch had had no attention for some considerable time, for its surface was partially obscured by overhanging branches, thick growths of weed and floating leaves and twigs brought down by the previous night's heavy rain. It would, Castle reckoned, have been possible for walkers, more concerned with where to take the next step than to look around them, to have passed by without noticing the horror almost literally at their feet. The thing might have lain undiscovered for days, even weeks, but for one woman's mishap.

They stood for several seconds without speaking. Jim felt an uncomfortable sensation in his stomach and even the hard-bitten Lord looked shaken. 'There is a willow grows aslant a brook,' the DCI quoted, half to himself. After a moment he added, 'I think I prefer the Millais version of the death of Ophelia.'

Castle took a deep breath. 'Me too,' he agreed.

Twelve

'The SIO says you're to keep off the footpath,' said the sergeant who was guarding the crime scene, 'and don't go tramping around under the trees either.'

Sukey and her fellow SOCO, Mandy Parfitt, exchanged glances. 'So how do we reach the body, Sarge?' Sukey demanded.

'Levitation?' he suggested, without a flicker of a smile.

'We've sent our wings to the cleaners,' said Mandy. 'Any other bright suggestions?'

'Or you can turn left on the other side of the stile,' said the sergeant, still poker-faced, 'and walk straight ahead till you come out of the wood. Make sure you keep close to the wall; there's to be a fingertip search of the area when you've done your stuff.'

'So how will we know where to look?' asked Sukey.

'Go along the edge of the field and a nice policeman will be there to tell you where the body is. Want a hand with your gear?'

'Thanks, Sarge.' They clambered over the stile and he handed them their equipment.

'There you go, ladies. Mind you don't get your feet wet . . . and don't go losing your heads!' This time he allowed himself a throaty guffaw.

Mandy rolled her eyes skywards as they set off. 'Sergeant Grymm, the original laughing policeman,' she sighed. 'Still, if you're stuck with a name like that, I suppose you have to keep your spirits up somehow.'

'I guess so,' Sukey agreed. They might find the waggish

sergeant irritating at times, but this was an occasion when the slightest touch of humour, however weak, was a help in preparing them for what they both knew would be a nerve-racking experience.

'I wonder if this is the missing wife?' said Mandy.

'You mean Janice what's her name? Could be. The absentee husband is a butcher, so he'd have the wherewithal to slice her head off.'

'I suppose the bastard reckoned it would make identification more difficult.'

They walked in silence for several minutes. The sky had cleared after the weekend's rain and the sun was still high, making the air hot and humid. The ground rose quite steeply in places and there was a considerable amount of undergrowth that made their progress, encumbered with their equipment, frustratingly slow. When they reached the field they ducked under the tape and followed it until, about a quarter of a mile ahead, they saw the two uniformed officers who had been guarding the spot until the process of securing the scene was complete and who had now withdrawn to the edge of the wood.

'It's just down there, in the ditch,' said one, pointing through the trees. 'The SIO said to check the path in both directions after you've taken your pictures of the body. That way –' he jerked his head towards the main road – 'the mud's been thoroughly churned up by the walkers, but he reckons you might still find the odd shoe print at the point where she entered the water that doesn't belong to any of them. There are a few clearer ones from the other direction that he wants recording.'

'How much further on does the path go?' asked Mandy.

'About a couple of hundred yards. It comes out by the entrance to some farm buildings.'

'And then what?'

The officer shrugged. 'There's a lane the other side. Whoever dumped her could have come from either direction. DCI Lord wants to know which looks the most likely, so see what you can turn up for him.'

'We'll do our best.'

Keeping their eyes open for anything significant, the two
SOCOs picked their way carefully through the trees until they
reached the path. The mud had been churned into a quagmire
and a wide lateral rut, heading straight for the edge of the
ditch, pinpointed the spot where the woman who found the
body had slipped and fallen.

'I suppose she stepped aside to avoid that tree.' Mandy indicated a young ash sapling leaning across the path, effectively
halving its width. 'You'd think she'd have gone to the other
side of it, wouldn't you?'

'Or at least hung on to it as she squeezed past,' said Sukey.
'We're going to have a job getting close enough to the edge
without falling in ourselves.'

'The others must have managed it when they pulled her
out. Their boots were caked in mud, but I didn't notice anyone
else who'd taken a ducking.'

'It looks as if they did it there.' Sukey pointed to a spot
further back towards the stile where weeds and mud at the
edge of the ditch showed signs of disturbance.

'I guess we'll have to get almost to the edge,' said Mandy.
'Why don't we put down a couple of stepping boards?'

They bridged the path with the boards they had laboriously
carried and, side by side, advanced cautiously until they had
a clear view down into the shallow water. Sukey's stomach
contracted and she swallowed hard; Mandy gagged and put a
handkerchief to her mouth. 'Poor cow!' she whispered.

'She looks like something out of a Pre-Raphaelite painting,'
said Sukey, unconsciously echoing Lord's initial reaction.

Mandy nodded. 'Or a water nymph in some Celtic legend.
Except for . . .' She turned away, unable to go on.

The woman lay full length on her back, her legs stretched
out in front of her and her arms by her side. Her body was
only just submerged and every detail was visible: the gingery
pubic hair; the full breasts; even the scarlet lacquer on her
toenails, highlighted by a shaft of sunshine glancing through
the trees. At first glance the figure had an almost surreal

beauty . . . until the eye registered the greenish colour of the swollen abdomen and the stump of neck where the head should have been.

Sukey swallowed again, took a deep breath and said, 'I suppose we'd better get on with it. Any ideas how I get near enough to take some shots without falling in?'

Mandy thought for a moment. 'Suppose I hang on to the tree with one hand and your waistband with the other, will that do it?'

'Let's give it a go.'

Ten minutes later, after one heart-stopping moment when Mandy almost lost her grip on the tree, Sukey declared that she had enough pictures. Thankfully, they retreated to firmer ground and waited there for a few moments to recover their breath and cool off. By now their sweat-soaked T-shirts were clinging to their bodies and their mouths were dry. They stood in the shade of the trees and slaked their thirst from the bottles of water they both carried.

'What now?' said Mandy, wiping her mouth with the back of her hand.

'Check for prints, I guess. All the walkers are women, so any larger than the others might have been left by the killer.'

'Or Messrs Lord and Castle.'

Sukey grinned. 'Good point.'

After a few minutes, during which Sukey photographed some prints that might or might not prove useful, they began checking in the other direction. They walked carefully through the carpet of weeds fringing the path, keeping a sharp lookout on either side.

'Looks like two people, probably a man and a woman from the size of the prints, walked this way from the farm end.' Sukey squatted down to take photographs. 'They had a dog,' she added, indicating a trail of paw prints. 'There aren't any going the other way, so they didn't go back. They must have plodded on as far as the stile.'

'Not much chance of picking out their prints in that morass,' Mandy commented.

'Anyone carrying a body would have left deeper prints,' said Sukey thoughtfully. 'Until they'd dumped her, of course, and then—'

Mandy chuckled. 'There you go again. You're supposed to collect evidence and leave the detecting to the detectives, remember? Shall we press on?'

'OK.'

A short distance further on they came to the yard and farm buildings the officers had mentioned. This too was cordoned off with blue and white tape and another officer was keeping guard. Here the ground consisted of hard core overlaid with coarse gravel. Apart from a few shallow puddles, it was dry.

'Not much chance of finding anything here,' Mandy commented.

'What about that?' Sukey had spotted a dark, iridescent stain on the gravel near the end of the track. 'Isn't that oil?'

Mandy walked over to inspect it. 'Looks like it,' she agreed. 'If the killer brought her this way, he'd probably have parked here. The oil could be from his car.'

They were getting fired up now. Sukey photographed the patch and collected samples of the stained gravel while Mandy took measurements and made a sketch. Then they walked a short distance along the lane in both directions to check the distance to the nearest dwelling and estimate the chances of anyone living there having noticed any unusual activity in the farmyard.

'If he did come this way, it must have been before the weekend,' Sukey said. 'It didn't start to rain until the small hours of Saturday morning.'

'What made him carry the body so far along the path?' Mandy wondered.

'I suppose he wanted it to remain undiscovered for as long as possible.' Sukey put her camera back in her bag. 'I guess that's all we can do for now. Shall we get back?'

'In a minute,' said Mandy. 'I need another drink.' She took out her bottle of water, sat down on a trailer and mopped her brow. 'Gosh, it's hot!' Her face was flushed and her short auburn curls clung damply to her forehead.

'It's getting really steamy,' Sukey agreed. She glanced up at the sky. 'It's clouding over; we could be in for more rain.' She took out her own water bottle and sat down. 'I wouldn't mind a nice cool shower.'

'Nor me,' Mandy agreed. 'I've been thinking,' she went on. 'We've assumed that as there weren't any likely-looking prints this end of the path, either the killer brought the body here before the rain or he came from the other end.'

'Right.'

'It would have been pretty risky heaving a body out of a car parked on a main road, even in the middle of the night. And we've found what could be traces of his car this end of the path.'

'So?'

'So maybe he didn't use the path at all. Maybe he humped it the short distance between here and where it was found by going through the woods. In which case he'd have been sure to leave traces.'

'Now who's playing detectives?' said Sukey mischievously. 'Are you going to mention it to DI Castle?'

Mandy grinned. 'Not likely. Leave it to the fingertip brigade to figure it out. Anyway, a lot will depend on Doc Hillbourne's estimate of how long she's been in the water.'

Sukey winced. 'You know what? I'll probably have to go to the morgue to take more shots of her. We'd better be getting back.'

When Sukey reached home that afternoon she was emotionally as well as physically exhausted. Photographing the headless woman through a veil of water had been harrowing enough; having to repeat the process in the clinical atmosphere of the morgue had been an even worse ordeal. Instead of going straight into the kitchen as usual to share a pot of tea and an account of the day's events with Fergus, she went upstairs, stripped off her clothes and stood for a long time under the shower until she felt at least partially cleansed. When she came downstairs Fergus took one look at her and said, 'Mum, you look shattered. Have you had a heavy day?'

'It has been pretty grim,' she said with a shudder, recalling the wrinkled, macerated flesh of the dead woman's hands, the discoloration of her decomposing flesh and, worst of all, the hideous stump where her neck ended, every detail of which the pathologist had insisted she record. 'We think we may have found the body of Janice Burlidge.'

'The woman who hasn't been seen since her husband did a runner to Spain?'

'That's the one. She . . . he'd cut off her head.'

'Gosh!' His mouth fell open. 'And you found her? That must have been nasty for you.'

Sukey grimaced. 'It's going to be even nastier for whoever finds the head.'

'I suppose they can't be sure it's her until it's found.'

'They can do DNA tests. I believe she's got a sister and a sixteen-year-old daughter – they can get samples from one of them. Anyway, let's not talk about it any more. Has anything interesting happened at the supermarket today?'

Fergus chuckled. 'Oh boy, did we have a drama! Our security guys arrested a shoplifter; he broke away, ran for it and tripped over a dog that had been tied up outside. He went sprawling and broke the bottle of Scotch he'd nicked.'

'I hope the dog wasn't hurt,' said Sukey.

'Not hurt, but not best pleased either; it took a nip at the thief's leg while he was lying on the ground. When he stood up he found he'd cut his hand on the broken glass and when they handed him over to the police he was threatening to sue the dog's owner and demanding compensation from the security company for his injuries.'

They laughed together at this absurdity and Sukey felt the tension subsiding. 'How about a cuppa?' she suggested.

'I'll make it,' said Fergus. 'Oh, by the way, there's a message from Elspeth. She still hasn't heard from Sabrina and she's in a fine old state. She says she must speak to you.'

'Oh no, now what?' Since Elspeth's agitated message a week ago there had been no word from her and Sukey had assumed that Sabrina had turned up without either of them bothering to let her know. 'OK, I'll call her while you make the tea.'

Elspeth sounded beside herself. 'I just don't understand it; I'm sure something's happened to her,' she said. 'I reported her missing last week; I told the police she'd gone to Bracknell but I didn't know why, and they said they'd found someone she'd spoken to – a schoolmaster they said – but he didn't know where she went after that. They really weren't very helpful at all.' Her voice rose to a thin, protesting squeak.

'I'm sorry to hear that,' said Sukey patiently, 'but unless there's something you haven't told me, or the police, there's nothing to suggest any harm's come to her. The thing is,' she went on quickly, before Elspeth could begin another tirade, 'you've only known Sabrina a very short time, and as far as the police are concerned you're not really in a position to officially report her missing.'

'That's more or less what they told me, so I thought I'd make some enquiries of my own,' said Elspeth. Her voice was firmer now, although slightly breathless. 'I went to her house and spoke to a neighbour.'

'And?'

'She said she saw Sabrina go out on Tuesday morning. She said she was out all day, at least, when she came home at eight o'clock her car wasn't on her drive, but it was there when she looked out of her window on Wednesday morning.'

'Well, at least she didn't have an accident on the way home.'

'So why hasn't she been in touch?'

'I don't know. Maybe she's decided it's all been a wild-goose chase and she's been making a bit of a fool of herself.'

'I don't believe it! You're being no help at all!' Elspeth said angrily and slammed down the phone.

'Oh dear!' Sukey went into the kitchen and reported the conversation to Fergus over their delayed cup of tea. 'I honestly don't see there's any more I can do to help,' she said.

'I've been thinking,' said Fergus. 'You'll probably think this is a daft idea, but this body you've been dealing with today – the one you're all assuming is Mrs Beef the Butcher's Wife. Suppose it turns out to be Sabrina?'

'Gus, get real. Someone who killed an old man by pushing him downstairs – even supposing that's what happened to Arthur Soames – is hardly likely to be a mad knifeman who carves up his next victim.'

Fergus grinned, a little sheepishly. 'I guess not.'

But a little later, as Sukey was preparing their evening meal, she found herself reliving her first sight of the murdered woman. She recalled her own remark, likening the figure to a Pre-Raphaelite painting, and Mandy's response: 'Or a water nymph in some Celtic legend.' She was conscious of a chill feeling in her stomach.

'Oh heavens!' She stopped dead in the act of scraping a carrot.

'What's up?' asked Fergus. She told him how Sabrina had come by her name. 'Wow!' he exclaimed. 'That's really spooky!'

Thirteen

The following day Sergeant George Barnes was in his most ebullient mood.

'Morning troops!' he said breezily as Mandy and Sukey entered the office. 'I'm afraid today's assignments aren't quite so exciting as yesterday's.'

'I think we can live with the disappointment,' said Sukey.

'And I'll be quite happy with a few break-ins with no damage to property and nothing missing,' said Mandy.

Barnes grinned. 'A bit tough on the nervous system, was it?'

Sukey winced at the memory of the previous day's experience. 'About the worst ever, I'd say.'

'Well, there's nothing in this lot to give you the willies.' He held out a sheaf of computer printouts. 'There you go. I'll leave you to sort out between yourselves which of you deals with what. If you're thinking of having a coffee before you set off . . .' he added hopefully, fishing out some coins from his pocket and offering them to Sukey, who happened to be nearest.

'OK, Sarge,' she said. 'I'll get them while you sort out the jobs, Mandy.'

They drank their coffee, divided the assignments between them according to their location and left the office. On their way down to the yard to collect their vans, Sukey told Mandy about the call from Elspeth and Fergus's semi-serious suggestion that the body in the ditch might have been Sabrina's. Mandy's initial reaction was the same as her own: even if they accepted that Arthur Soames' death was not accidental, the manner in which the unidentified woman had met her end was hardly in the same league.

'I'm sure that's right,' Sukey agreed, 'but later on I suddenly remembered how you'd compared the body to a nymph in a Celtic legend and it gave me quite a jolt. I'm not sure if I ever told you, but Sabrina says her aunt named her after a Celtic river goddess. It seems the old girl was superstitious and thought it might protect her niece against death by drowning.'

'What a bizarre idea.'

'According to Dalia Chen, she said it had something to do with the fact that her father told the aunt she could throw the baby in the river for all he cared.'

Mandy's eyes widened. 'The wicked old bugger!' she exclaimed.

'She says it was because her mother died when she was born and he blamed her.'

'It'd be ironic to end up dead in a ditch after all that.' Mandy shuddered. 'It's kind of spooky, isn't it?'

'That's what Fergus said.'

'But you don't seriously believe—'

'No, of course not, but somehow it seemed like a sort of omen. Maybe Elspeth's right, maybe something has happened to Sabrina.'

'Has she reported her missing?'

'Yes, but she says the police haven't been much help.'

'They probably don't consider she knows Sabrina well enough to say whether her silence is a serious cause for concern.'

'That's what I told her. She said they did take some action, but didn't get anywhere. I've a feeling they won't do any more unless she can produce some compelling reason to think Sabrina's come to harm.' Sukey glanced at her watch. 'Look, we'd better get on. I'll tell you more about it at lunchtime.'

As George Barnes had predicted, the morning's assignments presented few challenges. Among Sukey's were a smashed window and items stolen from a car parked at a well-known beauty spot, a garage broken into and a quantity of food stolen from a freezer, and a theft of cash from a small village shop. She spent some time there lifting prints from the counter and the till, watched in open-mouthed fascination by the proprietor's children.

'Well, it's given them a bit of excitement,' the woman remarked with a rueful smile as Sukey packed up to leave. 'They're dying to get back to school and boast about it to their friends. At least, he didn't get away with much – it was too early in the day. Now if it had been later . . .'

'Did they see it happen?' Sukey asked.

'No, and they're very miffed about it,' the woman said, looking fondly down at her offspring, who were clustered round her like chicks with a mother hen.

'Well, if we manage to get a lead on the culprit, we'll let you know,' Sukey promised.

The robbery at the shop was her last job. She called the office, learned that nothing more had come in and contacted Mandy on her mobile phone. 'I'm through for the moment,' she said. 'How about you?'

'I'm just about finished.'

'Let's meet somewhere for lunch. I want to talk to you.'

They ate their sandwiches sitting on a bench at the top of Crickley Hill while enjoying one of the most spectacular views in Gloucestershire. The late summer sun picked out glimpses of the River Severn; beyond it rose the Welsh hills, smoke-blue against a cloudless sky. While they drank coffee from their flasks, Sukey outlined the plan that had been slowly taking shape in her head during the morning.

'The more I think about it, the more I believe Elspeth is right,' she said. 'Something has happened to Sabrina.' She described the research that had led her and Fergus to the knowledge that Arthur Soames had been the history master at a school near Bracknell. 'Elspeth already knew that and she told the police she thought that's where Sabrina was going the day she disappeared. She said they'd spoken to someone at the school – presumably the headmaster – but they "weren't very helpful at all" as she put it. So she's been doing a bit of sleuthing herself.'

Sukey described Elspeth's visit to Sabrina's house and her conversation with one of the neighbours. When she had finished, Mandy said, 'If you ask me, she's realized she's been barking up the wrong tree and she can't bring herself to face anyone.'

Sukey nodded. 'I wondered about that, but I still think it's a cause for concern. Suppose she's in a serious state of depression . . . she might do something silly.'

'I don't see what you can do about it.'

'Things are pretty quiet at the moment. Suppose I tell George I've got toothache and my dentist has given me an emergency appointment. I could go and have a scout round at Sabrina's house, perhaps have a word with the neighbour Elspeth spoke to. Or maybe,' Sukey added as a further wild notion came into her head, 'Sabrina's left a window open somewhere; the weather's been pretty warm lately. If she is there, licking her wounds, I might persuade her to talk to me.'

Mandy's mouth opened and she stared at Sukey in consternation. 'Are you crazy?' she exclaimed. 'If anyone here got to know about it you'd be in all kinds of trouble, lose your job even.'

'All right, forget I said that. But you do agree there is some cause for anxiety?'

'I suppose so,' Mandy said grudgingly.

'So back me up when I call in tomorrow and tell George I've lost a filling.'

It seemed only fair to let Elspeth know of her plans, but Sukey was dismayed by her reaction.

'That's a wonderful idea!' she enthused. 'I'll come with you; I can introduce you to the neighbour and explain that you're with the police and—'

'I'm sorry, but no,' Sukey interrupted firmly. 'What I'm doing is completely off the record and this is strictly between ourselves.'

'But I want to help!' Elspeth's tone was almost piteous.

'I'm sorry,' Sukey said gently. 'Either I go alone or not at all.'

'Oh, very well,' Elspeth sighed. 'You will let me know what you find out?' she pleaded.

'Of course.' *Always supposing there is anything to find out,* Sukey added mentally as she put the phone down. Already, she was having second thoughts about the wisdom of what she was doing.

Although Sabrina's house had an integral garage, it appeared that – in common, Sukey observed, with several of her neighbours – she did not always bother to put her car away, for the sleek new Citroën was, as before, standing on the drive. An air of prosperity about the neighbourhood in general and Sabrina's house in particular seemed to support her claim that she was not motivated by a need to get her hands on her father's money.

Sukey walked up to the solid, white-painted front door and rang the bell; when there was no response she hammered on the heavy iron knocker, again without success. She checked the downstairs and upstairs windows; despite the warmth of the day, they were all tightly closed although windows of several of the neighbouring houses were open. The flowers in the hanging basket were drooping as if in need of water. It was safe to assume that there was no one in. *No one alive, at least,* said an uneasy voice in her head.

She decided to try the neighbour, whose name, according to Elspeth, was Mrs Wingate. Before she reached the front door it opened and a neatly dressed woman of about fifty appeared and said, 'If you're looking for Miss Soames, I'm afraid she isn't home. Are you a friend of hers?'

'Not exactly; I'm making enquiries on behalf of a mutual friend,' said Sukey. 'She's been trying for the past week to get in touch with Sabrina and she's afraid she might be ill or had an accident, or something.'

'Would that be the lady who was here the other day?'

'That's right.'

'Well, I don't know that I can tell you any more than I told her.' Mrs Wingate scrutinized Sukey with intelligent grey eyes. 'Are you some kind of detective?' she asked.

'In a way, but this isn't an official inquiry, I'm here as a favour to Elspeth . . . Miss Maddox,' said Sukey, hoping Mrs Wingate wouldn't press her further. 'I understand you saw Sabrina – Miss Soames – go out in her car on Tuesday morning.'

'That's right.'

'Do you happen to know what time she got back?'

'I'm afraid I don't. All I can tell you is that her car was there when I went out on Wednesday.'

'What time would that have been?'

'About half-past ten, I think. I can't be certain.'

'And you haven't seen or heard from her since?'

'No.' A troubled expression clouded Mrs Wingate's pleasant face. 'I've wondered once or twice whether I ought to pop round and see her, invite her round for a cup of tea or something. She has seemed very down lately, ever since her father died.'

'So I understand.' Sukey hesitated for a moment before saying, 'Forgive me for asking, but how well do you know her? I mean, does she ever confide in you?'

Mrs Wingate shook her head. 'Not really. We aren't what you could describe as close friends, just friendly neighbours. She's what people describe as a very private person.'

'She told me she does some work at home for a publisher of travel books and that she travels quite a lot herself. I take it she hasn't recently mentioned any plans to go away?'

'No, but I'm sure she would have done because I keep an eye on her house when she's away, pick up her post and so on.'

'You mean you have a key?'

'Well, yes.' Mrs Wingate hesitated. 'I've been wondering if I should go in and look around, just in case she's ill or something. Would it be all right, do you think? If you wouldn't mind coming in with me . . .'

As this was exactly what Sukey had in mind from the

97

moment the key was mentioned, she jumped at the suggestion. 'Yes, of course,' she said.

Mrs Wingate went back into her house and came back shortly
afterwards with two sets of keys. She used the first to lock
her own front door, explaining that, 'You can't be too careful
nowadays, there are some funny people about,' before joining
Sukey by Sabrina's front door. She opened it and stooped to
pick up several letters that lay on the mat before calling,
'Sabrina! Are you there? Are you all right? It's Pam.' There
was no reply. She called again with the same result. 'It's very
strange,' she said, looking down at the letters with a worried
frown. 'She never told me she was going away. What do you
think we should do?'

'I think perhaps we should take a quick look round the
house,' said Sukey. 'Just in case she's ill in bed and too weak
to answer,' she added, as Mrs Wingate appeared to hesitate.

'I'm not sure which is her room,' she said doubtfully. 'I've
never been upstairs.'

'We'll soon find it. You lead the way.'

Five minutes later they had checked every room in the house.
Everything was in perfect order and all the internal doors were
closed, but there was no sign of Sabrina. The windows were
securely fastened, the back door leading from the kitchen into
the garden was locked and the key hung from a hook beside
it. On a small table in one corner were a telephone, a small
personal directory and an appointments calendar, the latter
still open at July.

'Maybe this will give us a clue,' said Sukey. She ran her
eye over the few entries. 'On Tuesday the thirty-first, the day
you last saw her, she had an appointment with a Mr Bellmore
at Priory Park School. I presume that's in Bracknell – at least,
she told Elspeth Maddox that's where she was going.' Earlier
entries for the month included one reading 'EM, 7.30' on the
twenty-eighth and on the tenth a doctor's appointment with
'check-up' beside it. On the seventh was an entry reading 'see
MB' but no time or other information. She turned over the
page, but there were no entries for August.

'Do you happen to know what doctor she goes to?' she asked.

'I've no idea,' said Mrs Wingate. 'All I can say is that quite a few people round here are registered with the practice in Cherry Orchard Road.'

'If this is anything to go by, she didn't have much of a social life,' Sukey remarked. They went back outside and Mrs Wingate closed the door behind them.

'Well,' she said, her smooth brow puckered in a frown, 'she's obviously gone away again, but without her car. I can't understand why she never said anything to me,' she added with a touch of resentment.

'Are you sure the car hasn't been moved since Wednesday?'

'No, I don't think so, but . . .'

'But what?'

'Unless she's going out again, she usually backs it into her garage instead of leaving it on the drive, but as you can see, this time she drove it straight in. Still, if she got home very late on Tuesday night she was probably too tired to bother, or maybe she didn't want to make a noise opening and shutting the garage door.'

'The car looks brand new,' Sukey remarked. 'Has she had it long?'

'Only a few weeks, but I believe she's had some trouble with it already. Something about an oil leak. I'm afraid I don't know much about cars,' Mrs Wingate continued, almost apologetically. 'My husband used to do all the driving and since he died I've had to use taxis. The car's still in the garage and I keep telling myself it's a bit pathetic and I really should do something about it.' She chattered on about the possibility of taking driving lessons, but Sukey barely heard. The reference to an oil leak had been enough to switch her mind back to the stain that she and Mandy had noticed near the ditch where the headless and so far nameless body lay. A vague suspicion, barely considered seriously until now, began to harden into an ugly premonition.

'Do you happen to know where Sabrina kept her keys?' she said.

'I think she hangs them behind the front door. Why do you ask?'

'I'd like to check inside the car. If we could find the key . . .'

'Let's have a look.' Mrs Wingate made a move back towards the house and then stopped and turned back to the car. 'Oh, how silly of me! I never even checked to see if it was locked,' she said and reached for the handle of the driver's door.

'Don't touch it, please!' Sukey said sharply.

Mrs Wingate looked startled and her hand froze. 'Why not?' she said.

Sukey pretended not to have heard the question. 'I'm sorry, I'm afraid that must have sounded rude. May we please see if we can find the key?'

They found it on a small rack just inside the hall. Sukey was wearing her work clothes; among various small items that she kept in the pockets of her denim jacket was a pair of latex gloves. She put one on, lifted the key from its hook and went back to the car. She unlocked it and took a quick glance round. There was a faint, chemical smell characteristic of the interior of a new car and, as was to be expected, the upholstery and all the instruments and controls were immaculate. She took out a small flashlight and made a closer examination. Some fragments clinging to the mat in the driver's footwell caught her eye and she lifted a few of them with a pair of tweezers. 'Gravel,' she muttered under her breath. She found a small plastic envelope and dropped the fragments inside. Next she inspected the tyres, picked out several more pieces of gravel and bagged them up as well.

She squatted down and shone her flashlight under the front of the car; yes, there was a small patch of oil on one of the paving slabs. Finally, she opened the boot. All it contained was a first-aid kit; like the rest of the car, it smelled of newness. She closed the lid carefully and relocked the car.

'What is it?' asked Mrs Wingate, who had been standing by, watching Sukey's every move. 'You're looking very worried. Is there something seriously wrong, do you think?'

'I think there may be. The thing is,' Sukey said, choosing her words carefully to avoid causing unnecessary alarm, 'I'm beginning to think Sabrina didn't drive herself home on Tuesday night.'

'Oh dear! I wonder what that means?'

'It could mean one of several things. One possibility is that she was taken ill and someone drove her to hospital in her own car and then brought it home for her. If this is a spare key, he might have taken the other one with him so that he could use it to go and fetch her.' It was not, she felt, a particularly likely scenario, but Mrs Wingate accepted it without question.

'Well, if that's the case, they might have let someone know,' she said, a little huffily. 'Here we are, all worrying about her, just for the want of a phone call. Is there some way we can find out, do you think?'

'Leave it with me and I'll see what I can do.'

'I do wish you would. If I give you my phone number, will you let me know if you get any news?'

'Yes, certainly.' Sukey jotted down the number, thanked Mrs Wingate for her help and drove back to Gloucester. She spent the time it took to reach the station trying to decide what to do next.

Fourteen

O n Wednesday morning, while Sukey was using her ficti-
tious dental appointment to pursue her unofficial enquiries
into Sabrina's disappearance, DI Castle was summoned to the
DCI's office. Lord waved him to a chair.

'Morning Jim, sit down. We've had Doc Hillbourne's
preliminary report on the torso in the ditch. He estimates her
age as thirty-five to forty, but he hasn't been able to establish the cause of death yet. All he can be sure of is that it
wasn't by drowning.'

'I reckon that's a fair assumption,' said Castle drily.

'He adds that she'd had at least one pregnancy, but he can't
say whether it resulted in a live birth – and she certainly wasn't
pregnant at the time of death.' Lord handed the single type-
written sheet across the desk. 'Here, have a look for yourself.'

'I see he's taken samples for DNA and poison testing,' said
Castle after skimming through the report.

Lord nodded. 'We've asked him to do what he can to get
the results through quickly. As you can see from his notes,
he reckons the body was put in the water within hours after
death and had been there no longer than six or seven days.
Meanwhile we've got people out combing the area for the
head – sorry, no pun intended – but it's unlikely to be anywhere
near where the torso was found.' He took a slab of chocolate
from his pocket, broke off a section and popped it into his
mouth. 'What's the betting some poor sod walking his dog
will trip over it and have nightmares for weeks?' he added
with a touch of malicious glee.

'You'd have thought decomposition would have been further

advanced after a week in view of all the hot weather we've had lately,' Castle remarked.

'Yes, the Super raised that point. Hillbourne said the water would have had a cooling effect, which would slow things down. Plus all that rain over the weekend, of course.'

Castle handed the report back to Lord, crossed his legs and locked his thin fingers round his knee. 'Well Philip, from what we know so far, it could be Janice Burlidge, couldn't it?' he said.

'Could well be. The approximate time of death ties in with her disappearance, and she's the right age group.'

'It's a pity Hillbourne can't tell us how long ago she gave birth,' Castle remarked.

'Or whether she even gave birth to a live child,' Lord agreed. 'Still, it's a start.'

'I understand the fingertip search of the woods hasn't yielded anything.'

'Not a sausage. The patch of oil the SOCOs found suggests the killer accessed the path from the end furthest from the main road. I think it's safe to assume he dumped the body before the rain came and washed away any prints he might have left.'

'And no news of the husband?'

'Not a sniff.'

'Have the Spanish police been alerted?'

'Oh yes. They're being quite helpful, but no sightings so far.'

'Apart from the stretch marks on the abdomen there's no reference in the report to any distinguishing marks on the body – moles or scars for example.'

'That's something else the Super queried. It seems there are a few minor things that might mean something to anyone with what Hillbourne described as "an intimate knowledge of her body". The missing husband, for example.'

'Fat chance at the moment!' Jim commented. 'What about the other family members – or her GP?'

'There's only the sister and the daughter. The sister lives

in Canada; she's been told Janice is missing but hasn't any plans to come over to help with the search. I understand she's lived out there for years and they've never been very close anyway. Her GP couldn't help – Janice seems to have been a very healthy lady and there's nothing in her medical records to give us a clue. As for the daughter, looking at a headless torso would be a pretty harrowing ordeal for a sixteen-year-old, whether it turned out to be her mother or not. I think on balance it would be kinder to await the DNA results – unless, of course, the head turns up in the meantime.' Lord slid the report into the file on his desk and ate some more chocolate. 'So, what have you got to report, Jim? Has the Soames woman turned up yet?'

'No, but DS Chen has tracked down her GP and she had a word with him.'

'Was he able to help?'

'Not much. Dalia said he was quite definite that he knew of no reason why she should go walkabout. The last time he saw her was six months ago when she complained of difficulty in sleeping and he gave her a prescription.'

'What for?'

'He wouldn't say. Patient confidentiality and all that. Fair enough, I suppose; she isn't officially posted as missing.'

Lord frowned. 'So we're no further forward?'

'No, but Dalia said she had the impression that he was a bit uncomfortable at being questioned. Nothing she could put her finger on, just a feeling; she said he seemed relieved when she got up to go.'

'Well, we've done as much as we can in the circumstances.' Lord finished his chocolate bar and threw the wrapper in the bin. 'Tell the Maddox woman to let us know if she comes up with anything significant. My own feeling is that Sabrina has gone to ground for some reason of her own and she'll turn up again in her own good time. Right, Jim, I think that's all for now. Keep me posted.'

Castle emerged from Lord's room just as Sukey was walking along the corridor to report to George Barnes. 'Ah, Sukey!

I'd like a quick word with you,' he said in his official voice. 'Come into my office for a moment.' A little uneasily, she obeyed. Her disquiet increased when he asked, 'Have you had any further news from Elspeth Maddox? Has she heard from Sabrina Soames?'

'Not that I know of,' she said cautiously. 'Why do you ask?'

He repeated DCI Lord's conclusions and it was with considerable relief that she undertook to pass the message to Elspeth. Assuming that the brief interview was over, she moved towards the door, but he put a hand on her arm and said, 'How did you get on?'

She experienced a stab of alarm. Had he somehow got wind of the morning's escapade? Surely not. 'Get on?' she repeated.

'At the dentist? Was it painful?'

Her mind had been so focused on the morning's events that she had forgotten the pretext she had used for arriving late. 'Oh, that. Not too bad, thank you; it's just a bit tender.' By way of reinforcing the deception, she put a hand up to her face.

It was evident that he had noticed her momentary hesitation. He gave her a searching look and said, 'Is something else bothering you?'

His greenish eyes seemed to bore into hers and she found herself fumbling for a reply. 'No, nothing.' Conscious that the denial sounded unconvincing, she followed with a defensive, 'Why do you ask?'

'I just wondered.' His face was full of concern. 'You seem a bit worried.'

'Do I? It's probably because I'm not quite over the shock of Monday. It was all rather gruesome.'

He gave a sympathetic nod. 'I'm sure it was. Knowing what you were in for, I'd have given anything to have spared you from seeing it.'

'Thanks.' There was relief as well as gratitude in her smile. 'Have there been any developments?'

'It's all negative at the moment; we don't know who she

105

was or how she died. We're still working on the probability
that it's Janice Burlidge, but we can't make a positive ID until
the test results come back – or until we find the head, of
course.'

Mention of the missing head brought the whole hideous
memory flooding back. He was standing close to her and she
felt a sudden longing to lean on his shoulder and feel his
comforting arms round her. Knowing there was no chance of
anything of the kind taking place in the office, she said softly,
'Jim, is there any chance of seeing you soon? I feel in need
of a bit of TLC.'

In the corridor outside there was the sound of approaching
footsteps and he tensed visibly and made a move towards the
door, reaching for the handle in readiness to open it if anyone
should knock. 'How about this evening?' he said hurriedly.
'Can you feed me or shall I bring something in?'

The footsteps went on past and she had to hide her amusement at seeing him relax again. 'No need for that,' she assured
him. 'I've already made a chicken casserole. There's plenty
for three.'

'Wonderful. See you later.'

Before leaving at the end of her shift, Sukey went over to the
lab and had a word with one of the technicians, who, she knew
from experience, was not of a particularly curious disposition.
She gave into his keeping the samples of gravel she had taken
from Sabrina's car and asked him to compare them with
samples taken near the spot where she and Mandy had found
the patch of oil. He showed no reaction when she asked him
to give the results to her personally, and not to mention the
tests to anyone else.

'Elspeth rang at about half-past four,' said Fergus when she
arrived home. 'She sounded in a bit of a state. Maybe she's
only just heard about the mystery of the headless woman and
jumped to the conclusion it's Sabrina.'

'I'll give her a call in a minute. I have to speak to her
anyway; I've been unofficially instructed to tell her the police

don't intend to take any further action unless she can find some more evidence. She's not going to be best pleased to hear that.'

She moved to pick up the phone, but Fergus said, 'No point in calling yet; she was going out, didn't know what time she'd be back and she'll ring again later.'

'Damn!' She flung her bag on the kitchen table and went to the sink to wash her hands. 'Jim's coming to supper; what's the betting she'll ring when he's here?'

Fergus, busy with his customary task of making tea, gave her a curious look. 'What's going on that Jim shouldn't know about?' he asked.

'Sorry, Gus, I meant to tell you, but you were out late last night and there wasn't time this morning. I've been disobeying orders again.'

He listened with mounting excitement while she told him of her visit to Sabrina's house, her meeting with Mrs Wingate and the samples she had taken from the car.

'Gosh!' he exclaimed. 'That sounds like a real breakthrough. Why don't you want Jim to know?'

'Because it's all circumstantial and because I bunked off with a phoney story about the dentist.'

'But you can't leave it at that.'

'No, of course not. I've asked Adam in the lab to do a comparison, but he's not sure whether he can get hold of the originals.'

'Supposing he can't, what then?'

'I haven't thought that one through yet.'

'You could always go back to the same spot and pick up fresh samples,' he suggested.

Sukey gave an involuntary shudder. 'Perish the thought!' she said fervently.

'What if the body in the ditch is identified in the meantime?' Fergus went on.

'If it isn't Sabrina's I'll just forget it and hope no one finds out what I've been up to. If it is, I'll have to own up. Anyway, mum's the word for the time being.'

'If it does turn out to be Sabrina, you deserve a commendation for coming up with vital evidence,' he said proudly. 'You really are a whiz, Mum!'

'Thanks. Just remember, if the phone rings while Jim's here I'd like you to answer and if it's Elspeth say I'll call her back.'

'OK. Let's hope he doesn't smell a rat.'

A little after seven there was a knock at the door. When Sukey opened it and saw Jim she experienced a surge of emotion that took her completely by surprise. The events of the past few days had taken more out of her than she realized and she wept quietly on his shoulder while he held her close, stroking her head with one hand and murmuring, 'It's all right, it's a natural reaction.' Little by little she relaxed as her jagged nerves responded to his touch.

After a few moments she became calmer, dried her eyes and said, 'Sorry about that. Come in and have a drink. Dinner's almost ready.'

They sat in the kitchen while Fergus dispensed beer for himself and Jim and a glass of wine for his mother. Despite her warnings, he could not resist fishing for some information about the case that was uppermost in their minds. He picked up the evening's edition of the local paper and pushed it across the table. 'Are you really no further forward in the case of the woman in the ditch?' he asked, trying to sound casual as he indicated the headline reading, 'No Clues in Headless Torso Case'. 'Is it true you still aren't sure if it's the woman who went missing a week or so ago, Jim?'

'We're having to keep open minds; we think it may well be her, but so far we haven't found any hard evidence to back it up. We're waiting for the results of DNA and other tests.'

'How long will they take?'

Jim shrugged. 'We're trying to get them fast-tracked, but it could be several days.'

'Can't you tell us any more than that?'

'Gus, I think your mother has had enough of that particular case for the time being,' Jim said firmly. At that moment, the telephone rang and Sukey and Fergus exchanged glances.

'Will you answer while I dish up the veg?' said Sukey.

'Sure. I'll take it in the other room.' He returned a couple of minutes later; she gave him an enquiring look, but all he said was, 'It's the lady I told you about, the one who called earlier. It sounded urgent and I said you'd ring back as soon as possible.'

Fifteen

There was a moment's silence during which Sukey held her breath as she took a dish of carrots from the microwave and drained them at the sink. She braced herself for some searching comment or question from Jim, but none came. All he said was, 'Any chance of another beer, Gus?'

'Sure.' Fergus took a can from the refrigerator and handed it across the table.

'D'you want to put the lady out of her misery before we eat?' This time, Jim's voice sounded a little too casual. 'We don't mind waiting a couple of minutes, do we Gus?'

'Er, no, of course not,' said Fergus.

He shot an enquiring glance at his mother, but she shook her head. 'Not now,' she said firmly. 'I don't want the food to spoil. I'll call her later.'

Sensing that Jim had guessed that the caller was Elspeth, she was half expecting him to suggest she return the call once they had finished eating, especially in the light of their earlier conversation. It was, however, a relief that he did not refer to it again. Elspeth was undoubtedly impatient to learn the result of her visit to Bishop's Cleeve and fobbing her off without arousing suspicion could have been tricky. During the meal the subject of the body in the ditch had been carefully avoided and the conversation ranged over a variety of topics, but to Sukey's dismay, as soon as they were settled in the sitting room with their coffee, Fergus's insatiable curiosity got the better of him.

'Jim,' he said, 'how long d'you reckon it'll be for the test results to come through?'

'What test results?'

110

'About the woman in the ditch.'

Jim appeared to have forgotten his earlier refusal to answer further questions and replied without hesitation. 'They have to be sent away to a Home Office approved lab,' he explained. 'Normally they'd have to take their place in the queue, but the Super is pressing for them to be given priority. All I can add to what I already told your mother is that the pathologist says the woman had at least one pregnancy, which adds substance to the theory that it's Janice Burlidge. One thing we did learn during the afternoon is that there's been a possible sighting of the husband in a town on the Costa Brava.'

'Wow!' said Fergus. 'That sounds promising.'

'Maybe. We'll have to wait and see. A reported sighting's one thing; actually getting hold of the bloke for questioning is something else.' Jim glanced at the clock on the mantelpiece, put down his empty coffee cup and stood up. 'It's getting on for ten and I've still got things to deal with when I get home, so if you don't mind I'll be going now. Thank you for a wonderful meal, Sook – and thank you for being such a good barman, Gus.' By the front door, as Sukey helped him on with his jacket, he said, 'I've promised to visit my elderly aunt on Saturday, but maybe we can get together on Sunday?'

'That would be lovely.'

They clung together in a long, silent embrace. Then he said, 'Good night, love, see you Sunday,' and went to his car. With his hand on the driver's door he turned, opened his mouth as if to say something, changed his mind, got in and turned on the ignition. She waited until he had driven away before hurrying indoors and going to the telephone.

Fergus watched as she checked Elspeth's number before tapping it out. 'When that call came I was sure Jim would start asking questions,' he said.

'Me too,' she chuckled. 'I think he was going to say something as he was leaving, but he thought better of it.'

Elspeth had evidently been sitting by her phone waiting for

the call, for she answered immediately. Before Sukey had a chance to say a word she said angrily, 'Why didn't you phone before? Why didn't you tell me?'

'Tell you what?'

'That you've found Sabrina's body.'

'What are you talking about?'

'It's been on the television news – my neighbour told me. In a ditch, with her head cut off.' Elspeth's voice cracked and the sound of muffled weeping drifted over the wire.

'Now calm down, please,' said Sukey. 'The police are almost certain they know who the headless woman is, and it isn't Sabrina.'

'Are you sure?'

'As sure as they can be until there's been a positive identification. Didn't it say on the TV? It's in this evening's *Gazette* as well.'

'I'm only going by what Mrs What's-her-name told me. I didn't see the TV news and I don't read the local paper. What does it say?'

'The police believe it's the body of a woman who went missing about ten days ago. They think her husband is in Spain and the police there are looking for him.'

'Oh, thank God! I've been so worried. When you didn't phone I began to think the worst . . .' Elspeth was weeping again, but this time with relief.

'Yes, I'm sorry about that. I would have phoned earlier, but I've been a bit pushed for time.'

'Did you talk to Mrs Wingate?'

'Yes, and I understand the police have spoken to Sabrina's doctor. He couldn't explain her absence, but she doesn't seem to have had any health problems lately.'

'What's that got to do with anything? They aren't suggesting she's done some harm to herself?'

'No, but they seem fairly sure no one else has either. In fact, they've asked me to tell you they're confident she'll turn up soon.'

'You mean they've stopped looking for her?'

'I'm afraid so. They say there's not enough evidence for them to treat her as a missing person.'

'For goodness' sake! What does one have to do to be treated as missing?'

'It's a known fact that a lot of people disappear of their own accord.'

'But not Sabrina. She had a . . . a mission . . . it means so much to both of us!' Elspeth's voice threatened to break again, but she recovered and said, 'Did you and Mrs Wingate find anything interesting? Did you go into the house?'

'As it happens, we did; we were both concerned that Sabrina might have been taken ill.'

'And?'

'Everything was in perfect order and there was no sign of anything untoward having happened.'

'And you're going to leave it at that?'

'What else do you expect me to do?'

'I thought you were our friend . . . we trusted you to help us find out who killed Arthur and now—'

'Elspeth, believe me, I am your friend, but . . .' Sukey hesitated, at a loss as to what to say next. She had no intention of revealing the evidence she had collected from Sabrina's car until she had some positive results to report, yet she would have liked to give at least a small measure of reassurance that she was not abandoning the case entirely.

In the event, Elspeth solved the problem for her by bursting out, 'Oh, forget it, you're just like the rest of your lot!' and slamming down the phone.

The remainder of the week passed uneventfully. With the missing head as yet undiscovered and the results of the DNA and other tests still awaited, the police were unable to report any positive progress in their investigations and press interest switched to a gangland killing in another part of the county. The work of the Scenes of Crime Department returned to the normal series of minor incidents, of which the most spectacular that Sukey had to deal with was on Friday afternoon. A would-be burglar had fled empty handed after apparently cutting himself on the glass of the window he had broken to gain access to the house. This gave her the excuse she needed to visit the laboratory with the blood samples, but to her disappointment Adam was not on duty, so her hopes of a quiet word with him on the subject of gravel were dashed for the time being.

There was no further word from Elspeth, but on Friday evening Sukey was surprised to receive a telephone call from Mrs Wingate.

'I'm not sure whether I've done the right thing,' she began, a little nervously, 'and of course, there may be nothing in it, but . . .' She hesitated for a moment before saying, 'I think I might have a clue to where Sabrina has gone – or rather, to someone who might know.'

'Really?' Sukey said eagerly. 'Tell me more!'

'I'd been racking my brains ever since your visit, trying to think of anything that would help us trace her.'

'And?'

'As you know, I have her key and I keep an eye on her house and pick up her post when she's away and so on. This morning, I . . .' She hesitated again. 'I went into the house to . . . well, to have another look round. I hope you won't say anything to the police about this,' she hurried on. 'Perhaps I shouldn't have . . . I didn't poke around or disturb anything.'

'I'm sure you acted perfectly properly,' Sukey assured her. 'After all, she did trust you with her key.'

'Yes, she did, didn't she? So you think it's all right?'

Sukey felt her patience beginning to wear thin. 'Mrs Wingate, what is it you're trying to tell me?'

'There's a picture postcard from someone who's sent her cards before, someone who addresses her as "Auntie Sab" and signs herself "Annie Bee". That's B double E, like the insect,' she added helpfully.

'Where do the cards come from?'

'Different places. They're holiday postcards – this one's from Greece.'

'You're saying you think this Annie Bee might have some idea where Sabrina's gone?'

'It's possible, isn't it? The trouble is, I've no idea where she lives.'

'Does Sabrina keep a personal directory by the phone? Maybe she's in there – have you looked?'

'Well, no – I didn't like to. I was wondering if you . . .'

Sukey's interest had been quickening by the minute. 'You want me to come with you?'

'Would you?'

'Yes, of course. How about tomorrow morning?'

'When did this latest card arrive?' asked Sukey.

Mrs Wingate looked embarrassed. 'Actually, it was among the letters I picked up the day you were last here,' she admitted. 'I didn't think to look through them at the time . . . they seemed to be mostly junk mail . . . you know how it is.'

'Never mind.' Sukey studied the card a little more closely. It was a picture of the Parthenon, postmarked Athens and posted about two weeks earlier. The message was brief and uninformative: *Dear Auntie Sab, Having a brill time, weather fab but a bit too hot the day we climbed up here. I've had my first swig of ouzo (Dad wouldn't let me have a whole one to myself!). Lots of love, Annie Bee.*

'It doesn't tell us much, does it?' said Mrs Wingate.

'Annie sounds fairly young,' said Sukey thoughtfully. 'Her language and her handwriting are quite childish.'

'I suppose Bee is a nickname?' Mrs Wingate suggested.

'Or B might be the first letter of her surname,' said Sukey. 'Maybe there's another Annie in her form at school and her friends use it to distinguish between them. Let's check in Sabrina's phone book.' She picked up the personal directory that lay beside the telephone and checked under B. 'It's not much help,' she sighed. 'There's only one entry and that's a Dr Brinton. Would he be a partner in the practice you mentioned last time I came?'

'Yes, of course he is; I see him myself.' Mrs Wingate waxed

enthusiastic. 'He's such a wonderful doctor, and such a nice man. His wife's nice too, and they have a lovely little daughter . . . she's about six, I think, and the image of her Daddy.'

'You've met his family?'

'Oh no, but he has a picture of them on the desk in his surgery. I always enquire after them when I visit him . . . I think doctors spend so much time listening to other people's troubles and they appreciate it when someone shows a little interest in them.'

'Quite.' Sukey was beginning to find Mrs Wingate's loquacity a little wearing. 'I don't suppose you happen to know the little girl's name?'

'I'm afraid I don't. I could ask him on Monday if you like; I have an appointment to see him in the morning. It's just a routine check-up,' she ran on. 'He likes to see his woman patients of a, well you know, a certain age every so often, just to make sure everything's in good order.' She gave a self-conscious titter and then added earnestly, 'He's such a caring doctor and all his patients think the world of him.'

'I'm sure they do,' said Sukey. She had been riffling through the pages of the book while Mrs Wingate was speaking and was surprised at the small number of entries.

'Have you found something interesting?' asked Mrs Wingate on seeing her jotting down some of the numbers.

'I don't know until I've checked.' Sukey closed the book and put it back in its place. 'Thank you for your help. I hope your check-up is OK, and if your doctor's daughter's name is Annie, would you let me know?'

'Of course I will.' Mrs Wingate clapped her hands and beamed. 'Isn't this exciting? I'm so glad I phoned you – and I *do* hope Dr Brinton is able to help.'

'I hope so too,' said Sukey. She recalled that it was DS Dalia Chen who had spoken to Sabrina's doctor, and she resolved to have a quiet word with her as soon as possible. In the meantime, there was Sunday to look forward to.

Sixteen

It was one thing to resolve to speak to Dalia Chen about her visit to Sabrina's doctor; it was quite another to raise the subject without having a valid reason for doing so. If Dalia suspected Sukey of carrying out some unofficial enquiries into Sabrina's disappearance, she would almost certainly report her suspicions to DI Castle. And apart from not wanting any hint of her continued interest in the case to reach Jim's ears unless and until there was something concrete to report, she wanted even less to give Dalia the opportunity of any confidential chats with him.

She was so preoccupied with the problem that she twice failed to answer Fergus, first when he offered to make her some toast and later when he asked if she wanted tea or coffee.

'What's up with you this morning, Mum?' he asked. 'You're not sickening for anything, are you?'

'Huh?' She gave a start and dragged her mind back to the present. 'Sorry Gus, I was miles away. Coffee, please, and make it strong. Maybe a shot of caffeine will stimulate the little grey cells.'

'Have you got a problem?'

'In a way. I'm trying to figure out an excuse to call on Sabrina's doctor, but that isn't the real problem. It's Dalia – she's already been to see him and I'd really like her impressions, but I don't want her asking questions.'

'Why do you want to talk to him if Dalia's already eliminated him?'

'It's not a question of elimination. It's never been suggested that he had anything to do with Sabrina's disappearance. It's just that I think he may have known her personally.' She gave him an account of her visit the previous morning and Mrs Wingate's subsequent telephone call.

'And you don't want Dalia to know what you're up to because she's sure to go telling tales to your Mr Wonderful,' said Fergus flippantly.

'If you mean Jim, then yes.' Sukey gave an involuntary sigh. 'I wish I didn't like Dalia; it would be so much easier if I could hate her.'

'You don't really think he's attracted to her, do you?' said Fergus. This time there was a note of genuine concern in his voice.

'No, but I'm sure she's interested in him, and she sees much more of him during working hours than I do.'

'You're worried he might be susceptible to the oriental charm?'

'Maybe he – oh, I don't know!' Sukey made an impatient gesture. 'Let's not talk about that. Anyway, it's not the immediate problem.'

'You should have told me last night. I could have brought my massive brain power to bear on it and probably solved it for you by now.'

'I would have, but you were out on the tiles till some unearthly hour.'

'It was Saturday,' he pointed out. 'I went clubbing with some of the lads and I offered to be the driver.' Fergus had recently acquired an elderly but still serviceable Ford Escort of which he was inordinately proud. 'Don't worry, I was on fruit juice all evening,' he added virtuously as he put a mug of black coffee in front of her. 'Try that for strength.'

'Thanks.' She took a mouthful and gave an appreciative nod. 'Just what I needed. What are your plans for today?'

'Spending it with Anita. We're going to Stratford in the evening with her parents to see *Macbeth*. How about you?'

'Jim's coming round in the morning and we're going for a country walk and then having a pub lunch somewhere.'

'Sounds like fun. We're free during the day; would you like us to join you?'

'Er . . . if you really want to.'

Fergus burst out laughing. 'Oh Mum, if you could have seen the look on your face! I was only kidding.' He hesitated for a moment before saying slyly, 'I'm sure you'll find a way of taking Jim's mind off the lovely Dalia.'

She pretended to cuff him round the ear. 'That's enough of your lip, my lad.'

In the event, the problem was solved for her. It was Jim who raised the subject when, after a brisk walk in the Cotswolds and lunch at a village pub, followed by a blissful afternoon indoors, he went downstairs to put the kettle on.

As they sat on the edge of Sukey's bed drinking tea, he said casually, 'I don't suppose Elspeth's heard from Sabrina?'

'Not that I know of. I haven't spoken to her since last Wednesday. She was in a bit of a state because she was convinced the headless torso was Sabrina, but I managed to reassure her on that point. Then I gave her your message and she took it very badly. I tried to explain there was nothing more the police could do but she wouldn't listen; she just hung up on me.'

'Do you reckon she might be doing a bit of ferreting around on her own?'

Sukey gave him an enquiring look. 'What gives you that idea?'

'She didn't strike me as someone who gives up easily.'

'Jim, are you saying you think there may be something suspicious about Sabrina's disappearance after all?'

He hesitated before replying. After a moment, he said, 'Not exactly, but I keep remembering something Dalia said, after she'd spoken to Sabrina's GP.'

Sukey stiffened inwardly at the mention of Dalia's name, but replied calmly enough, 'Oh? What was that?'

'It was just that she had a feeling he wasn't happy at being questioned. "Uncomfortable" was the word she used.'

Sukey felt her pulse rate quicken. 'Did she have any theory about why this should be?'

'We didn't really discuss it, but it has crossed my mind since that perhaps he might have been giving Sabrina some treatment that he wouldn't want made public.'

'You mean over a drug addiction?'

'Or possibly an abortion.'

Sukey shook her head. 'That never occurred to me, but I suppose it's possible,' she said slowly. 'I certainly never noticed anything about her that suggested a drug problem, although she was in a highly emotional state. I suppose she might have been in the early stages of pregnancy, but I don't see why that should make Dr Brinton uncomfortable, unless—' She broke off suddenly and put a hand to her mouth as an entirely new thought struck her.

'You were going to say, "unless he's the father", weren't you?' said Jim quietly.

'That did occur to me.'

'It occurred to me as well. If the General Medical Council found out he'd had a relationship with a patient, he could be struck off.'

'Jim, you're surely not suggesting—'

'That he's had anything to do with Sabrina's disappearance? No, I'm not saying that, but he may know the reason and is protecting her, and possibly himself.'

'It doesn't really add up though, does it? As far as we know, all she and Elspeth are concerned about is finding out why Arthur Soames died.'

'That's true. The last we heard of her was that she had a meeting with someone in her dad's old school in Bracknell. It's just been niggling at the back of my mind, that's all. As if I didn't have anything else to think about,' he added with a rueful grin.

'Perhaps you'd like me to do a bit of detecting for you?' Sukey kept her tone light, but inwardly her excitement was mounting. It was fairly certain from the evidence of the post-card that the doctor and his family knew Sabrina personally.

Why, if the relationship was a perfectly innocent one, had he not been more open about it during Dalia's visit? All of a sudden, she was beginning to see him in a different light.

Jim drained his cup and leaned across Sukey to put it on her bedside table. Then he took her cup from her hand and put it beside his own, pulled her into his arms and began gently fondling her breast. 'Let's forget about detective work and talk about something else,' he said softly. 'Or better still, let's not talk at all.'

On Monday evening Mrs Wingate called Sukey to say that Dr Brinton's daughter was called Annie. 'He said – without my having to ask – that they call her Annie Bee because she's always busy at something. I asked him where he and his family went for their holiday,' she went on excitedly, 'and they went to Greece. Isn't that amazing? You are so clever, Mrs Reynolds. He said they'd had a wonderful time and Annie was just of an age to take an interest in the history and the culture and so on. It must be such an advantage to children whose parents take the trouble to show them these wonderful places. It all helps to widen their experience.'

'Did you happen to mention the postcard to Sabrina?' asked Sukey the moment she had a chance to get a word in.

'No, I didn't like to. Do you think I should have done? I thought it would have sounded as if I was being, well, nosey you know.'

'I'm sure you're right.'

'What are you going to do next? Please let me know if I—'

'No, that's fine, you've done brilliantly,' Sukey assured her. As tactfully as possible and after promising to let Mrs Wingate know if there were any developments, she brought the conversation to a close.

'Brinton.' The voice was clipped, impersonal.

'Dr Brinton, my name is Susan Reynolds,' Sukey began. 'You won't know me, but I'm a—'

'How did you get hold of this number?' Brinton interrupted. 'It's ex-directory.'

'I got it from Sabrina Soames,' Sukey said quietly.

Her reply brought about an immediate change in his manner. 'You've heard from her recently?' he said sharply.

'No. I was wondering if you had.'

'Not for some time.' He sounded deflated, almost disappointed. Then he reverted to his initial aggressive attitude and snapped, 'Anyway, what's your interest?'

'I believe you already know that her friends are very worried about her. She is trying to find out more about her father's death and we understand she recently made a visit to a school in Bracknell where he used to teach. That was two weeks ago and no one has heard from her since. Her friends reported her disappearance to the police and I understand one of their officers paid you a visit.'

'That's correct, although I don't see what it has to do with you. I told them that the last time I saw her was about six months ago when she came to my surgery for a prescription and I knew of no reason why she should disappear.'

'If that's the case, can you explain why there's an appointment in her diary to see you for a check-up on the tenth of July? There was also a reference to someone with the initials MB whom she was seeing on the seventh; would you have any idea who that is?'

He did not answer immediately and when he did he ignored the second question. 'She might have seen one of the other partners,' he said dismissively. 'I've been on holiday.'

'Ah yes, in Greece – but during the second half of the month, I believe, when your daughter sent a postcard from Athens to her Auntie Sab?'

This time the silence went on for so long that Sukey began to think the line had gone dead. Eventually he said in a low voice, 'I'd prefer not to continue this discussion on the telephone. Would you be willing to meet me somewhere?'

'How about at your surgery?'

'No, not there.' The suggestion appeared to fill him with

alarm. 'Do you know the Castle Hotel on the Evesham Road?'

'Yes.'

'Let's see, what time is it now? Seven o'clock. I have some things to attend to for an hour or so . . . can you be in the lounge bar at about eight thirty?'

'Yes, I can manage that.' Sukey jotted down the details. 'How will I know you?'

'I'm tall with grey hair and I'll be wearing navy cotton trousers and a linen jacket over a blue open-necked shirt. And you?'

'I'm five feet three with short dark curly hair and I'll be wearing a blue denim skirt and a white top.'

'Right, I'll see you then. And please don't mention this arrangement to anyone else.' He didn't add, 'the police, for example', but she was fairly certain that was what he had in mind.

'I don't like it,' said Fergus.

'Why not?'

'He may be up to something.'

'What sort of something?'

'I don't know. Suppose Sabrina was pregnant and was threatening to tell his wife? He might have killed her to shut her up and protect his professional reputation. Now you've let him know you've found out he knew her, he'll be afraid you're going to dig deeper and he might decide he's got to do away with you.'

'Well, he can hardly top me in the lounge bar of the Castle Hotel, can he?'

'No, but he might spin some yarn in the hope of putting you off the scent and then follow you when you leave to find out where you live . . . or run you off the road or something.'

'Gus, I think you're getting a bit melodramatic.'

'Am I?' His young features were taut with anxiety. 'I know you, Mum; you've stuck your neck out before and nearly come to grief.'

'Only nearly,' she retorted. 'But just to keep you happy,

I'll let him know before I leave him that you know where I am and who I've been meeting. That should put paid to any murderous ideas he may be harbouring.'

With that, Fergus had to be content.

Seventeen

If it was true that Sabrina had been having an affair with Dr Brinton, it was, Sukey thought, hardly surprising. He had the kind of features that would cause most women from eighteen to eighty to stare in open-mouthed admiration: chiselled, classical, aristocratic – and sexy. When he rose from a seat facing the door to greet her she felt the magnetism from the other side of the room. As they exchanged formal greetings and shook hands his steady grey eyes locked on to hers, but they held no trace of a smile.

'Please sit down, Ms Reynolds,' he said. 'What would you like to drink? I'm on vodka and tonic,' he added, indicating the glass on the table in front of him. Sukey noticed that it was already almost empty, although she had arrived punctually. Either he had been there for some time, or he was on edge and needed steadying.

'I'd prefer a glass of red wine, please,' she said.

'Coming up.' He went to the bar and gave the order. She glanced round; the lounge bar was almost deserted, probably because most of the guests were in the restaurant. Unusually for a hotel there was an absence of piped music, but from some other part of the hotel she detected the distant sound of a piano playing a theme from *Les Sylphides*.

Brinton came back with her wine and a refill for himself. He tipped the remainder of his first drink into the fresh glass, made a show of lifting it and said 'Cheers!' in a tone lacking cordiality. He took two long swallows before asking, 'How long have you known Sabrina? I don't recall her ever mentioning anyone called Susan.'

'Only since the death of her father.' Sukey hesitated for a moment before continuing, uncertain how much she was prepared to reveal. 'I happened to be at his house the day he died and I came into contact with her as a result. As I said, she's been badly affected by his death and I've been trying—'

'Yes, I know all about her problems – probably better than you do,' he cut in. His tone was curt to the point of rudeness. 'So what are you – a social worker?'

'No, not exactly.'

'What then?' His eyes had an almost mesmeric quality and she found herself shifting uneasily under their gaze. It was obvious from his next remark that, having had time to recover from the initial jolt the extent of her knowledge had given him, he had decided it was his turn to call the shots. 'I warn you,' he said in a voice as smooth and hard as tempered steel, 'that I'm not prepared to go on with this discussion unless you tell me exactly what your game is.'

Sukey glanced round the room. The few remaining drinkers, having been discreetly summoned by a waiter, had departed for the dining room and the only occupant was a bored-looking youth who was languidly polishing glasses behind the bar. Her son's misgivings came into her mind and in a sudden moment of panic she visualized herself being firmly escorted out of the room, bundled into a car, driven to a deserted spot and summarily despatched. Then she told herself not to be an idiot; Brinton's manner might be unnecessarily aggressive, but he was entitled to know what gave her the right to question him.

'All right, I'll come clean,' she said. 'I'm here because Sabrina and Elspeth – she's the woman who—'

'Yes, I know who Elspeth is,' he interrupted again. 'Just stick to the point; I haven't much time.' He glanced at his watch as he spoke and she guessed that he had arranged this meeting without his wife's knowledge.

'All right. They wouldn't accept the coroner's verdict and insisted there was something suspicious about Arthur Soames' death. When the police refused to open an investigation they – Sabrina and Elspeth, that is – asked me if I could help them.'

'You're a private detective?'

'I have been following some lines of enquiry on their behalf, and one of them has led me to you.'

'You haven't answered my question.'

'All right,' Sukey said again, 'if you must know, I work for the police. I'm a civilian Scenes of Crime Officer.'

'I see. I suppose that's how you came to know your employers paid me a call after Sabrina was reported missing? I let them believe that we had a normal doctor–patient relationship, told them she hadn't consulted me for six months and that I had no idea she was missing. Then you found Annie Bee's card and put two and two together.'

'That's about it, but the police don't know I'm making these enquiries.'

'I see.' Brinton appeared to relax on receiving this information and Sukey felt immediately that it had been an unwise thing to say. 'But my son knows about this meeting,' she added quickly.

He responded with a smile that was almost a sneer. 'So if you don't check in by a certain time he'll have half the police in the county searching for you!'

'Something like that,' she responded defiantly. 'And since your time is so limited, perhaps you can give me one good reason why I shouldn't inform them that you lied to Detective Sergeant Chen when she came to see you. I'm sure they'd be very interested.'

The directness of her retort brought another change of attitude. He lowered his gaze and fiddled with his glass before saying, 'The fact is, Sabrina and I . . . well, something happened between us that is frowned upon between a doctor and his patient. Something that could get me struck off the medical register if it came out.'

'You had an affair with her?' His shoulders twitched in a semblance of a shrug. 'And is that why she's gone into hiding . . . because she's pregnant?'

'Oh no! This was a long time ago. I don't know any more than you do about where she is and I'm as concerned as anyone. I swear to you that she hasn't told me anything about these enquiries you claim to be making, but I did see her on the days you mentioned and I gave her some mild tranquillizers because she was sleeping so badly.'

'Which you told DS Chen was six months ago.'

'I suppose it was an unwise thing to do. I don't know why I said it unless . . . I suppose it was because I was afraid something might come out about – oh, my God!' As he was speaking, a small tidal wave of little girls in ballet dresses erupted into the room from a door in the far corner and headed for the exit. There was an excited scream of 'Daddy! You came after all!' and one of the dancers broke ranks and headed for their table. Brinton's eyes seemed to glaze over as she rushed up and embraced him.

'I . . . yes, that is I . . .' For a moment he could do nothing but stare helplessly over the child's head at the slight, grey-haired woman who had followed her and was now wearing what Sukey described to Fergus later as a 'you'd better have a good story' expression. Then he remembered the proprieties, got to his feet and said, 'Jennifer, this is Susan Reynolds. Ms Reynolds, my wife Jennifer.'

The two women exchanged nods; Jennifer fixed her husband with a frosty stare and said, 'Good evening, Mark. No doubt you didn't expect to see us here.' He made a vague gesture. 'It's very simple,' she went on, 'the venue for the competition had to be changed at a moment's notice because the room at the Community Centre was double-booked. Fortunately, our pianist knows the manager here and she was able to fix it.'

'That was lucky,' he muttered.

'Yes, wasn't it? What's your story?'

'I'll tell you later.'

'Too right you will.'

Annie Bee, apparently oblivious to the acrimonious nature of these exchanges, was tugging at her father's arm. 'Didn't

I do well?' she said eagerly. 'Aren't you proud of me, Daddy?
Did you see me dance too, Susan?'

'You did brilliantly, chick!' he assured her. 'Ms Reynolds
is a friend of Sabrina's,' he went on. Turning to Sukey, a little
desperately it seemed to her, he said, 'Maybe you'd like to
tell Jennie about your, er, investigation.'

'You're a friend of Auntie Sab? Have you seen her lately?
Did she get the card I sent her from Athens?' The little girl
was hopping from one foot to the other in her excitement.

Sukey barely heard the questions. Her brain was reeling as
she looked down at Annie Bee. She was, as Mrs Wingate had
said, 'the image of her Daddy' – except for the eyes. His were
grey; hers were large and round and china-blue, like Sabrina's.

Explanations were obviously called for – explanations which
could hardly be given in front of Annie Bee. Five minutes
later Sukey found herself reluctantly agreeing to join the
Brinton family at their home in a village north of Bishop's
Cleeve. They travelled in three cars; Jennifer was on her own
as Annie Bee insisted on riding with her father and Sukey had
declined the offer of a lift despite a promise to drive her back
to the hotel afterwards to pick up her own car. As she followed
Jennifer out of the car park with Mark bringing up the rear,
she had a sense of being trapped, like a prisoner under escort
to some unknown destination. She knew that both Fergus and
Jim would thoroughly disapprove of what she was doing and
for a moment, as Jennifer turned off the main road into a quiet
lane, she was tempted to drive straight on as far as the next
junction and find an alternative route back home. Then she
reminded herself that it was Jennifer Brinton who had insisted
on the meeting while her husband had shown a distinct lack
of enthusiasm for the idea. She had to admit the woman had
a point. Any wife, in similar circumstances, would have felt
entitled to be told the full facts of what, on the face of it, was
a highly compromising situation.

On arrival at the house, Mark ushered Sukey into a comfortably but unostentatiously furnished sitting room and offered

her a drink, which she declined in favour of coffee. Murmuring something about putting the kettle on, he disappeared; Jennifer entered the room a moment later with Annie Bee, who had insisted on giving Sukey a message for Auntie Sab. 'Do tell her about how I won the competition, won't you?' she pleaded, and Sukey promised to give her the news the very next time she spoke to Sabrina.

'Do you think she'll be away for long?' the child asked, her smooth brow puckered with anxiety. 'She usually tells us where she's going.'

'She's been very sad after losing her Daddy,' Sukey explained gently. 'I expect she wants to be alone for a while.'

'Come along now, young lady, it's time you were in bed,' said her mother and hustled her out of the room. She returned a short while later to report that Annie, quite worn out with the excitement of the evening, was already fast asleep. Mark brought coffee on a tray and served it before sitting on the couch beside her, with Sukey facing them.

'Right, so who's going to start?' asked Jennifer. Her gaze moved from her husband to their visitor and back again.

She was not, Sukey sensed, a woman to be trifled with. 'I will if you like,' she said, as her husband showed no sign of volunteering. 'And I'll begin by assuring you, Mrs Brinton, that I'd never set eyes on Mark before this evening. I hadn't even spoken to him until I telephoned earlier. I've been trying to find out what has happened to Sabrina Soames and my enquiries – such as they are – have led me to him. He was, I think, on the point of telling me about his relationship with her when you arrived so unexpectedly.'

Jennifer rounded on him. 'Is this true?' she demanded.

'Of course it is,' he replied. 'You know I'd never—'

'Never be unfaithful to me? Never again, that is. How can I be sure? Once bitten, twice shy.' She was on the verge of tears and he moved closer and reached for her hand, but she snatched it away.

'Jennie, I swear to you—'

'Please, you must believe him,' Sukey interposed, 'and as

for further explanations, I don't really think I need any. Having seen Annie Bee, it all seems pretty obvious. Her eyes give it away – I spotted the resemblance immediately. She's Sabrina's daughter, isn't she?'

There was a long silence. As before, Jennifer was the first to break it. Her voice, which had been strong until now, became unsteady. 'I suppose it was my own fault,' she said. 'I was so much in love . . . so desperate to marry Mark . . . I never told him I couldn't . . .' she swallowed hard, fighting back tears before continuing, 'that I couldn't have children.'

He put an arm round her shoulders and this time she did not repulse him, but leaned against him, quietly sobbing. 'I was as much to blame as you, love,' he said gently. 'If I hadn't flown into a rage . . . if I hadn't said all those cruel things . . . there was no excuse for that.'

Sukey sat drinking her coffee in an embarrassed silence. They seemed to have forgotten her presence and she was uncertain what to say or do until Jennifer sat up, dried her eyes and said, 'You probably get the picture – we were estranged for a while and Annie Bee was the result.'

Little by little, the sad story came out. Sabrina, unable to face the prospect of single motherhood, begged the childless couple to bring the baby up as their own while allowing her to keep in regular touch with her by assuming the role of a friend of the family and a surrogate aunt to her own daughter.

'So you adopted her?' said Sukey as, having made the revelation, the couple fell silent.

'There's no need for you to know the details,' said Mark, somewhat evasively it seemed. 'I won't deny we had very strong misgivings, but Sabrina was, to put it mildly, in a highly emotional state and threatening to make our affair public if I didn't agree to her demands. I'd only just joined the practice; it would have done immeasurable damage to my career and besides, Jennie and I both wanted children.'

'But surely,' said Sukey, 'Annie Bee will find out the truth sooner or later.'

'We'll deal with that in our own way, when the time comes.'

His manner hardened again and she felt the veiled threat behind the words.

Unless, of course, something happens to Sabrina before Annie Bee becomes old enough to spot her own resemblance to her so-called 'Auntie Sab' or someone else remarks on it, was the terrifying thought that came into Sukey's head. Almost as if he had read her mind, he continued, 'Well, now you've wormed our secret out of us, you might as well leave, but you'll keep it to yourself if you know what's good for you.'

Eighteen

'Certainly I'll leave, and I'm truly sorry if I've caused you any distress, but—' Sukey was about to add, 'you could have spared yourself all this if you'd told the truth about when you last saw Sabrina,' but remembered just in time that it was not the lie that had brought her here but Annie Bee's card. She stood up and made a move towards the door, but Brinton was there first, barring her way. His eyes were as hard as flint.

'Not until you give me your word that you will not reveal to anyone, least of all the police, what you have learned this evening,' he said. 'Jennifer and I –' he gave his wife a swift glance before turning back to Sukey – 'have been through a great deal of trauma over this business and, as you've already pointed out, we face some difficult decisions in the future. We are not prepared to stand by and allow you or anyone else to make things even more complicated, or to destroy the family life we've established at such a great emotional cost.'

Sukey quailed inwardly at the implied threat, but she stood her ground. She struggled to keep her voice steady as she said, 'Dr Brinton, I'm interested in only one thing, and that is to find out what has happened to Sabrina. You claimed a while ago to be "just as concerned as I am" about her disappearance, but you disclaimed all knowledge of her personal life when the police came to see you.'

'I thought I'd explained that.'

'Oh yes, you thought you were protecting yourself. I can't say I admire you for it, but I can understand it. What bothers me is that you say you know nothing about the enquiries I've been making, but you haven't asked me a single question

133

about any progress I might have made, or shown any real concern for her safety.'

For a moment she thought she had provoked him to anger; his jaw set and his mouth hardened and then, without warning, he sat down again and put his head in his hands. 'You're right,' he admitted. 'I don't have any excuse, except that it's been such a fight to keep the thing from falling apart, trying to let Sabrina have plenty of contact with Annie Bee without letting our other friends see them together in case someone spots the resemblance . . . it's been a continuous strain and it can only get worse as Annie gets older.' He raised his head and looked Sukey directly in the face. 'And besides,' he went on with a nod in the direction of his wife, who sat with her eyes cast down and her hands folded in her lap, 'it's been particularly difficult for Jennie; I didn't want to, well, give the impression that—'

'Don't tell me you were trying to spare my feelings,' she cut in. 'I've known all along that you care for Sabrina more than you've ever cared for me. She was the one who was able to give you a child, not me, not your wife, not—' The outburst ended in a choking sob and she got up, pushed past him and rushed out of the room.

'Jennie, please!' he called after her before turning back to Sukey with a helpless expression. 'You see how it is,' he said. 'Outwardly we're the perfect family, but behind the scenes we're living on a knife-edge.' His demeanour had undergone a radical change; he was no longer threatening, but beseeching. 'Ms Reynolds, I beg of you, don't make things even more difficult for us all.'

'That's the last thing I want to do,' Sukey said earnestly. She took one of her business cards from her handbag, wrote her mobile number on the back and offered it to him. 'You've known Sabrina for a long time and I think it's possible she's told you things about her past life that might help Elspeth and me find out what has happened to her. If you're sincere when you claim to be concerned for her welfare, will you call me at this number any weekday evening after five o'clock and answer a few questions?'

'I doubt if I can be of much use, but . . . all right, I'll try and call you tomorrow.' Mechanically, he took the card and put it into his pocket. 'Now, if you'll excuse me – ?'

'Yes, of course. I'll see myself out.'

The moment he heard the sound of her car on the drive, Fergus emerged from the house and opened the garage door. 'Mum, I've been so worried about you!' he exclaimed as she got out of the car. 'I was going to give you till ten o'clock and then call Jim.'

'Well, thank goodness you didn't.' Sukey went into the kitchen, flopped on to a chair, sat back and closed her eyes. 'I've got a serious problem.'

'Which is?'

'To tell or not to tell.' Fergus listened in growing bemusement as she outlined the saga of the Brinton family. 'Part of me wants to believe he's telling the truth, that he's truly concerned about Sabrina and has no idea what's happened to her. On the other hand . . .'

'Did he decide that she was becoming a threat to their cosy family life and had to be eliminated?' he finished as she left the thought hanging in the air.

'Exactly.' She got up and went to the sink for a glass of water. 'I saw two sides of him this evening: one, the doctor who had a fling with a patient, got more than he bargained for in the way of consequences and will go to any lengths to avoid damage to his reputation, either as a doctor or as the ideal family man.'

'And the other side?' he prompted as she sat thoughtfully sipping the water.

'Someone who is genuinely penitent, who cares deeply about his wife and child and is desperate to protect them from further hurt. It seems to me,' she went on between sips of water, 'that Sabrina has been a threat from several points of view.'

'How d'you mean?'

'It was obvious from the way Jennifer reacted that she's still deeply unhappy about the situation and what led to it.

135

Being forced to have regular contact with her husband's former mistress can't have made it any easier for her.'

'Mum, are you suggesting that Jennifer had a motive for killing Sabrina?'

'It wouldn't be the first time a wronged wife has murdered the other woman. Jennifer has had over six years of living with a daily reminder of her husband's infidelity and if it's been festering all this time – well, something might have snapped. Another possibility, of course, is that Brinton decided to eliminate Sabrina. That would solve both problems at a stroke; with her out of the way it would give him a chance to improve his relationship with his wife and at the same time remove the risk of Annie Bee ever finding out the truth.'

'There is a third possibility,' said Fergus.

'You mean, they might have conspired to kill Sabrina? Or one of them did it and the other helped cover it up?'

'Something like that.'

Sukey shook her head. 'If they were guilty they'd have been very careful not to show private feelings in front of me. As it was . . . if you had seen the bitterness in that woman's eyes . . .'

'Just the same, the fact that you've found out the truth makes you a threat, Mum. You gave him your phone number, so he could find out your address and—'

'Only my mobile number,' she pointed out. 'You can't trace an address from that.'

'So what? He knows where you work; he could lie in wait for you, follow you when you leave and track you down that way. Mum, you could be in deadly danger; you've got to tell Jim.'

'Oh, for goodness' sake, Gus, stop being so melodramatic! I told him you knew I was coming to see him and he must know that if anything happened to me he'd be number one suspect.'

'All right, but why don't you just let Jim decide whether it's worth following up.'

'Gus, those two are living under a terrible strain. I don't want to add to it any more than necessary.'

'But—'

'Listen. We're forgetting what started all this. Sabrina was last heard of visiting a school in Bracknell where her father used to be a teacher. I'm hoping that Dr Brinton will have some idea about why she went there, that's all.'

'We know why she went and we know she came back.'

'We don't know the details. As for coming back, it's true her car was on the drive next day, but there's no proof she was the one who drove it there.'

'Did you tell him that?'

'I would have done, but his wife threw a wobbly and he asked me to leave so that he could go and comfort her. In the circumstances, I did what seemed the best thing – gave him my mobile number and asked him to call me.'

'You won't meet him again alone, will you?' Fergus pleaded.

'Not unless he insists, and then I'll be sure to let you know exactly where.'

'Suppose he doesn't phone? Will you tell Jim then?'

'Yes, of course – but I'm pretty sure he will.'

Sukey had guessed correctly. At a quarter to five the following afternoon, Brinton phoned.

'I hope this isn't too early,' he began. 'Evening surgery begins at five and I—'

'No problem,' she assured him. 'This shouldn't take long.'

'What exactly do you want to know?'

'Whether Sabrina ever confided in you about her relationship with her father. There isn't time to go into all the details now, but it's become clear during the past few days that he was a pretty devious character. Did she ever hint at anything like that?'

'Not that I remember. All she said about him was that he rejected her at birth and she'd been trying for years to establish a loving relationship with him, without success.'

'Would you say she had an obsession about it?'

He hesitated before replying. Eventually he said, 'I wouldn't normally discuss this, but in the circumstances it's only fair to say that, in my professional opinion, she suffered serious psychological damage as a result of her father's attitude.'

'Did you ever suggest any treatment?'

'If you mean psychiatric treatment, no – at least, I did hint at it once but she rejected it out of hand. All I could do for her was give her antidepressants from time to time.'

'Did you never suspect that she might have harmed herself in any way?'

'No. She had Annie Bee to live for.'

'Did she ever mention that she thought her father might have been known to the police?'

'Certainly not. Where did you get that idea?'

'She said as much to Elspeth – and to me – before going off to Bracknell.'

'What on earth was she doing in Bracknell?' He sounded genuinely surprised.

'Her father used to teach at a school there. We know she made contact with someone at that school and we believe she returned home the same day, but nothing has been seen or heard of her since.'

There was a brief silence at the other end of the line before he said, 'I'm sorry, but I have absolutely no idea what reason she had for going.' There was another pause before he added, 'If that's all, I really have to get ready for surgery.'

'Yes, of course. Thank you for calling.'

'Well?' said Fergus, who had been standing by, listening to his mother's end of the conversation.

'He claims not to have known about a possible connection with the police, but he didn't ask any questions. Come to think of it,' Sukey went on, 'he didn't even ask me to let him know if I find out anything further about Sabrina's whereabouts.'

'Because he already knows the answer,' said Fergus grimly. 'Mum, you've simply got to tell Jim. If you don't, I will.'

'Maybe you're right, although I'm not convinced he's guilty.'

'You can't afford to take a chance – and besides, you promised Jim.'

'That's true. OK, I'll tell him, but I'll need time to think what I'm going to say.'

Nineteen

Sukey was not normally given to bad dreams or broken nights, but when she fell into bed that evening it was some time before she fell asleep, despite being physically tired. Every time she closed her eyes the scene in the Brintons' sitting room seemed to dance on her retina like a shot in a video when the pause button is pressed. She recalled the pain in Jennifer's eyes as she was forced to suffer the humiliation of her inability to bear children, and the complex web of deceit it had brought in its train, laid bare before a stranger.

Even more chilling was the memory of the menace in Mark Brinton's icy stare and the threatening words that accompanied it. It was just talk, she told herself a dozen times as she tossed and turned, a gut reaction following the realization that she had – albeit unwittingly – forced them to disclose the family secret. Despite her assurances that she had no wish to cause them further pain, that her sole interest was to find Sabrina, she could not rid herself of that image. Although she eventually fell into a restless sleep she awoke with a feeling of unease that she found impossible to shake off.

She made an effort to appear normal when checking in for work the following morning, discussing the assignments handed out by George Barnes and exchanging the usual office banter, but Mandy had evidently noticed the preoccupation lying just beneath the surface. As they went down into the yard to pick up their vans she said, 'Something on your mind?'

'Why do you ask?' Sukey responded defensively.

'You don't normally ask twice where a place is – in fact, as it was Rayleigh Court we were talking about you wouldn't

140

normally need to ask once, seeing as it's only just round the corner from where you live.'

'Oh gosh, did I do that?' said Sukey in dismay. 'I must be slipping. I did have rather a restless night.'

'Any particular reason?'

'Well, yes, in a way.'

'Want to tell?'

It occurred to Sukey that part of her restlessness had been due to the internal tussle she had been having with herself, which, in a nutshell, was how much – if anything – she should tell Jim. The thought was followed immediately by the realization that she needed to confide in someone other than Fergus, who was motivated solely by concern for her safety. Mandy could be relied on to take a more objective view of the situation.

'I've been landed with a rather knotty problem,' she said after a moment's thought. 'I'd like your opinion, but there isn't time to tell you now – can we meet at lunchtime?'

Mandy shook her head. 'Sorry, I've got to take Mum to have her feet done. Why don't you pop round for a cuppa after we finish? Don't worry about her listening in,' she added as Sukey hesitated, 'all she wants to do when I get her home from the day centre is flop down in front of the telly and put her feet up. They keep the old dears on the go all day; "keeping their minds occupied" they call it. Mum enjoys all the activities, but she comes home pretty tired. She'll nod off within five minutes of kicking her shoes off.'

'In that case . . . yes, I'd love to.'

Although she and Mandy had been friends ever since they joined the SOCO team some four years previously, it was the first time that Sukey had been invited to Mandy's home to meet her mother. She knew, of course, that although the old lady was able to move around the specially adapted bungalow with the aid of a walking frame, she was dependent on her daughter for many of her daily needs. It meant that Mandy's life was severely restricted, but she seldom complained and always spoke of her mother with love and compassion.

Mrs Parfitt was slight and frail looking, but her eyes were bright like a bird's and her short sparse hair still bore traces of the coppery lights she had bequeathed to her daughter. The hand she held out was so delicate that Sukey was almost afraid of crushing it, yet it took hold of hers in a close, warm grasp.

'I'm so glad to meet you, my dear,' she said in a voice as firm as her handshake. 'Mandy's told me so much about you. How's that son of yours getting on?' She sipped her tea and chatted with animation for several minutes before giving a sudden, uncontrollable yawn. 'Oh, excuse me!' she apologized. 'I usually have a little nap when I get home, but as you were coming—'

'Please, don't mind me,' Sukey assured her.

'We'll go into the kitchen while you have your kip,' Mandy said briskly, 'and when you wake up we'll have a little snifter . . . She so looks forward to her glass of plonk in the evenings,' she added in a low voice as she escorted Sukey to the kitchen and closed the door behind them. 'I'm not sure her doctor would approve, but the poor old thing doesn't get much in the way of treats. Right,' she went on, perching on one of two stools at the breakfast bar and motioning to Sukey to take the other, 'what's the problem?'

She listened without interruption while Sukey recounted the events of the previous evening. Eventually she said, 'I suppose you're asking yourself whether you think Sabrina represented a strong enough threat to give Brinton a motive for topping her. The trouble is, of course,' she went on without waiting for Sukey to comment, 'he must know that sooner or later, even with Sabrina out of the way, they'll have to tell Annie Bee she's adopted and she's going to want to know who her birth mother was.'

'I'm none too sure she has been officially adopted,' said Sukey. 'When I mentioned it, he avoided giving a direct answer.'

'I wonder if they managed to pass the child off as Jennifer's,' Mandy speculated.

'How in the world could they have done that?'

'You'd be surprised what can be done if you know the right people. As a doctor, that wouldn't have been a problem for Brinton, provided he had enough of the ready.'

'Gosh!' Sukey felt her mouth open in disbelief. 'If you're right, and anyone found out, they could be in serious trouble.'

'And you have found out, so you represent a very real threat.'

'Theoretically, yes, but he knows I work for the police and that if anything happened to me—'

'You know as well as I do that people sometimes do desperate things when they're cornered.' A troubled look clouded Mandy's pale, freckled face. 'I really think you should tell the boss – only I advise you to choose your time. I heard on the grapevine that he's not in the best of moods at the moment.'

'Oh, why's that?'

'Haven't you heard? The results of the DNA tests in the headless corpse case have gone astray and will have to be carried out all over again.'

'Wow! Someone's going to get their knuckles rapped over that,' Sukey remarked. She felt a pang of resentment that she had not been party to the information. Normally, Jim would have confided in her, but she had hardly set eyes on him since the weekend. Determined not to let her disappointment show she said casually, 'Talking of tests has just reminded me. I asked young Adam to run some for me and I'm still waiting for the results. I'll chase him tomorrow.'

'What tests were those?'

'You remember I went to Sabrina's house? I found grit in the tyres of her car that I thought might match the samples we took near the spot where the headless corpse was found.'

'Interesting,' Mandy commented. 'Let me know what he says. And we still don't know who the headless corpse is,' she went on. 'The plot thickens. If it should turn out it isn't Janice Burlidge it could be Sabrina, in which case your friend Mark Brinton would be slap bang in the middle of the frame. You *definitely* need to tell the boss.'

'I suppose so,' Sukey sighed. 'Thanks for the advice, and thanks for listening.' She slid off her stool and picked up her handbag. 'I'd better be going. Say goodbye to your mother for me,' she added as they tiptoed past the slumbering figure on their way to the front door.

'Will do. See you tomorrow.'

To her disappointment, Sukey found no opportunity to talk to Jim the following day. He had made no effort to contact her since Sunday and so far as she knew had spent most of his time out of the office. This was by no means unusual; like most of his fellow officers, he carried a heavy workload, but just the same she felt unreasonably put out at his silence and unavailability.

Shortly before four o'clock, as she finished her day's report and was preparing to leave, one of the civilian secretaries popped her head round the door and said, 'Chief Inspector Lord would like a word with you, Sukey.'

The summons was so unusual that Sukey felt a pang of apprehension. Had he somehow found out about yesterday's visit? Perhaps Mark Brinton had phoned to complain . . . but no, the last thing he would want was to attract the attention of the police. Just the same, she felt distinctly uneasy as she knocked on Lord's office door.

He had obviously been consuming biscuits; an empty packet lay on the desk and the front of his shirt was speckled with crumbs, which he was busy brushing away as she entered in response to his summons. He tossed the packet into the waste bin and waved her to a chair.

'Sit down, Sukey,' he said cordially. 'Everything going all right?'

'Yes, thank you, sir.'

'No problems?'

'No, sir.'

He must have noticed her slight hesitation, for he gave her a searching look and said, 'You don't sound very sure.' When she did not reply, he said, 'Young Jim not been paying you enough attention lately? Oh, I know it's supposed to be a great secret, but you know what it is in a place like this . . . rumours get around.'

Sukey felt herself turning pink. 'We try to be discreet, sir,' she said demurely.

'Quite right too. Thought I'd better mention it because I'm afraid you won't be seeing much of the lad for a couple of days. I've packed him off to sunny Spain. We're still awaiting the results of the DNA tests, but in the meantime the police in Barcelona have pulled Burlidge in and they've agreed to let a couple of our officers question him about his wife's whereabouts.'

'I see. Well, sir, thank you for telling me, but—'

'You're wondering why he hasn't told you himself? To tell the truth, he's a bit embarrassed. The thing is, I had to send a DS with him. I'd have sent Andy Radcliffe, but he's on leave, so it's had to be DS Chen.'

'Dalia!' Sukey was unable to conceal her dismay. Jim was going to spend two or three days in the heady atmosphere of one of the most romantic cities in Spain, a city that the two of them had often promised themselves they would visit together . . . and he was going with Dalia. The knowledge that it was official business didn't make the hurt any less.

As if he could read her thoughts, Lord went on, 'He wasn't best pleased, said you wouldn't like it either, but there wasn't much I could do. In the end, he asked me to break it to you and say he hoped you'd understand.'

'Thank you sir, I appreciate that.' Sukey felt a stinging sensation behind her eyes and got up to leave, anxious not to make a fool of herself in front of Lord.

'Least I could do,' he said, 'and don't you worry about him. Thinks the world of you, he does.'

Then why didn't he have the guts to tell me about this trip himself instead of fobbing me off on to DCI Lord? Sukey found herself thinking resentfully. *And now*, her thoughts ran on, *I've got to sort out this Brinton thing by myself and it's all his fault. I could at least have had the benefit of his advice if I'd had the chance to ask for it.* This, she knew, was unreasonable in the light of her earlier ambivalence about the whole situation, but she brushed reason aside and concentrated on feeling wounded. *I'll jolly well carry on with the hunt for Sabrina on my own*, she resolved as she headed for the laboratory to find out if Adam had anything of interest to tell her.

Twenty

'Sorry it's taken so long,' said Adam. 'We've been rushed off our feet for the past week and with people being on holiday we've got a bit behind. Anyway, here's your stuff at last.' He opened a metal cabinet and took out two transparent plastic sample sachets, each attached to a printed sheet, and handed one of them to Sukey. 'I think you'll find the results quite interesting. Read that one first.'

'Thanks, Adam.' As Sukey scanned the report she felt a twinge of mingled excitement and apprehension. As she had half expected, half feared, it confirmed a match between the fragments of grit she had taken from the tyres on Sabrina's car and those she and Mandy had found near the scene where the headless corpse had been discovered.

'Don't get excited, it's not conclusive,' said Adam. 'You'll find similar samples in the yards of sand and gravel merchants all over the county.' He handed her the second report. 'Now have a look at that.'

She read the printed sheet with rising interest. It referred to additional material found clinging to the grit that appeared to have come from a different source. 'Cotswold clay?' she said. 'Are you sure?'

'Reasonably sure. If it turned out to be crucial we'd need far more information about a possible source, but it's fairly typical of the region. I'd say it was picked up after recent rain; if it was in dry conditions and only minute quantities were collected I'd probably have missed it.'

'Well, thanks very much, Adam.'

'No problem.'

Sukey drove home with her brain in turmoil. Last week she had been able to assure Elspeth that the headless corpse, while not yet having been positively identified as that of Janice Burlidge, could not have been Sabrina's for the simple reason that according to the pathologist's report the dead woman had borne a child. That explanation had been blown out of the water with the revelation that Sabrina was the mother of Annie Bee. The results of Adam's tests gave a further twist to the mystery of her disappearance. Surely, it was now her duty to inform the police of what she had unearthed as a result of her activities during the past week?

With Jim unavailable, DCI Lord was the obvious person to approach. Once, in the past, when she had overstepped the accepted limits of a SOCO's function, Lord had brushed aside Jim's reservations, praised her detection skills and even hinted that she might at some time consider rejoining the force with a view to a career in the CID. She had no doubt that he would take her findings seriously, but hard on this thought came another. There was no question of telling him only part of the story. Features detailed in the pathologist's report on the headless corpse might very well have applied to Sabrina, but for that one significant fact that had appeared to eliminate her. Either she would have to take her enquiries a stage further on her own, or cause irreparable harm to the Brinton family by revealing their involvement in the deception over Annie Bee's birth.

There had been no word from Elspeth since the day she had slammed down the phone in a temper after being told the police were making no further enquiries into Sabrina's absence. Perhaps now was the time to re-establish contact to see if there had been any further news. She would look pretty foolish if she went running to Lord with her story if Sabrina had turned up in the meantime and neither woman had thought it necessary to tell her.

When she reached home Fergus pounced on her and said, 'Where have you been? Jim's been calling you; he says he's at the airport. He sounded quite upset when I told him you weren't home yet.'

'Too bad,' she said acidly. 'I'm surprised he bothered.'

Fergus stared at her. 'What do you mean? What's going on?'

'He and the lovely Dalia are off to Spain to interview the husband of Janice Burlidge and he was too chicken to tell me himself, so he got DCI Lord to do it.'

Fergus whistled in astonishment and then said hastily, 'Well, he's obviously feeling unhappy about it or he wouldn't be trying to contact you.'

'So he jolly well should.'

'You could try calling him back,' Fergus suggested. 'He said they were loading but the flight might not have taken off yet.'

'I'm not going to bother. Anyway, mobiles have to be switched off once you're on board the plane.'

'But Mum, you're not going to take it out on him just because . . . I mean, it's an official trip and he couldn't choose who to take with him, surely.'

'I suppose not, but—'

'And I'm sure he'd much rather have you with him than Dalia.'

'Only I'm not a DS, am I?' she said waspishly. She spread her hands in a gesture of resignation. 'Oh, it's not that, of course, it's . . . oh hell, it's sod's law! Just as I've got to the point when I need to talk to him about something he goes swanning off with her, of all people.'

'He's only obeying orders.'

'Yes, but why couldn't he tell me himself?'

'He probably knew you'd hit the roof.'

'Yes, I might well have done,' she admitted. 'Gus, it's been quite a day. Let's have a drink while I tell you about it.'

They sat in the garden, Sukey with a glass of wine and Fergus with a beer, while she brought him up to date. When she had finished speaking they both fell silent for a few minutes. Then Fergus said, 'If Adam is right about there being Cotswold

149

mud in Sabrina's tyres, where do you suppose she picked it up?'

'Not from anywhere near the Brintons' home,' she said. 'They live miles from the Cotswolds.'

'I'm still not convinced they had nothing to do with her death,' said Fergus. 'Suppose Brinton arranged to meet her in some remote hilltop village? Maybe she wanted to keep their affair going and he had made up his mind to end it?'

'You aren't seriously suggesting he arranged a tryst up some muddy farm track in the pouring rain, killed her by cutting off her head with a saw he carries in the boot for just such an eventuality, drove her body down to the A38 in her own car, stripped off her clothes and dumped her in a ditch? How do you suppose he got rid of the evidence, namely one woman's clothes and her severed head, before driving her car back to her house, leaving his own car behind?'

'He had an accomplice to help him dispose of the body and then drive him home from Sabrina's place.' Fergus was evidently reluctant to exonerate Mark Brinton.

'Mrs B, for example?' Sukey said with mingled scorn and amusement.

'Why not? We've already agreed she had a motive for wanting Sabrina out of the way.'

'Oh Gus, get real. It sounds like an episode from a third-rate TV series. Let's go over the facts again. We know Sabrina's car has an oil leak, and there was a patch of oil on the gravel near where the body was found, but it doesn't follow that it came from her car. That's a thought.' She got up and went into the house, returning a moment later with a pad and a pen. 'I'll make a note to find a moment to pop back to her house and collect a sample of oil for comparison.'

'You could check for traces of blood in the boot,' Fergus suggested.

'I did have a quick glance and it all looked quite clean. Still, if we need to make a closer inspection we'll have to bring the car in and that would mean making it official.'

'Which you're thinking of doing,' he reminded her.

'I haven't made up my mind yet. Where were we? Let's assume for the moment that the oil did come from her car. If so, then the chances are that the body in the ditch is hers and her car was used to carry it from wherever she was killed.'

'Which might be somewhere in the Cotswolds.'

'If that's the case, it would seem to rule out the Brintons.' Sukey felt her spirits lift slightly at the thought.

'Not if my theory is correct,' Fergus said stubbornly. 'Well, some even more unlikely things have been known to happen,' he persisted, seeing her dismissive shake of the head. 'You came round to my way of thinking about a possible enemy from Arthur Soames' past being his killer,' he pointed out.

'So I did, but there's nothing to link him with the Brintons.'

'Nothing that we know of, but there are lots of things we don't know about any of them. And don't forget, whoever topped Sabrina had to be someone who knew where she lived.'

'Not necessarily. She probably carried some kind of ID; her driving licence, for example.'

'I suppose so,' he conceded grudgingly. He emptied his glass and said, 'Is it OK if I have a refill?'

'So long as you're not going out in the car later on.'

'No, I've got some reading to do. Do you want a top-up?'

'No, thanks. Just leave me to think for a moment. I want to get things into chronological order.' Sukey put down her wine glass, picked up her pen and began making notes. When Fergus came back she said, 'Sabrina went off to Bracknell, interviewed someone at her father's old school and wasn't seen again. By all accounts the interview didn't last very long and Bracknell can't be much more than a couple of hours' drive from Bishop's Cleeve, if that. Yet she still wasn't home when her neighbour went to bed that night, so she must have gone on somewhere else, possibly somewhere in the Cotswolds.'

'To meet Brinton,' he suggested. 'Maybe she learned something that linked him with her father, something that he was desperate to hide. She called him to find out more, he panicked and—'

'Will you shut up about Brinton for a moment? I'm still inclined to believe he and his wife are telling the truth when they claim to know nothing about her disappearance. But you could be right; maybe she did learn something at the school, something the person the police spoke to didn't consider worth mentioning, but which in some way meant something to her? She went there because she thought the visit might lead her to her father's killer, don't forget. That's something we've tended to lose sight of. Suppose she picked up a clue that led her to him and she very rashly went and confronted him?'

'I reckon she did just that and we know what happened then—' Fergus began, but she cut in sharply.

'We don't *know* anything of the kind. This is all pure guess-work. It's still possible the headless corpse is Janice Burlidge's and if it is and her butcher husband killed her, cutting off her head in an attempt to conceal her identity makes sense. If it's Sabrina's and Brinton killed her, as a doctor he might well have a sharp enough instrument to do the job with, and he could have used her car to dispose of her, but I don't believe he did.'

'So what are you thinking of doing next?'

'Before I do anything else I'm going to have a word with Elspeth.'

'And then what?'

'Assuming there's still been no word from Sabrina, I'll try and make contact with the head of Arthur Soames' old school.'

'But the police have already tried that and got nowhere.'

Sukey shrugged. 'Maybe they didn't dig quite deep enough. Anyway, I'll see what Elspeth has to say.'

She half expected a cool reception, but Elspeth not only welcomed the call, she fell over herself to apologize for her display of ill temper.

'I've wanted to call you every day since, but I thought you wouldn't want to bother with me – with us – any more after the way I hung up on you. You've tried so hard to be helpful and . . .' Her voice was unsteady, as if she was fighting tears.

'There's no need to apologize,' Sukey assured her. 'I'd have come back to you sooner if I'd had any news. I take it Sabrina hasn't been in touch?'

'No.' The monosyllable was flat, expressionless. 'I've just about given up hope; any day now I expect to hear her body's been found. I feel so wretched, I can't sleep without pills and I miss Arthur so much, and my mother . . .' This time Elspeth's voice broke altogether. It was in stark contrast to her demeanour during their first meeting. Then, she had seemed so poised and controlled, only later revealing herself as a vulnerable woman who had seen her last chance of happiness snatched away from her.

'I'm sure you're finding it all a terrible strain,' Sukey said. 'Have you seen your doctor?'

'Yes, and he's been very kind, but he can't bring Arthur back.'

'No, of course not. If it's any comfort, I haven't given up my search for Sabrina. I haven't got very far, but there is one more avenue I can explore if you want me to go on trying. I just wanted to be sure she hadn't turned up in the meantime.'

'If only!' Elspeth exclaimed piteously. 'Please, please, Sukey, do go on trying.'

At around noon the following day, Sukey drove to a quiet spot, parked her van and called Priory Park School in Bracknell. A woman who identified herself as the head teacher's secretary answered almost immediately.

'I'm afraid Mr Bellmore is out this afternoon,' she said in response to Sukey's request. 'If it's about an admission for next year, we already have a full intake and several on the waiting list.'

'No, it isn't that; in fact it's a rather delicate matter.'

'Does it concern one of our pupils?'

'No, it concerns a former teacher at your school, Mr Arthur Soames.'

There was a brief silence at the other end of the line before the woman said guardedly, 'Mr Soames retired a long time ago, so I think it's unlikely Mr Bellmore can help you as he's only been here about five years.'

'Yes, I've already been told he didn't know Mr Soames personally, but I would like to have a word with him just the same.'

'Do I understand you've made this request before?'

'Not exactly.' Sukey had already decided to avoid mentioning the police if possible. 'Actually, I'm trying to contact Mr Soames' daughter. I believe she came to see Mr Bellmore a couple of weeks or so ago, but it appears she didn't return home and I'm trying to find out where she is. I want to speak to her rather urgently and—'

'Excuse me,' the woman cut in, 'but I fail to see why you think she would have told Mr Bellmore anything about her future movements. He had never set eyes on her before.'

'So you remember her visit?'

'I didn't meet her personally, no, because I was on holiday at the time, but he did mention it when I returned. He also said something about one of her friends having reported her missing.'

'Did he make any comment about her visit?'

'It seems her late father took early retirement and for some reason or other she wanted to know why. Naturally, Mr Bellmore was unable to help her as it was so long ago and he said she became rather agitated and hinted that he was concealing something from her. He said he had quite a job getting rid of her.'

'You mentioned that you were on holiday at the time so presumably the school was closed, but—'

'The school never closes completely. Most of the children go home for the holidays, but we have a few boarders who for various reasons have to stay on, so we maintain a skeleton staff. We have a deputy head who takes charge when Mr Bellmore is on holiday and Mrs Unwin, his former secretary, comes in to keep the office running while I'm away.'

'His *former* secretary?' Up till now, Sukey had felt she was merely raking over ground that had already been explored and found sterile. Suddenly, a new possibility appeared to open up. 'Does that mean she's retired?'

'That's right. She retired two years ago.'

'Would she have been at the school at the same time as Arthur Soames?'

'It's possible, I suppose.'

'And she was there when Sabrina Soames came to see Mr Bellmore?'

'I imagine so.'

Sukey felt her optimism mounting by the second. She grabbed her notebook and a pen from the dashboard. 'Could you possibly give me Mrs Unwin's phone number?'

'Without her permission? Certainly not.'

'Then if I give you my number, would you be kind enough to ask her to ring me – or allow me to ring her? Please,' Sukey begged, 'it is quite important.'

'All right,' the woman said with evident reluctance. 'I'll see what she says, but I can't make any promises.'

Twenty-One

It was after eight o'clock that evening when Sukey's telephone rang. Her first thought was that it might be Jim calling from Spain; when an unfamiliar woman's voice asked for Mrs Susan Reynolds she felt a sharp stab of disappointment as she answered, 'Speaking.'

'My name is Lucinda Unwin,' the woman said. 'I had a call this afternoon from the secretary to the headmaster of Priory Park School, who said you would like to speak to me. I understand you have been making enquiries about a former teacher at the school, the late Mr Arthur Soames.'

'That's right. Thank you so much for calling.'

'What is it you want to know?'

'I believe you were the former headmaster's secretary before you retired. Do you remember Mr Soames?'

'I do.'

The tone was neutral, yet its noticeable lack of warmth suggested a latent reserve that aroused Sukey's interest. 'I understand you were on duty at the school when his daughter called to see the present head, Mr Bellmore, recently,' she continued.

'I was only working in the morning that day and she called in the afternoon, so I didn't actually meet her.'

'But you heard about her visit from Mr Bellmore?'

'He mentioned it, yes.'

'Can you remember what he said?'

'He said her father had been found dead in his garden, apparently as the result of a fall, but she did not believe his death was accidental. He said she seemed convinced –

156

"obsessed" was the word he used – that someone with a grudge against him had killed him and she wanted to find out more about his past associates. She seemed to think one or other of his former colleagues might be able to help her, but Mr Bellmore said that none of his present teachers had been at the school long enough to have known him personally and he was not prepared to divulge the names and addresses of former staff. He said she became very upset and he suggested that if she had doubts about her father's death she should take them to the police. At this point she all but accused him of being part of some kind of conspiracy and he ordered her to leave.'

'That's more or less what I've heard, except it's the first time a conspiracy theory has been mentioned,' Sukey said. 'All I know is that both Sabrina Soames and the lady who was engaged to marry her father are convinced that there was something suspicious about his death, although the coroner was in no doubt that it was accidental. Whatever the truth of the matter, the point is that Sabrina hasn't been seen or heard of since she called on Mr Bellmore and we – that is, the late Mr Soames' fiancée and I – are very concerned about her.'

'You're surely not suggesting that Mr Bellmore had anything to do with her disappearance?' Lucinda Unwin sounded profoundly shocked. 'I can assure you—'

'I'm not suggesting anything of the kind,' Sukey said hastily.

'Was this reported to the police?'

'Naturally, and I understand they did send an officer to the school to check that Sabrina had called there. The problem is that they don't accept that there's any serious cause for concern. They say there's nothing to suggest that any harm has come to her; they point out that people often go missing voluntarily for a variety of reasons and they seem to think this is true in her case. They believe she's simply gone off somewhere to grieve in private and that she'll turn up again "in her own good time" as they put it.'

'But you're not satisfied that's the case?'

'We do have serious doubts about it.'

'I take it you've checked with her relatives?'

'So far as we know she has no other relatives since her father died, and by all accounts her relationship with him was not very close.'

'What about her other friends?'

'She doesn't seem to have any – or at least, none that we know of. We've spoken to her next-door neighbour and her doctor, but we haven't been able to trace anyone else who knew her personally.'

'I see.' There was a short pause, as if the speaker was weighing up the situation. Eventually she said, 'So how do you think I can help?'

'It's the past I'm interested in. You knew Sabrina's father and you were at the school when he took early retirement. Do you happen to know why? Was it on health grounds?'

There was another pause before Mrs Unwin said, 'That was the reason given.'

'Do I understand that you have some doubts?'

'Before we go any further, may I ask why you are interested? Have you known Miss Soames a long time?'

'I never set eyes on her before her father died. She came to ask for my help after the inquest; she was upset at the accidental death verdict and begged me to make some enquiries on her behalf.'

'You're a private detective?'

'No. I work for the police, but this inquiry is entirely unofficial.'

'I see. Well, I did hear a suggestion, but it was never made public, that . . .'

'That what? Please tell me; it could be important.'

'I think perhaps it would be better if we were to meet. I don't like discussing sensitive matters on the telephone, especially with a perfect stranger. Would you be willing to come and see me?'

'Certainly.' Sukey felt her synapses humming with anticipation. Was this a breakthrough at last? 'I could come tomorrow if it's convenient.'

'Yes, I can manage that.' Mrs Unwin dictated the address and gave directions. 'Shall we say about two thirty?'

'That will be fine. Thank you very much.'

Sukey put down the phone with a feeling of mingled optimism and frustration. More than anything at this moment she needed someone to talk to about this latest development. It was Friday evening; Fergus was out with his friends and not expected home until after eleven, and there was no means of contacting Jim. She considered calling Elspeth, but decided not to. She would be sure to want to go to Bracknell with her and whilst on the one hand it would have been nice to have company, if Elspeth lost her cool as she had done earlier, the interview could go badly wrong. She spent the next hour making notes of questions to put to Lucinda Unwin before switching on the television and restlessly surfing the channels without finding anything to hold her interest. She was about to give up and get ready for bed when, a little after ten o'clock, she was surprised to hear a key in the front door.

'What's up? Did the pub run out of beer?' she asked flippantly as the sitting-room door opened and Fergus and another lad of about the same age entered. She gave a gasp of alarm at the sight of her son's badly swollen, half-closed eye and the bloodstained handkerchief he held to his cheek. 'Gus! Have you had an accident? Come and sit down and let me have a look.'

'No accident, just a bit of a punch-up,' he said, sinking into the nearest chair. 'Richard drove me home in my car; he'll need a lift back if you don't mind, Mum.'

'Of course, if he doesn't mind waiting while I clean that cut. It's not very deep, thank goodness, but that's a real shiner you've got there.' She bustled out of the room and came back a few minutes later with a bowl of warm water and a towel. 'How on earth did you get involved in a punch-up?' she went on as she sponged the wound and washed away the blood. 'It's not like you.'

'Some guy who'd had a bit too much to drink took a swipe at me,' Fergus said, wincing as she patted his face dry. 'It's no big deal.'

'Without provocation? That's dreadful! Were the police called?'

'I doubt it. There was a bit of an argument and we were all chucked out of the pub,' Richard explained. 'It happened in the car park.'

'Didn't you get the name of the guy who hit you? He should be nicked,' she insisted.

'Oh for goodness' sake, stop fussing, Mum,' said Fergus testily. 'I'm all right, it's only a bruise.'

'You could have sustained serious damage to your eye. As it is, I think we should go to A and E and get someone to look at it.'

'I'm all right, I tell you.'

'At least let me put a cold compress on it.'

'Please, just take Richard home; I'm going to bed.' He got up and went out, slamming the door behind him. Sukey looked enquiringly at his friend, who was standing just inside the room looking a shade embarrassed.

'Are you going to tell me what happened?' she demanded.

Richard shrugged. 'It's like he said; the guy had had too much to drink. His friends took him away before it got seriously out of hand.'

'But why pick on Fergus?' Even as she spoke, Sukey was conscious that the incident was so typical of scuffles that occurred regularly on Friday and Saturday nights that unless there was a serious disturbance it would have caused little comment. It was unlikely that the police would have been called just because a handful of young drinkers exchanged a few punches in a pub car park before dispersing. But this was different; it was her son, her only just eighteen-year-old child, who had been attacked, and all her protective maternal instincts were roused.

She looked appealingly at Richard, but all he said was, 'I'm sure he'll tell you about it himself after I've left, Mrs Reynolds. If you wouldn't mind running me home, please?'

'Yes, of course. I'll just get my keys.'

The light in Fergus's room was still burning when she

returned. She tapped on the door and said, 'Gus, can I come in?'

'What do you want?'

'I want to know more about what happened.'

'I told you.'

'You didn't tell me anything. What did you do to antagonize this chap?'

'It's none of your business.'

'Don't speak to me like that!' she said angrily. 'If you're in any kind of trouble, of course it's my business.'

'I suppose you're afraid it'll damage your career if you have a son who gets drunk and fights in pubs.' He spoke in an angry, resentful tone that she had never heard from him before and she was at a loss to know how to respond.

After a moment she said quietly, 'I'm sure you know that isn't true, Gus. I'm just concerned for your safety.'

'You needn't worry. He doesn't know where I live. Just forget it, will you.'

'Can't I get you anything? How about some tea or hot milk?' There was no response. 'Are you in any pain?'

'Will you please stop fussing. I've taken a couple of aspirins and I want to sleep. I'll be OK in the morning.'

Sukey spent a wretched night. The meeting with Lucinda Unwin, which held out at least some hope of progress in the search for Sabrina, now seemed of minor importance compared with the possibility that her son was in serious trouble; worse, that he might have suffered permanent injury to his eye. They had had plenty of minor spats in the past; teenagers of both sexes were notorious for flying off the handle, but she could not recall a single occasion when he had been so secretive, or spoken to her so rudely and aggressively. It crossed her mind to speak to his father, but, knowing Paul, he would almost certainly avoid involvement in anything that threatened to disturb his comfortable existence. If only Jim were there – but the thought of Jim reminded her that he was in Spain with Dalia and made her more miserable than ever.

The following morning, heavy eyed after only a few hours

161

of troubled sleep, she went downstairs to make tea. Fergus, habitually an early riser, would normally have been there before her; it being Saturday, they would have chatted amicably about their respective plans for the weekend. But there was no sign of any movement from his room and after much deliberation she decided to leave him to sleep for the time being. If he did not appear by ten o'clock, she promised herself, she would take him a cup of tea, check on the condition of his injuries and hope to find him in a better mood. So she showered, dressed and did some housework while trying to decide how to approach him when he finally made an appearance.

A little after nine o'clock Elspeth rang. 'Oh Sukey,' she said, and there was a catch in her voice that hinted at recent tears. 'You'll never guess what I've just heard. One of my neighbours went away on a cruise the day Arthur had his fall and she didn't even hear about it until yesterday. She came round to see me and say how sorry she was and . . . this is the awful thing . . . she said, "To think Dr Gardner was actually a few doors away that day. I remember seeing his car; he must have been visiting another patient." Oh Sukey, if he had only known, if he could have got to Arthur before I did . . . he might have been able to save him.'

'I think that's very unlikely,' Sukey said gently. 'All the medical evidence showed that Arthur's death was instantaneous. But it's possible Dr Gardner might have seen something, maybe something that seemed insignificant at the time, that could help us find out what really happened.'

'Do you really think so?'

'I'm only saying it's possible, although I wouldn't pin too much hope on it. On second thoughts, if he'd spotted anything unusual that morning, I'm sure he'd have mentioned it at the inquest.'

'But it might be worth asking him. Should I speak to him, or will you? I would so like to do something to help. Have you made any progress, by the way?'

It was such a relief to have someone to talk to that before she realized it Sukey found herself telling Elspeth about her plan to call on Mrs Unwin. Elspeth was naturally excited at the news, but to Sukey's surprise she did not demand to accompany her. Instead, she said almost humbly, 'I expect you'd prefer to go alone, but I'll come with you if you like.'

'That's all right, but thanks anyway. Are you going to be at home this evening?'

Elspeth gave a sad little laugh. 'Where else?'

'In that case, I'll come straight to your house after I leave Bracknell to let you know how I got on.'

'That would be wonderful; thank you so much.'

Sukey had barely put down the phone when Fergus appeared. She saw with relief that the swelling over his eye had begun to subside and the cut on his cheek showed no sign of infection. 'Good morning, Gus,' she said brightly, determined to sound normal. 'How are you feeling?'

'Not bad, bit of a headache that's all.'

'No sickness or double vision?'

'No, I'm fine. Who was that on the phone?'

'Elspeth, wanting to know if I had any news.'

'And have you?'

'As it happens, I have. I'd have told you last night, only—'

'I'm sorry I was so rude . . . it was just—'

'I know, Mummy making a fuss in front of your friend—'

'It wasn't that so much; I felt embarrassed at having been such a prat in the first place.'

'You don't have to tell me if you don't want to.'

He sat down and fiddled with the mug of coffee she put in front of him. His face was scarlet and he avoided her eye. 'I know it was a daft thing to do,' he began, 'but the fact is . . . well, I started chatting up this bloke's girl in the pub. She'd had a spat with him and she was giving me the come-on, just to wind him up, I guess. Anyway, the boys dared me to follow it up, the bloke took exception and, well, you can guess the rest.'

He looked so sheepish that Sukey burst out laughing. 'You

163

idiot!' she exclaimed. 'I'm not surprised he took a swipe at you. That'll teach you not to mess with another man's girl.'

'All right, don't rub it in,' he said with a rueful smile and then added anxiously, 'You won't tell Anita, will you?'

'Of course not.'

'So what's the news you were telling Elspeth? Is it about Sabrina?'

'It is. Drink your coffee while I give you the low-down.'

Twenty-Two

Sukey was about to begin telling Fergus about her conversation with Lucinda Unwin and the planned visit to Bracknell that afternoon when the telephone rang again. Her spirits soared as she heard Jim's voice.

'Sukey? This is just a quick call to let you know I'm back.'

'Back where? At home?'

'No, Heathrow. Dalia's gone to pick up a car and we're going straight to headquarters. We should be there in a couple of hours. How are you?'

'I'm fine. When can I see you?'

'I'm not sure. There have been some pretty dramatic developments in the Burlidge case and I have to see DCI Lord and probably the Super as soon as we get back.'

'What sort of developments? Did you speak to Mr Burlidge?'

'Oh yes, we spoke to him all right. We spoke to his wife as well.'

'What?'

'They've got some kind of scam going. I'll tell you more when I see you.'

'Oh, my God!' Sukey exclaimed. 'That means . . . Jim, there's something I have to tell you.'

'Can't it wait till I get back?'

'No, Jim. Please listen, this is important.'

'Can't hear you; you're breaking up.'

'I must talk to you. Are you still there? Can you hear me now?' She was shouting into the phone, but there was no response and after a moment the line went dead. 'Either his battery's run out or he's lost the signal,' she said, switching off in exasperation.

'Maybe he'll call back in a moment,' said Fergus. 'What was all that about anyway?'

'Janice Burlidge is alive and well and up to no good with her husband in Spain,' she said.

His jaw dropped. 'Gosh!' he exclaimed. 'Then the body in the ditch has to be Sabrina's, and it's obvious who killed her. What are you going to do? You have to tell Jim about the Brintons now.'

'Yes, of course; that's what I was trying to do when we lost the connection. I've no means of contacting him now until he gets back to within reach of a land line.'

'What about Dalia? Have you got her mobile number?'

'No.'

'Maybe he'll get her to call you. Or you could leave a message at HQ.' At that moment the phone rang for the third time and Sukey grabbed it.

'Jim?' she said eagerly, but her hopes faded as a gentle voice the other end said, 'Is Fergus there, please?'

'It's Anita for you.' She handed him the phone. 'Keep it short,' she mouthed and put a finger to her lips. He gave a nod of comprehension as he wandered out of the room. He was back after a few minutes, wearing an expression of profound relief.

'What a bit of luck!' he exclaimed as he returned the instrument to its cradle. 'Anita's having to go away with her parents to visit her granny, who's fallen over and broken her hip. They'll be gone the whole weekend so I won't have to face her looking like this.'

'Well, bully for Granny!' said Sukey with heavy irony. 'I hope you didn't allow your delight to show.'

He had the grace to look abashed. 'I suppose that did sound a bit callous, but you know what I mean. Anyway, you were saying . . .?'

'Darned if I know what to do next. I don't want to cancel my appointment with Mrs Unwin because she may know something that will help me trace Sabrina's movements after leaving the school. That's going to be more important than ever now.'

'Do what I suggested – leave a message with someone in CID asking him to ring you a.s.a.p. He can call you on your mobile if you've left home before he gets back to the police station.'

'That's true. If he rings here after I've gone, ask him to do that, will you?'

Mrs Unwin lived in a quiet street on the outskirts of the town, in a modest, brick-built end-of-terrace house with a bay window on the ground floor and a pocket-handkerchief-sized front garden. She had evidently been looking out for her visitor, for the door opened as soon as Sukey, having parked her car in one of the few available spaces a short distance away, opened the wrought-iron gate. She was a heavily built woman with short, straight grey hair and dark-rimmed glasses that gave her a slightly forbidding appearance.

'How good of you to be so punctual,' were her first words in response to Sukey's greeting. 'It's so annoying, isn't it, when people keep one hanging about, waiting for them to turn up?' she went on as Sukey murmured a polite response. 'Builders and electricians and so on can be so tiresome; sometimes they're hours late, or don't even turn up at all. Do come in.'

She marched ahead of Sukey along a short passage and ushered her into a cosily furnished sitting room. French windows opened on to a colourful display of flowers and shrubs that caused her to exclaim, 'What a pretty little garden!'

'It is lovely, isn't it?' Mrs Unwin's homely features lit up in a beaming smile and for the second time within two minutes, as she later reported to Fergus, Sukey felt she had scored Brownie points. 'This is Miss Fennell,' her hostess went on, gesturing towards a slim, petite woman with small features and smartly styled pepper-and-salt hair, who was seated in one of a pair of cretonne-covered armchairs grouped round an old-fashioned fireplace. 'She teaches music at Priory Park.'

'How do you do, Mrs Reynolds,' said Miss Fennell. She appeared to be several years younger than Mrs Unwin, and in contrast to the latter's brisk, clipped tones she had a softer voice and a gentler manner.

Sukey took her proffered hand and said, 'How do you do. Please, call me Sukey.'

'Thank you, Sukey. I'm Barbara. I hope you won't think I'm intruding, but Lucinda and I had a long chat after she spoke to you and we agreed that I might be able to help you with your enquiries. I happened to be at the school when your friend called. To be frank, I've been concerned about her myself, and we're both anxious to help you trace her.'

'It's rather delicate,' Lucinda began as she waved Sukey to the second armchair and sat down heavily on a couch. 'It was all swept under the carpet at the time . . . it would have been so damaging to the school's reputation if it had come out. Everyone was very concerned to avoid publicity and there seemed no doubt that early retirement was the best solution.'

'When Mr Soames' daughter turned up after all these years wanting to know why her father had taken early retirement, I was in a quandary,' Barbara explained without giving Sukey an opportunity to put in a question. 'It happened years before Mr Bellmore's time, so of course he knew nothing about it and he sent her away, rather unkindly, I gather. I found her wandering in the corridor in some distress and she told me how her father had died in a fall and she was convinced it wasn't an accident and no one would believe her. She was trying to make contact with people who had known him while he was a teacher at the school. I must say,' Barbara continued, 'it struck me as a little odd that, so far as I could make out, she knew little or nothing about his life at the school.'

'The fact is, she had a very difficult relationship with her father,' said Sukey. 'Without going into a lot of detail, it appears that it had quite a profound effect on her psychologically, but the sad thing is that she felt they were beginning to get closer when . . .' She hesitated for a moment, wondering whether to bring Elspeth into the discussion at this point, but Lucinda made the decision unnecessary by breaking in.

'Poor child!' she exclaimed earnestly. 'Poor, poor child! Priory Park has had many such cases to deal with over the years. I'm sure Mr Gladwin – he's the former Head – had no idea that there was one amongst his own staff. In fact,' she went on, 'he might not have known Mr Soames had a daughter. I certainly did not.'

'Did you have much contact with Mr Soames?' Sukey asked.

'A certain amount, mostly about administrative matters, but I never got to know him well. In fact, I don't think he formed any close friendships among the staff, although he was highly regarded as a teacher and also as a scholar. I believe he had several history textbooks published.'

'As a matter of fact, it was reading the introduction to one of his books that put us on the track of your school,' said Sukey.

'I wonder if it would have made a difference to the way Mr Gladwin handled his case if he'd known about his family problems,' said Barbara thoughtfully.

'Oh, I doubt it, dear,' said Lucinda. 'He had all the other children and the reputation of the school to consider.'

'Excuse me,' said Sukey, 'do I understand that Mr Soames left under a cloud?'

'I'm afraid he did. As I said before, it was all rather delicate.'

It was not difficult to guess what had led to Arthur Soames' abrupt departure. Just the same, Sukey felt it was important to put the matter beyond doubt.

'Was he suspected of child abuse?' she asked.

Barbara Fennell shifted awkwardly in her chair. 'Nothing was ever proved,' she said, 'but Mr Soames used to give private history tuition to some of the children and one boy alleged he had been . . . interfered with. Naturally, Mr Soames strongly denied that anything improper had taken place.' Her manner suggested that she had been inclined to believe the belea-guered teacher.

'Was there just the one complaint?'

'If there were other victims we never heard about them. It was just this one boy who was so seriously upset that he told his uncle, who immediately brought the matter to the head-master's attention.'

Lucinda Unwin took up the story again. 'Mr Gladwin was absolutely horrified at the accusation; at first he was reluctant to believe it, but the boy's uncle – the parents were dead and the uncle was his guardian – insisted he would not have made it up. He said his nephew had been badly traumatized by the experience and he threatened to report the affair to the police unless Mr Soames was immediately dismissed. The last thing Mr Gladwin wanted was to have the police round asking questions and giving rise to gossip and scandal, so he persuaded Mr Soames to take early retirement.'

Sukey turned to Barbara. 'So, how did you respond to Sabrina's – Miss Soames' – questions?'

'I was at a loss to know what to say. I felt she was entitled to some explanation but I didn't feel it was my place to tell her the unpleasant details. After all, he was her father, and he had so recently died . . . I didn't want to add to her grief.'

'So Mr Soames retired without a stain on his character, and never mind other potential victims so long as the school's good name was undamaged.' Sukey found it difficult to keep the scorn out of her voice.

'We don't *know* that there were other victims,' said Barbara with a hint of reproach in her gentle voice, 'and the good name of the school was terribly important to Mr Gladwin. We specialize in caring for children who have lost one or both parents, or suffered some other trauma; he founded it after his wife died and his own son found it difficult to attend a normal school. Naturally, the thought of anything so dreadful as sexual abuse happening to an already traumatized child filled him with horror.'

'I take it Arthur Soames didn't threaten to sue for wrongful dismissal,' said Sukey.

Lucinda gave a sniff of contempt. 'Oh no! He was probably only too relieved that the matter wasn't taken any further.'

'As a matter of fact,' said Barbara, 'I suspect, although I can't be certain of this, that Mr Gladwin paid Mr Soames a considerable sum by way of compensation for losing his job, probably out of his own pocket.'

'And did you decide after all to tell Sabrina the whole story?'

'Not exactly, but as I said, I felt she was entitled to some explanation after all the trouble she had taken to get this far,' said Barbara. 'I concocted some tale about a serious disagreement with one of the parents which got out of hand, and as her father was approaching retirement age anyway it was thought better that he leave early.'

'And did that satisfy her?'

'Far from it. She demanded the name and address of the parent and she began to get very agitated again, so in the end I—' Barbara broke off and glanced almost guiltily at Lucinda. 'I know it was a bit unethical, but I felt so sorry for her.'

'You told her what she wanted to know?' Sukey said eagerly before Lucinda had a chance to say anything.

'The school was half empty and Mr Bellmore had gone to lunch. I know where the records of former pupils are kept, so I gave Miss Soames a cup of tea, left her in the staff room and went to the archive room to look up the boy's address. I recalled his name – Harry Ashton – so I was able to find it quite easily.'

'Was his guardian called Ashton as well?'

'No. I believe Harry was his sister's son, so the name would have been different. He was a doctor; that I do remember, and I think Harry called him Uncle Mark. I should explain that we have two separate filing systems; the pupils' names and addresses are kept on a card index for quick reference, but their school records, medical reports and details of the family history and so on, are considered more confidential so they're kept in a locked filing cabinet. I don't have a key to that; I'd have needed Mr Bellmore's permission to open it.'

'It doesn't matter for the moment.' The mention of Uncle Mark who was a doctor had set Sukey's spine tingling. She had guessed Mark Brinton to be in his mid-forties; it was feasible that he could have assumed guardianship of a ten-year-old boy

171

fifteen years or so ago. 'I take it you gave Sabrina Harry's last known address?' she added, doing her best to conceal her excitement.

Barbara nodded. 'Yes, I did,' she said. 'Of course, I pointed out that Harry was in his mid-twenties by now and there was no guarantee that either he or his uncle was still living there, but at least it gave her something to go on . . . and it got rid of her, which was a relief.' Barbara ended with an embarrassed laugh.

'Did she make any comment before she left about what she was going to do next?'

Barbara frowned and pursed her lips. 'I don't recall her exact words,' she said after a few moments' thought, 'but the gist of it seemed to be that she would be calling at the address to find out if they were still there, or where they'd gone if they'd moved.'

'Do you have the address with you? Would you give it to me?'

Barbara drew a slip of paper out of her handbag. 'As I said, all this happened many years ago, but for what it's worth . . .' She held out the paper and Sukey took it with mounting anticipation. Her pulse quickened as she read what was written on it. The address was of a house in a village in the Cotswolds, less than ten miles from Gloucester.

Twenty-Three

S ukey put the paper in her pocket, thanked the two women for their help and got up to leave. They pressed her to stay for tea, which she politely declined, saying that she wanted to pursue her enquiries without further delay. They said they quite understood, that it had been a pleasure to meet her and they hoped she would soon find her missing friend. As they parted on the doorstep, Barbara Fennell offered the suggestion that if Sabrina had in fact uncovered the true facts behind her father's early retirement, the shock and shame might well have caused her to go away somewhere remote while she came to terms with it. This of course was in line with the police conclusion, reached without the benefit of these further revelations, yet it did not tie in with Sukey's deeply held conviction that some harm had come to her. Now that Janice Burlidge had been found alive, the possibility that the body in the ditch was Sabrina's became stronger than ever. She glanced at her watch on the way back to her car. It was ten past three; the interview had taken less than forty-five minutes but it was long enough for the whole picture to have changed.

She drove a short distance, pulled into a lay-by and switched off her engine. If Mark Brinton was indeed the guardian of Harry Ashton, and if the boy had been so badly damaged by his experience at the hands of a suspected paedophile as to make normal relationships difficult or even impossible, this might well constitute a motive for murder. But why wait fifteen years? It was conceivable, of course, that Soames had felt so threatened that he had left the neighbourhood as quickly and quietly as possible and that it had taken his killer – for by now, Sukey was beginning to share Sabrina's conviction that his death had not been an accident – all that time to track him down.

There was, of course, a further possibility to be considered. Despite Barbara's defensive attitude, it was unlikely that such a man would have confined his disgusting practices to just one victim. There might well have been others who, through shame or shyness, had never come forward. Had one of them been so affected by his experience that in adult life he had felt impelled to seek out and face his tormentor and, moved by an overwhelming sense of rage and injustice, somehow caused that fatal fall?

Sukey pulled out a notebook and jotted down a few facts. According to the obituary of Arthur Soames that had appeared in the local paper, he had been living in Gloucester for some ten years, yet according to what she had learned today he had left Priory Park School fifteen years ago. Where had he been during those five years? Everything she had learned about him prior to today suggested that since moving to Rosemount Villas he had led a blameless life, tending his garden, serving the church as a sidesman and member of the PCC, and more recently planning to marry Elspeth Maddox. The engagement, it was true, had caused some eyebrows to be raised, mainly on account of the disparity in age. But could there have been a more sinister reaction from some hitherto unnamed person? Perhaps another woman in the parish had cherished an ambition to become Mrs Soames? It was hard to visualize Arthur as the victim of a *crime passionnel*, yet stranger things had happened. The more Sukey thought about it, the muddier the waters seemed to become.

A further point to consider was that Sabrina had hinted to Elspeth that her father might at some time have been in trouble with the police. And shortly after making that cryptic remark, she had made her way to Priory Park School, obtained from Barbara Fennell the last known address of one of Soames' victims, and quietly disappeared. Barbara was quite definite that she had not told her the true facts behind her father's early retirement, merely hinting at some altercation with a parent that had 'got out of hand' and possibly, by implication, threatened the good name of the school. It would, however, have been perfectly natural for her to want to seek further information. Having received so little support from the police, had she then visited the address Barbara had given her, come face to face with Harry Ashton or his uncle, and learned the dreadful truth about her father?

Sukey's thoughts went racing ahead as she tried to visualize what might have happened next. Had Sabrina indeed met her death at the hands of her father's killer and her body been mutilated and transported by him to that watery grave? There could be no answer to that question until the body had been positively identified unless in the meantime she turned up elsewhere. Despite Elspeth's insistence and Sukey's own inner conviction that she had come to some harm, there was as yet nothing to disprove the police theory. The possibilities seemed so numerous and so contradictory that her brain reeled with the effort. She needed to talk to Jim; surely he would have called her home number by now and Fergus would have told him that she wanted to speak to him urgently. And at that moment her mobile rang and he was on the line.

'Sukey, I'm sorry it's taken so long to get back to you. Things have been moving so fast here that I haven't had a moment. Where are you? Fergus said you had something urgent to tell me.'

'I'm a couple of miles outside Bracknell.'

'What on earth are you doing there?'

'Trying to trace Sabrina Soames' last known movements.'

'But we've been up that road and drawn a blank.'

'Yes, but I've gone a little further. The officer who visited the school where he used to teach spoke only to the headmaster about Sabrina's visit, but he or she didn't trouble to ask if she spoke to any other member of staff.'

'And did she?'

'Oh yes, and I tracked down that person and uncovered some very useful information.'

'Just a moment. The message I got from Fergus was that you were trying to tell me something important when I called you from Heathrow and the line broke up. That was before your trip to Bracknell. Are you saying this is something different?'

'Yes, but let's get back to the most important thing. If the body in the ditch isn't Janice Burlidge, then it could be Sabrina's.'

There was a pause while Jim considered this assertion. Then he said, 'I don't think so, Sook. The pathologist was pretty certain that the woman in the ditch had borne a child, remember? Sabrina—'

'Has a six-year-old daughter,' Sukey broke in, unable to contain herself a moment longer. 'And there's something else I've discovered only this afternoon; the father of that child is, I have reason to believe, the former guardian of a boy called Harry Ashton, who was sexually abused by Arthur Soames when he was a teacher at Priory Park School.'

'How in the world do you know all this?'

'It's a long story. When can I see you?'

'Are you coming straight home?'

'I'm going to make a short detour to a village called Birdcombe, which is where Harry Ashton lived when he was at the school. It's just possible he may still be living there.'

'Hold on a minute!' A familiar note of alarm came winging over the wire. 'You aren't planning to confront this chap, are you?'

'No, of course not. I just thought it would be useful to know if he's still around or if anyone remembers him. There might be a village shop where I could enquire.'

'I'd be much happier if you came straight home and told me the full story before you go blundering into a potentially dangerous situation,' he said urgently.

'Oh please, give me credit!' she retorted, stung by the term 'blundering'. 'I'll see you later; I should be back by five thirty.'

'All right, but do take care. By the way, is there any chance you might feed a hungry DI who's been missing you like hell?'

'I'll think about it. Oh, one other thing; when you see Fergus, don't ask him how he got his black eye. He's very embarrassed about it.' She explained, and he gave a great shout of laughter.

'Just the sort of daft thing I might have done at his age,' he said and rang off.

Sukey consulted the gazetteer at the back of her road atlas and gave a little grunt of satisfaction as she found what she wanted. She tore a page from her notebook and wrote down an address. Then, having checked the most direct route to Birdcombe, she started her engine and drove off with the words 'missing you like hell' ringing sweetly in her ears.

Birdcombe was a typical Cotswold village nestling in a fold of the hills. It was approached along a narrow, steeply descending lane with open grassland on either side where grazing sheep raised their heads to gaze curiously as Sukey drove by. She drove slowly down the hill past a scattering of houses on either side until she spied a modern building with the legend 'Birdcombe Village Hall' carved in stone over the door and a sign on the wall indicating a free car park. She pulled into the gravelled enclosure, cut her engine, got out of the car and glanced round. It was evidently a popular starting point for walkers; a dozen or so assorted vehicles were already lined up against the boundary fence and the most recent arrival, a slightly harassed-looking young mother, was in the act of decanting an excitedly prancing dog and a handful of children of assorted ages from a people carrier. She gave Sukey a friendly nod and a wave before locking the car and following her brood towards the far corner, where a stone stile gave access to a footpath leading across a field towards some woods.

It took Sukey less than ten minutes to walk the length of the village street. A number of people whom she took to be visitors like herself were sauntering along in the sunshine, admiring the colourful displays in the well-tended front gardens, pointing cameras and binoculars in various directions at the surrounding countryside or browsing among the gravestones in the churchyard. There was no sign of a village shop, but a fingerboard pointing off to the right led her to the Farrier's Arms, whose doors stood invitingly open. Business was evidently brisk, for every table on the forecourt and in the adjoining garden seemed to be occupied. Sukey went inside and ordered a glass of lemonade from a cheerful-looking man with a glistening bald head and bare brawny arms.

'This seems a very popular village,' she commented as he served her. 'Is it always as busy as this at weekends?'

'When the weather's this good.' He took her money and handed over her change. 'You're not from these parts then?'

'No, I live in Brockworth, but I'd simply love to have a house in a village like this. In fact –' she took the slip of paper from her pocket and pretended to consult it – 'I'm told there's a cottage for sale here. The Old Barn; do you know it?'

'The Old Barn on the market?' The man looked surprised. 'Not that I know of. You know anything about Harry Ashton moving, Renée?' he added, turning to a plump young woman who had just dumped a tray of empty glasses on the counter.

She raised an eyebrow and shook her head. 'Can't say as I have. Not that he'd tell the likes of us.'

'Are you sure you've got the right address?' the barman said to Sukey.

'I think so.' She showed him the paper; he peered at it and then gave a loud guffaw. 'If I had a fiver for everyone who's made that mistake I could afford to retire,' he said. 'This is Birdcombe; the house you're looking for is in Bird*field*.'

'Oh dear, so it is.' Sukey pretended to check the address again before putting the paper back in her pocket. 'Has this Mr Ashton lived here a long time then?'

'Grew up here, so I understand,' said the barman. 'A very shy young gentleman, hardly speaks to anyone and doesn't welcome callers. The house is tucked away at the end of the village so no one ever sees his comings and goings.'

'Bit of a mystery man, you could say,' Renée added.

'Oh well, I've obviously had a wasted journey,' said Sukey. 'Is Birdfield far from here, by the way?'

'About twenty miles, on the other side of the river,' said the barman with some relish. 'Good luck with your house-hunting!'

Sukey thanked him, downed her drink and then, feeling like a bloodhound on the scent, set off in search of The Old Barn, Birdcombe.

Twenty-Four

I t was not difficult to find. On the very edge of the village,
just before the road crossed a stream and began a gentle
climb up the other side of the valley, she came to a substan-
tial stone house, identified by a wooden sign on the five-barred
gate as Waterside Farm. Next to the farmyard was a small
paddock and beyond that a second gate bore the name The
Old Barn. A gravelled drive full of potholes, bordered on one
side by wooden fencing and the other by a dry-stone wall, led
alongside the paddock, curved away to the left and disappeared behind a clump of trees. The house was invisible from
the road and there was no sign of any human activity. Sukey
stopped for a moment, debating whether it was wise to go on.

Curiosity triumphed over prudence. She unfastened the
latch on the gate and pushed it open. It had a strong spring
and as she stepped through and released it, it swung to behind
her and closed with a sharp metallic clang that made her
jump. She half expected dogs to start barking, but apart from
a couple of horses in the paddock that raised their heads briefly
before resuming their grazing, nothing stirred. After a moment
she began walking along the drive until the cottage came into
view. It was a single-storeyed stone building with a roof of
Cotswold tiles that had probably once housed animals. It
looked neat and well maintained; climbing roses and clematis
made a colourful display on the walls and to the left of the
white-painted front door a graceful weeping tree cast dappled
shade over an ornamental stone birdbath. A small paved patio
area to the right was ringed with shrubs of differing shapes
and shades of foliage in terracotta and ceramic containers,

evidently selected and arranged by someone with artistic flair. There was no garage; a blue Ford Fiesta that had seen better days was tucked away, almost out of sight at the side of the cottage.

Beside a lounger on the patio was a small table on which stood an empty glass and a book, suggesting that the occupant was not far away. Despite her promise to Jim, Sukey was toying with the idea of knocking on the door and trying the same technique as she had used at the Farrier's Arms in the hope of coming face to face with Harry Ashton, but at that moment a young man in jeans and an open-necked shirt appeared from behind the cottage, trundling a wheelbarrow. He was wearing a portable CD player, which meant he had probably missed the sound of the gate closing. The assumption was confirmed by his reaction on seeing her, for he stopped dead and stood staring at her with an expression of mingled astonishment and apprehension, still gripping the handles of the wheelbarrow.

She took a couple of paces forward, pulled out the paper with the false address on it, assumed her most beguiling smile and said politely, 'Good afternoon! I'm sorry if I startled you, but I understand—'

She got no further. He dropped the wheelbarrow and dragged off the headphones as if they had suddenly become red-hot. He took a couple of paces towards her, putting his hands out in front of him as if warding off an attack.

'Go away!' he said in a trembling voice. 'Please, go away!'

'That's all right,' she said soothingly. 'I can see I've called at an inconvenient time. I apologize for disturbing you. I've been admiring your beautiful garden and I was wondering—'

Slowly, so as not to alarm him by any sudden movement, she took another couple of steps forward, but he repeated in a hoarse, unsteady voice, 'Didn't you hear me? I said go away.'

There was obviously no point in remaining. She made a gesture of compliance with one hand, turned away and began

181

retracing her steps. Halfway to the gate she stopped short and stared at the ground, struck by something she had not observed before. There had been rain the previous night and although it had mostly dried up there were still patches of yellowish mud beneath the gravel in some of the deeper potholes. There were similar traces on her shoes. Cotswold mud, such as Adam had found in the sample she had taken from Sabrina's tyres.

She was about to bend down to take a closer look when she heard footsteps crunching on the path behind her. They seemed to be increasing in pace and she glanced nervously over her shoulder to see Harry Ashton running towards her, clumsily on account of his heavy boots but closing the distance between them at a frightening rate. At the sight of his expression, she fled. She was still ahead of him when she reached the gate, but in her panic she fumbled with the catch. He was almost on her; she put a foot on one of the bars and attempted to climb over, but he grabbed her by the ankle, dragged her back and pinned her against the gate by her upper arms.

'Who are you and what the hell are you doing here?' he panted. 'What do you mean by poking your nose in, asking questions—'

'I haven't asked you any questions.' There was something manic in his gaze that filled her with terror, but she tried to speak quietly. 'You told me to leave, and I was leaving.'

'That's no answer! I want to know why you're here.'

'It's quite simple. I was told this house was for sale and—'

'For sale? This house?' He gave a wild burst of laughter. 'At least, that's a better story than the other one tried, but I still don't buy it.' He shifted his grip on her arms; his hands moved towards her shoulders so that his fingers brushed her neck. He brought his face down level with hers. 'You're dangerous,' he said softly. 'Do you know what happens to dangerous people?'

Her heart was thumping as if it was trying to escape through her ribs. 'What makes you think I'm dangerous?' she faltered.

'I just know it.'

'I promise you I mean you no harm. Please,' she pleaded, 'let me go, you're hurting me.'

'That's nothing to what I could do.' His hands crept round her throat and his eyes blazed with hatred.

It was time for desperate action. He was standing so close to her that she had little room for manoeuvre, but his legs were wide enough apart to allow the knee she directed at his crotch to reach its target. The effect was dramatic; he gave a sharp grunt, released his grip and fell to the ground, where he lay curled in a foetal position whimpering like a child. Sukey vaulted over the gate and without a backward glance raced back up the lane towards the village as if the Furies were after her, almost running into the path of a car coming from the opposite direction. The driver braked, swerved and shouted angrily at her from his open window, but she took no notice and ran blindly on. By the time she reached the car park, which by now was almost empty, she was virtually winded and her legs felt like jelly. She unlocked her car with shaking hands, sank into the driver's seat and collapsed over the wheel.

It was several minutes before she recovered her breath. She took a long drink of water from the bottle she kept in the car, wiped the sweat from her face with a tissue and checked the time. It was a little after five o'clock and the remaining few walkers were rejoining their cars and leaving. The last thing she wanted was to be alone in the car park; as soon as the pounding in her chest had subsided she started her engine and joined the queue for the exit. As she waited to pull out on to the road she gave a nervous glance back along the way she had come, but there was no sign of Harry Ashton or his blue Ford Fiesta. By the time she reached the junction with the main road there were two or three cars behind her, soon to be joined by others as the evening rush-hour traffic built up, but she paid no particular attention to them. She failed to notice the one that followed her at a discreet distance for the rest of her journey. Even had she done so, it would not have concerned her since, after slowing down behind her while she

183

Betty Rowlands

turned right into Bramble Close, it continued straight along the main road towards the city.

She arrived home still feeling shaken. She found a plaintive message from Elspeth demanding to know why she hadn't been in touch. The message ended with the news that she would be out for the evening and would call tomorrow. That was a relief; Elspeth was the last person she wanted to speak to at the moment. Fergus had also left a message saying he was playing tennis and had been invited to supper at Richard's house. She poured herself a stiff drink and then took advantage of his absence to make some written notes to add to the dossier she had been keeping on her earlier enquiries. It was almost seven o'clock when Jim arrived, by which time she had showered, changed and begun work on preparing dinner.

'Darling, you look wonderful!' he exclaimed as she opened the door.

As she had taken particular pains with her appearance she felt this was no more than she deserved. 'Is that the best you can do after your trip to the city of romance?' she taunted him, stepping back to evade his outstretched arms.

'Don't be coy, woman,' he said, grabbing her. 'It seems a lifetime since I saw you.' There was a long silence before he said, 'I've missed you so much, Sook. I kept thinking of the times we've promised ourselves to do that trip, and it seemed so ironic—'

'That you left it to someone else to tell me you were doing it with another woman,' she interrupted, trying to rekindle some of her earlier resentment and failing dismally.

'It was all arranged in such a rush and there was no opportunity to tell you in private,' he protested, 'and to barge into the SOCOs' room to announce it would have been a dead giveaway. I mean, there was no reason connected with work for you to be told about the trip, so I thought as DCI Lord is the only one apart from Andy Radcliffe who knows about us . . .'

Sukey looked away to hide a smile. Was he really that naive, she wondered indulgently, or just deliberately kidding himself?

184

'All right, I forgive you, so long as you've brought me a present,' she said graciously, eyeing the duty free airport carrier he had deposited by the front door.

'Two bottles of Rioja and some posh French perfume,' he said, handing them over. 'Sorry I didn't have time to gift-wrap them.'

'Lovely! Thank you, darling. Now come in and open one of those bottles while I tell you about my afternoon's sleuthing.'

He listened attentively while she told him what she had learned from Lucinda Unwin and Barbara Fennell. He said, 'Clever girl!' on hearing of the ruse by which she had established that Harry Ashton still lived in Birdcombe, but although she deliberately made light of Harry's hostile reception and glossed over the physical attack, his admiration swiftly turned to irritation. 'For God's sake, Sukey, having tracked the chap down, why couldn't you leave it at that? He sounds seriously disturbed; anything could have happened.'

'I suppose I wanted to be absolutely sure it was him,' she said, feeling suddenly foolish. 'I wasn't planning to ask if Sabrina had been there, but I'm pretty sure she had because when I gave him the spiel about the house being for sale he said that was a better story than the other one had told. And then there was the evidence from Sabrina's tyres—'

'What evidence? Something else you haven't told me? And what's all this about Harry's uncle being the father of Sabrina's child?'

'I don't have any proof of that, but there are several rather odd coincidences that I think are worth checking. I've been ferreting around for ages and I've tried several times to tell you what I've discovered, but I could never contact you because you were always off on some other case and you wouldn't take me seriously when I said I thought something had happened to Sabrina.' The stress of the afternoon was beginning to have its effect and Sukey could hear her voice wobble.

Jim put an arm round her and held her close for a few moments. 'I'm sorry, darling, I know I've been a bit out of touch lately,' he said gently, 'but remember, I did admit sharing your doubts, and it so happens that DCI Lord does as well although he agrees that without some evidence of foul play that's hardly a reason to start an investigation.'

'I know.'

'Anyway, I'm taking you seriously now, so tell me every-thing.'

'What about dinner?'

'I can wait a bit longer if you can.'

'All right. I've made a few notes; I'll go and get them.'

He read through them, asked a few questions and then sat without speaking for a while. At last he said, 'Well, now we know the body in the ditch isn't Janice Burlidge, I reckon we have to work on the possibility that it's Sabrina, but to prove it we're going to need a DNA sample from the kid.'

'That's what I was afraid of,' Sukey sighed. 'It's going to bust that family apart.'

'I'm afraid that's a risk we have to take,' said Jim. 'I'll see Philip Lord about this at the first opportunity. Meanwhile, what's for dinner?'

Twenty-Five

Sukey's pursuer had taken the opportunity of a break in the traffic to make a U-turn. Although his practice did not extend this far he knew the district well, knew that Bramble Close was a cul-de-sac of no more than ten pairs of semi-detached houses and bungalows. He pulled into the kerb, got out of the car and strolled back the way he had come. He was in no particular hurry; in his experience, most of the residents of such developments used their garages for storage and left their cars on the drive, and he was banking on Sukey doing the same. In this he had at least partially miscalculated; being security conscious, and because now and again she carried police property in her car, Sukey was meticulous about putting her car away. On this occasion, however, he was in luck; the brown Astra he had followed all the way from Birdcombe was still on the drive at number 6 while the woman who had all but blundered into his car and whom he had instantly recognized stood in front of the garage chatting with her next-door neighbour. He had seen all he needed and he turned and walked back to his car at the same unhurried pace, confident that Sukey had not so much as glanced in his direction.

He had achieved his immediate objective, but the problem of what to do next tormented his brain for the entire return journey. First, he must get the truth out of Harry, find out exactly what he had done to cause the woman to lash out at him, leaving him curled up on the ground sobbing his heart out. 'She hurt me here, she hurt me *here*!' he was moaning, clutching his genitals, and back came the recollection of the day fifteen years ago when the headmaster of Priory Park

187

School had telephoned. 'I'm afraid your nephew has suffered some serious psychological disturbance,' he said. 'He's utterly distraught; we've tried to get him to tell us the problem, but all he keeps saying is, "Uncle Mark, I want Uncle Mark." Can you possibly come and talk to him?' And so had begun the chain of events that had led to Arthur Soames' enforced retirement.

Soames, of course, had got away with it unscathed, established a fresh life for himself and eventually become a highly respected member of his new community. He hadn't even bothered to change his name, while his victim – probably one of many – had to live the rest of his life haunted by the memory of the degradation suffered at his hands. Some might have been able to put the experience behind them and, after time and therapy, establish normal relationships, but not Harry Ashton. The man who had accepted responsibility for the only child of his late sister had watched a bright, promising but hypersensitive and already emotionally scarred lad become a near recluse, unable to trust anyone but his only living relative. Fifteen years on, the pain was never far from the surface. Harry's only interests were those he could pursue in solitude, chiefly his books and above all his garden. It was ironic, Mark reflected grimly as he turned off the main road into the lane leading to the village, that his principal source of comfort had in the end turned out to be his undoing.

There was no sign of Harry when he reached the cottage. The windows, which on such a warm day would normally have been standing open, were tightly closed and the curtains drawn. He let himself in and called softly, 'Harry! Where are you? It's Uncle Mark.'

He had to call several times before a weak, subdued voice replied, 'I'm in my room. Has she gone?'

'Yes, she's gone.'

'Are you alone?'

'Of course I am. Are you all right? Shall I come up, or will you come down?'

'I'll come down in a minute.'

'I'll make some tea.'

'That would be nice. Thank you, Uncle Mark.'

The voice was that of a grown man, but the words and the attitude were those of a desperately vulnerable child. As had happened so many times before, Mark experienced a wave of fierce anger against the creature who had brought him to this. Dead the man might be, and good riddance, but his destructive influence lived on.

While he was making the tea, Harry came softly downstairs and entered the kitchen. He was a handsome young man, tall, well built and the image of his mother. At least, Mark reflected for the thousandth time, she had been spared the knowledge of the further pain her child had suffered, was still suffering and would, unless a miracle happened, go on suffering for the rest of his life.

'I'm sorry, Uncle Mark,' he said humbly. 'I lost my rag again. I know I shouldn't have, but she was up to something, I know she was, just like the other one. Why can't they leave us alone?'

'They want to know how Arthur Soames died.'

'Everyone knows how he died. He fell down the stairs in his garden and broke his neck. What else is there for them to know?'

'I'm afraid they believe there was more to it than that.' Mark filled two mugs with tea and put them on a tray. 'Shall we have this on the patio?'

'Are you sure it's safe?'

'Of course it's safe. I'm here to look after you.'

'I only feel safe when you're here. I wish you could be here all the time.'

'You know that isn't possible.'

'I know. All right, let's go outside. I'll fetch another chair.'

They settled down to enjoy the late-afternoon sun. Several minutes passed before Harry said, 'Most of the time it's OK. No one comes here but the postman and the milkman and the people from the farm, and I don't mind them. It's just that when a stranger comes along asking questions, it all comes back. Like last time.' He passed a hand over his eyes, trying to blot out the memory. 'That was terrible. I wish it hadn't happened.'

'It's too late to worry about that now. Tell me exactly what happened this time.'

'I told her to leave. At first, she wouldn't go and she had this piece of paper.'

'Did she show it to you? Did you see what was on it?'

'No. I told her again to go, and this time she did start walking back towards the gate and I thought, it's all right, she's going . . . and then she stopped and started staring at the ground and I got worried in case she'd seen something.'

'What could she have seen?'

'I don't know, but I felt myself getting angry, so I ran after her to chase her away . . . and she started running . . . and I got angrier still . . . and I caught up with her and she pretended she was here because she wanted to buy the cottage and I just knew she was lying . . . and then she . . .' Harry's voice failed; he put down his half-finished mug of tea and covered his face with his hands. 'I didn't mean to hurt her, I only wanted her to go away,' he moaned. 'Why did she have to do that to me?' He rocked to and fro in his anguish. As for Mark, black despair seemed to engulf his very soul.

After a while Harry said in an almost inaudible voice, 'Do you know who she is, Uncle Mark?'

'Yes, Harry, I think I do.'

'Do you suppose she'll complain to the police about me?'

'Yes, Harry, I'm afraid she will and I have to do something about it.'

'There won't be any more killing, will there? I don't want there to be any more killing.'

'So, your trip brought an unexpected result. A good one from our point of view, of course. It's up to the Spanish police to sort it out now.' DCI Philip Lord closed the file on his desk and sat back with a satisfied smile. 'Except for the kid, of course. What d'you suggest we do about her, Jim? She's caused us to waste a hell of a lot of time and resources.'

DI Castle shrugged. 'Search me, sir. I don't think we can blame the poor girl for fearing the worst. Burlidge is her step-father, of course – we already knew that – and she never really took to him. The mother was supposed to have gone to Spain first and start looking at properties while father tied up the sale of the business here before following a few days later. The story was they'd send for her as soon as they found a suitable house. They didn't leave an address, didn't respond to text messages or otherwise keep in touch after they left. When she didn't hear from them she got the idea into her head that something had happened to her mum and simply panicked. She had no idea what the pair of them were really up to – she thought they were all going to a new and glamorous life on the Costa Brava.'

'Poor kid!' Lord chewed his moustache and considered. 'Well, it looks as if the parents will be in a Spanish nick for some time to come, so she can't go out there now. I suppose we'll have to call in the social services.' He sighed and took a bag of mint humbugs from a drawer, popped one into his mouth and offered the bag to Jim. 'Want one?'

'No thanks. Not good for the teeth.'

'That's what the wife tells me.' Lord put the bag back in the drawer. 'Right, that's the Burlidges sorted.' He threw the file into his out tray and sat back. 'So now we have the problem of an ID for the lady in the lake – or shall we say, the dame in the ditch.' He gave a wheezy chuckle at his own witticism. 'Any ideas on that, Jim?'

'I rather think I have, sir. Sukey thinks it might be Sabrina Soames.'

'Does she, by heck?' Lord sat up with a start and took the file Castle handed him. 'Been doing our job for us again, has she?' He sat noisily crunching the humbug while he read through Sukey's notes. When he had finished he said thoughtfully, counting off the points on his stubby fingers, 'One, the late Arthur Soames was a paedophile. Two, Sabrina learns the identity of some parent who lodged a complaint against him fifteen years ago. Three, her car is on her drive next day, but no one saw her put it there and she hasn't been seen or heard of since. Four, Sukey picks up the trail, goes to call on Soames' alleged victim and gets a lively reception.' He sat back and fingered his moustache. 'This puts a different complexion on the matter, doesn't it? I reckon your significant other could be on to something, Jim. Establishing an ID might be tricky; as I understand it, the Soames woman has no living relatives we can apply to for help in carrying out a DNA comparison. We'll have to check in the house; there's probably a hairbrush or something that'll yield a sample. If we draw a blank there, I suppose as a last resort we'll have to apply for an exhumation order.'

'Not necessarily.' Castle took a second set of notes from his briefcase and handed them over. 'Have a look at this.'

Lord whistled softly through his teeth as the significance of what he read dawned on him. 'So Sabrina had a child by her doctor, eh? No wonder he wants that kept quiet – but it would hardly be in her interests to blow the whistle, so on the face of it he had no motive for killing her on that score. But then she starts asking questions about her father's death and uncovers an episode from his past that provides a direct link with the father of her child. We have to assume that she did the same as Sukey did – called at the last known address of the abused child, found he was still living there and . . . well, we can only guess what happened next. If Sukey's experience is anything to go by, she certainly wouldn't have been welcome.'

'She'd also have been pretty distressed at what she had found out about her father,' said Castle. 'Sukey was prepared to walk away when she realized she wasn't getting anywhere with Ashton, but that didn't stop him attacking her. If Sabrina had been more persistent, things might have turned very ugly.'

'You're suggesting he killed her?'

'He might well have done; he seems to be liable to fits of uncontrollable rage.'

'If the headless torso in the ditch is Sabrina, he couldn't have got her there by himself – or cut off her head so cleanly either for that matter,' Lord observed. 'The fact that it looked like a professional job made us suspect it was Janice Burlidge because her husband was a butcher.'

'So Harry sends a frantic SOS to his doctor uncle,' Castle suggested. 'He comes along with his surgical saw, does the necessary and together they transport the body to where it was found.'

'I wonder why they took it so far away?' Lord mused, gnawing at his moustache and looking gloomy. Then he brightened. 'Maybe they buried the head in the garden,' he suggested. 'I reckon there's enough here to justify interviewing young Ashton, and his Uncle Mark, and then maybe applying for a warrant to do a spot of gardening.' He scooped up Sukey's notes and handed them to Castle. 'Get on with it, Jim, and report back to me a.s.a.p.'

'Yes, sir.'

The telephone on Lord's desk rang as Castle got up to leave. He had no reason to stay and listen to the conversation, but he had been back in his own office for only a few minutes before his own phone rang. It was Lord summoning him back.

'I've just heard from the chap who's been carrying out the DNA test on our headless torso,' he said as Castle walked through the door, 'and guess what, they've found a match with a Scottish prostitute who went missing about the same time. And to put the matter beyond doubt, the woman's head has turned up on a rubbish dump somewhere near Derby. Badly decomposed, of course, but no doubt about the ID.'

The two men stared at one another in silence for a second or two before Castle muttered, 'So where the hell is Sabrina?'

Twenty-Six

He slept badly and woke before dawn. It was becoming part of an established pattern that began the day Sabrina Soames arrived at The Old Barn seeking information about her late father. There had been overnight rain but it had cleared by morning, giving way to a day of unbroken sunshine that gave everything a freshness and sparkle, unusual for late summer and almost dazzling in its brilliance. Harry had been in a particularly happy mood, proudly showing him the first apples from his little orchard. And then came the ring at the bell and the living nightmare began.

It was a shock for both of them, of course, that moment of mutual recognition. Explaining his presence there and his relationship to Harry was straightforward enough. She was sympathetic at first, but the atmosphere grew tense when she demanded to know the precise nature of the complaint he had lodged against her father all those years ago, a complaint so serious that his career as a teacher had been prematurely ended. She had a fixation that his death had not been accidental and refused to accept the coroner's verdict. She became less and less rational; she had even come out with some preposterous theory about possible collaboration with the police in a hunt for criminals. There might, she said, have been drug dealers who were targeting children at the school and whom he had helped to bring to justice – potential enemies who, after serving long prison sentences, had tracked him down to exact revenge. She begged him to try to remember anything, any tiny scrap of information that might have seemed irrelevant at the time but could just possibly help her arrive at the truth.

It was all self-delusion, of course, but he had felt sorry for her in her distress. He had done his best to assure her that none of this was true, that he knew of no such circumstances and that the accidental death verdict was the right one. He had glossed over the real nature of his complaint about her father with some vague psychobabble about failure to empathize with young, traumatized children. He still felt he might have persuaded her had not Harry, who had sat silent during her tirade, suddenly burst out, 'Why don't you tell her the truth, Uncle Mark? The bastard tried to bugger me!'

She flew into a rage, declaring that the allegation was false. He insisted, gently at first but with increasing vehemence, that he was satisfied beyond doubt that his nephew had been seriously abused and was suffering a lifetime of trauma as a result. He admitted with hindsight that he should have reported the matter to the police, but had been persuaded by the headmaster of the damage it would do to the school. So there had been the eventual compromise arrangement, whereby her father would take early retirement.

She became hysterical, flinging out wild accusations of her own. Harry's story was a malicious attempt to wreck the career of an innocent man. It was well known that children who for some reason bore their teacher a grudge told a pack of lies about supposed abuse as a form of revenge. Now, she declared, she knew why her father had sent her away; it was to protect her from the poisonous rumours they were spreading around. They had murdered her father and she was going to report them to the police.

What happened next was a blur; one minute she was halfway out of the room on her way to the front door, the next she was lying dead at their feet. That moment of incredulity was followed immediately by the need for self-preservation. They had to be practical. Sabrina had not known of his relationship to Harry; it was unlikely that anyone reporting her missing would pick up the connection. It was a chance they had to take. They conceived their plan and put it into action with an almost military precision. The next few days had been nerve-racking; trying to appear normal before his family and his patients had called for reserves of strength and self-control that he hardly knew he possessed. But as time passed without an enquiry or visit from the police, he had begun to relax. Harry seemed to have shut the whole episode from his mind and carried on with his normal life as if nothing untoward had happened. And now this other woman had picked up the trail and tracked them down. Well, he knew what he had to do.

Slowly and cautiously he got up, gathered together the clothes he had worn the previous day and stole from the room. At the door he turned and looked back, but there was no movement from the bed. His wife had always been a sound sleeper, although if their daughter woke in the night she too was awake in an instant. He lingered for a moment, straining his eyes; through the grey light of dawn he could just make out the shape of her body beneath the covers and the outline of her cheek against the white pillow. He tiptoed bare-footed along the landing; hardly daring to breathe, he put his head round the half-open door to the next room where his daughter lay in the deep, untroubled sleep of childhood. He crept downstairs and got dressed in the cloakroom before going into his study to pick up his bag and the keys to the surgery. The car was on the drive; he always left it there to save time in case of an emergency call. He released the handbrake and allowed it to roll down the slight incline and along the road for a short distance before starting the engine.

'Come in, come in, gentlemen!' Superintendent Wells greeted DCI Lord and DI Castle with a rare smile and – even more rarely – an invitation to sit down. His manner was unusually benign. 'I've been reading the report on the Burlidge case. Nothing against the couple in this country, so all we have to do is hand our file over to the Spanish police and the kid to social services. Very well done, a most satisfactory outcome.'

'Thank you, sir,' they replied dutifully in chorus.

'And now the headless torso's been identified and it looks as if the donkeywork will land in someone else's lap there as well. It gets better, doesn't it?' He sat back in his chair and rubbed his hands together. 'Very satisfactory,' he repeated. 'So, what was it you wanted to talk to me about?'

At a signal from Lord, Castle handed the Superintendent a file labelled *Sabrina Soames*. 'We think it's time we treated this woman officially as a missing person, sir,' he said.

Wells scanned the report and gave a short bark of mocking laughter. 'So your SOCO lady has been playing detectives again and got herself into another scrape. Quite a glutton for punishment, isn't she?' He reread the report, frowned and said, 'Why the hell wait till now to treat this woman as a misper?'

'We did make tentative enquiries, but we came to the conclusion that she had probably disappeared deliberately,' said Lord. 'There was no reason to suppose she was in any danger and it's not as if she's a vulnerable teenager, just a rather neurotic and obsessive woman approaching middle age.'

'But nevertheless she's been reported missing,' said Wells, thumping the desk with his fist.

'By a woman who had only known her a matter of days,' Lord pointed out. 'She was hardly a reliable witness to her behaviour or general character.'

'Not good enough,' snapped the Superintendent. His bonhomie had vanished like the sun behind a cloud. 'I'm surprised at you both. This poor woman may have had a breakdown or be suffering from amnesia or living rough. She may need help. I don't suppose that occurred to you, did it?'

This display of humanitarian concern was so out of character that neither Lord nor Castle could think of anything to say. Fortunately, Wells did not appear to expect a reply. 'It's obvious this chap in – what's the name of this God-forsaken village – Birdcombe has something to hide and it's possible the "other one" he referred to is the missing woman, so you'd better send someone to have a word with him right away. And go and talk to Uncle Mark as well.' He threw the file on the desk and reached for the telephone, his standard method of indicating that an interview was over.

Outside, the two detectives exchanged glances. 'You know

what,' said Lord as they made their way along the corridor towards their respective offices. 'If we'd reported that we'd spent umpteen hours of police time trying to track down Sabrina without a result we'd have got a bollocking for wasting resources.'

'Can't win, can we?' Castle agreed. He paused outside the SOCOs' room. 'If it's all right with you, I'll let the girls know the latest developments. They'll be interested to know who the headless woman is.'

Sukey found it surprising that Elspeth had not been in touch with her again to enquire about her visit to Bracknell. She had taken the precaution of asking Jim how much she should reveal about the latest developments and he had told her quite firmly that if asked she should say that certain information had come to light which she was unable to divulge and the police were making further enquiries. When at lunchtime on Monday he dropped into the SOCOs' office to inform them that the body in the ditch had at last been identified, their immediate reaction was the same as that of the two detectives had been: Where, then, was Sabrina Soames? Had she gone into hiding, unable to show her face after discovering her father's true nature? Worse, had she found life unbearable and decided to put an end to it? Jim, of course, had no answer to either question; all he would say was that he and DCI Lord had only a few minutes previously referred the matter to Superintendent Wells and been instructed that from now on, Sabrina was officially classed as a missing person.

'Wish I'd been a fly on the wall during that interview!' said George Barnes after the door had closed behind him. 'Whatever reasons they gave for whatever they did or didn't do, I'll bet Wells shot them down in flames.' The Superintendent, transferred from the Met a few months before, had not endeared himself to his subordinates although it was noticeable that he managed to ingratiate himself with his superiors.

Sukey kept her thoughts to herself. It seemed inevitable now that enquiries about to be set afoot would result in the Brintons' carefully guarded secret being exposed. It was almost certain that in covering up the true circumstances of Annie Bee's birth they had entered into a highly irregular, possibly illegal arrangement. Even if it turned out that Mark Brinton had nothing to do with Sabrina's disappearance, irreparable harm would have been done. She wondered if Jennifer Brinton knew about Harry Ashton's history and thought she probably did. That would have been another person she had to share her husband's attention with. The poor woman hadn't had an easy time, and things were going to get a great deal harder for her.

Sukey was dying to know what form the enquiries would take and who would be interviewed first. It was unlikely that Jim would tell her; the less she knew, the less chance there was of her 'poking her nose in' as he might put it. It was frustrating, but she would simply have to wait. When she got home, she rang Elspeth, but got no reply. When Elspeth returned her call an hour later, she was not in the best of tempers.

'I've been trying to contact you all over the weekend,' she complained.

'I got your message, but I was out quite a lot of the time—' Sukey began, but Elspeth didn't wait for her to finish.

'Of course you were, you were at Bracknell. That's what I wanted to talk to you about, but I had to go away at short notice and I didn't have your number with me and directory enquiries wouldn't give it to me. I explained it was urgent, but it didn't make any difference.' She made the refusal sound like a personal snub.

'I'm sorry about that,' Sukey said patiently. 'I've been ex-directory for a long time; it's official policy.'

'Well, it was very inconvenient. And on top of that, I've just come back from the surgery; I had an appointment to see Dr Gardner and he wasn't there for some reason so I was fobbed off with another doctor. They said he'd been called to an emergency.'

'Well, that sort of thing does happen from time to time. Wasn't the other doctor able to help you?'

'Of course not. Don't you remember? I particularly wanted to ask Dr Gardner if he'd noticed anything unusual when he was in Rosemount Villas the day Arthur died.'

'Oh, er, yes that's right.' Sukey realized rather guiltily that this detail had slipped her mind. 'Never mind, you can always make another appointment.'

'I tried, and they said they weren't booking any more appointments for him until he'd cleared today's backlog and rescheduled his appointments for the rest of the week. They weren't at all helpful.' Elspeth's voice was shaking; evidently her nerves were at breaking point and this comparatively minor setback was almost the final straw. 'Anyway,' she went on, 'tell me about your trip to Arthur's old school. Were they able to help you?'

'They did give me certain information that I've passed on to the police, but I'm afraid I can't—'

'Oh, for goodness' sake!' Elspeth's voice rose in pitch and Sukey could tell she was on the verge of breaking down. 'Surely you can tell me!' she pleaded tearfully.

'Just keep calm and listen. There is one thing I can tell you, which may be of some comfort. We now know the identity of the woman in the ditch, and it isn't Sabrina.'

'So you think she's still alive?'

'We can't say for certain, but the police haven't given up hope that she'll be found safe and well.'

Twenty-Seven

'I'm a bit concerned about how we tackle this chap, Andy,' said Castle as he and Detective Sergeant Radcliffe made their way downstairs. 'According to Sukey, he's quite well built and he's only a comparative youngster. If he gets stroppy we may have to call for assistance.'

'That occurred to me,' said Radcliffe, 'especially as Sukey will be with us. The sight of her might be enough to set him off again. I can't understand why Lord agreed she should come with us,' he went on, frowning. 'SOCOs don't usually get involved in interviews with suspects.'

'It is irregular,' Castle agreed, 'and I can't say I'm happy about it either but you know what she's like when she sets her mind on something. The way she put it to the DCI is that she's not going as a SOCO but as a private citizen who was subjected to an unprovoked attack. Of course, if the chap is there and she can make a positive ID, that'll be all the justification we need to pull him in for questioning.'

'So what line are you going to take?'

'Bearing in mind that he's a bit unstable, I'm going to go softly-softly at first. I'll tell him the lady we've brought along with us claims he used unnecessary force to get her to leave his property and see what he has to say about it.'

'Are you going to question him about Sabrina Soames?'

'That will depend on how he reacts.'

Sukey was waiting for them at reception. They got into Radcliffe's car, with Castle sitting beside him in the front passenger seat and Sukey in the back. Apart from a few desultory remarks on the weather (brilliant) and the state of the traffic (heavy, with holidaymakers towing caravans making overtaking difficult) there was little conversation until they reached Birdcombe. Radcliffe pulled into the car park and they got out.

'It must be all of thirty years since I was here!' the sergeant exclaimed, surveying his surroundings with a mixture of pleasure and appraisal. 'There have been quite a few changes; I noticed several new houses and that village hall wasn't there either, or the car park. Visitors had to leave their cars in the lanes in my day and the locals used to make a great to-do about it at parish council meetings.'

'You used to live here?' asked Castle.

'No, I lived near Stroud, but I often came here for the cricket. Our team was top of the village league for three seasons in a row,' he added with a touch of pride. 'We had the deadliest seam bowler in the county.'

'Very interesting,' Castle agreed absently. He too was looking around, taking his bearings. 'Where do we go from here, Sukey?'

She pointed towards the centre of the village. 'That way. There's a turning to the right leading to the pub and the house is a couple of hundred yards further on, at the very end of the village.'

'Ah yes, the old Farrier's Arms.' Radcliffe was still in nostalgic mode. 'I've sunk many a pint of the local ale in there after a match.'

'OK, Andy, save the reminiscences till later,' said Castle with a touch of impatience and the three of them once more fell silent.

Sukey felt on edge; DCI Lord had clearly been impressed by the tangle of relationships she had unearthed and it had not been too difficult to persuade him to allow her to come on this mission, but now she was beginning to have second thoughts. The memory of Harry Ashton's hands sliding round her throat still had the power to raise a shudder. Despite the unprovoked attack, she had made it clear that she would prefer not to press charges against him, but Jim had managed to get Lord to stipulate that if she wanted to go with them she would have to play the role they had assigned to her. It was part of the strategy they were using to deal with an individual who, although evidently disturbed, might be in a position to give them vital information about a missing person.

Castle meanwhile was mentally considering their options. Ashton had over-reacted to Sukey's unexpected appearance; had Sabrina Soames met with a similar, possibly even more violent reception? So far there was not a shred of evidence that any harm had come to her yet his instinct, developed after many years of CID work, told him that all was not well. If they could persuade Harry Ashton to tell them what had prompted his unprovoked attack on Sukey, maybe they could get him to reveal something that would help them track Sabrina down. And despite his claims to know nothing about her present whereabouts, Dr Mark Brinton, when questioned about his relationship to Harry Ashton, might have to change his story. DS Dalia Chen and DC Tony Hill were at this moment on their way to have a word with him. It would be interesting to know what sort of reception they got.

When they reached The Old Barn they found the gate propped open with a heavy piece of rock. They walked up the drive without speaking until the cottage came into view.

'Pretty,' commented Castle.

'The sort of thing wealthy townies pay an arm and a leg for to use as a weekend retreat,' said Radcliffe, a trifle sourly.

'Well, at least this one's permanently occupied,' said Castle.

'It looks as if he's in; his car's still there.' Sukey pointed to the blue Fiesta. 'And he seems to have a visitor.' She indicated a second car, half hidden behind a low hedge.

'I wonder if it's Uncle Mark,' said Castle. 'That would make things easier for us.'

'It's not Mark Brinton's car,' said Sukey, 'not unless he's changed it within the past few days.'

'Maybe his own car's being serviced and the garage have lent him that one till it's ready,' Castle suggested.

Radcliffe shook his head and went to take a closer look. 'I'm pretty sure I've seen it before,' he said.

'Any idea where?'

'I'm just trying to think. Yes, I remember. It was parked outside the church hall where they held the inquest on Arthur Soames.'

'*Was* it?' Castle felt a stir of anticipation. 'The plot thickens. Come on, let's hear what they have to say!'

They went up to the front door and Radcliffe pressed the bell.

Jennifer Brinton eyed the warrant cards the two detectives held out and put a hand to her throat. She was obviously nervous.

'My husband isn't here,' she said.

'We called at his surgery, but he isn't there either,' said DS Chen.

'He hasn't got a surgery today.'

'So can you tell us where he is, please?'

'He went out. He didn't say where he was going.'

'Did he say when he'd be back?'

'No. I'm afraid I can't help you. Please call later.'

She was on the point of closing the door, but Hill stepped forward and said, 'May we come in for a moment, please? We think you may be able to help us.'

'I'd rather not answer any questions without my husband being present.'

'This won't take long.'

With evident reluctance she stood aside and allowed them to enter. Dalia Chen noticed that she cast anxious glances at the houses on either side, as if fearful that a neighbour might observe what was going on. She showed them into the sitting room where, not so long ago, she and her husband had reluctantly revealed to Sukey Reynolds the secret that they had fought for so long to conceal. Out of politeness she asked them to sit down while she perched on the edge of a chair, showing every sign of being ill at ease.

'We're looking into the disappearance of a lady called Sabrina Soames,' Dalia began. 'I believe you know her.' Jennifer gave a mute nod. 'We have traced her movements as far as an address in Birdcombe where we understand she spoke to a man called Harry Ashton. Does this name mean anything to you?' Jennifer shook her head. 'Your husband has never mentioned this man to you?'

'Not that I remember. Who is he? Is he one of Mark's patients?'

'You are absolutely sure you have never heard of him?'

'Quite sure.' Jennifer sounded a fraction less tense, but her eyes were wary. 'I'm afraid you'll have to speak to my husband. If you'd like to leave a telephone number?'

'Of course.' Dalia handed over one of her cards. 'Will you ask him to contact me or DC Hill as soon as possible, please?'

'Certainly.' She was plainly relieved to see them go and even managed a polite smile as she showed them out.

Back in the car Dalia said, 'Did you notice the change of attitude when we started asking about Ashton?'

Hill nodded. 'She was like a cat on hot bricks at first, but when the questions switched from Sabrina to Harry Ashton she seemed to relax a shade. She was still on her guard, though. Very interesting.'

'You think she was telling the truth when she said she didn't know Ashton?'

'Hard to tell. I'm not so sure about not knowing where her husband is either. What do you reckon, Sarge?'

'We'll have to wait until we can interview the husband. There's nothing more we can do here, so we might as well go back. Maybe there'll be some news from Birdcombe.'

There was no response to the first ring, but a movement behind the curtains showed that someone was in the house. Radcliffe rang again; after a few seconds the curtain was pulled aside and a face peered out. Castle turned to Sukey, who was standing behind him, and mouthed over his shoulder, 'That him?' She nodded. The two detectives held up their warrant cards; the curtain dropped and the face vanished. Radcliffe rang again; when there was still no response he put his foot to the door. After a couple of kicks it flew open to reveal Ashton cowering behind it. His face was white with fear and he was visibly shaking.

'What the hell do you want?' he demanded. 'You've no right—' He backed away along a narrow passage; Castle and Radcliffe followed, keeping their distance to avoid alarming him further while Sukey brought up the rear. 'Don't touch me!' he whined. 'Leave me alone!'

'It's all right, Harry, no one's going to hurt you,' Castle said gently. 'We just want to ask you one or two questions. Shall we go in here?' He moved towards a door to the right of the passage, but Ashton sprang in front of him, spreading his arms to bar their way.

'Not in there! You can't go in there!' he shouted.

'All right, you show us where.'

'This way then,' he said sullenly, indicating another door at the end of the passage. As before, he led the way, moving backwards as if fearing a rearguard attack. He even reached behind him to open the door, which led into a kitchen with windows overlooking a well-tended garden.

'What a lovely view you have, Harry,' said Castle. 'Why don't you sit down?' he went on, pulling up a chair, one of several grouped round a table.

Until that moment, Sukey's diminutive figure had been virtually concealed behind the two men. Castle's move towards the chairs left her for the first time fully visible to Ashton. At the sight of her, his features contorted and he let out a howl of fury. 'You bitch!' he screamed. 'I knew I should have finished you off last time!' The change in his demeanour was so sudden that the two detectives were caught off guard. Before either of them could move he had leapt at Sukey and locked his hands round her throat.

He was squeezing her windpipe, choking the life out of her. She clawed frantically at his fingers, but to no effect. She tried to scream to the men for help, but could only utter a strangled croak. She was dimly aware of raised voices shouting commands and oaths, but the intolerable pressure went on increasing. There was a drumming in her ears; lights flashed before her eyes; she felt herself losing consciousness. Then came the sound of a blow followed by a grunt and a thud, and it was all over. Jim's arms saved her from falling and she sagged against him, dragging in lungfuls of precious, life-saving air.

When she was able to speak she said weakly, 'You took your time, didn't you?'

'He's as strong as an ox,' said Jim. His voice was unsteady and she could tell that he was almost as shaken as she was. 'Andy had to slug him; it was the only way to get him off you.' He pointed at the floor behind her, where the sergeant was snapping handcuffs on a dazed-looking Ashton. He was a sorry spectacle as he lay there making soft moaning sounds. Tears were running down his cheeks and mingling with the blood coming from his mouth, yet his eyes were full of help-less fury.

'What do we do with him now, Guv?' asked Radcliffe.

'You'd better call for reinforcements,' said Castle. 'He's still a bit groggy, but he could well give us trouble in the car on the way back.' A snarled threat from Ashton seemed to confirm this possibility. 'You stay there and keep an eye on him for the moment,' Castle went on. 'I'm going to have a look round, especially in the room he was so anxious to keep us out of.'

'I'll come with you, if you don't mind,' said Sukey. To remain in that room with Harry's baleful gaze fixed on her was more than she could stand.

To her relief, he did not argue, but turned and led the way back along the passage to the door that Ashton had forbidden them to open.

Twenty-Eight

The curtains were drawn, but the light from outside was strong enough to penetrate the unlined fabric. It fell on a room comfortably furnished in traditional cottage style, with two deep armchairs covered in old-fashioned flowered cretonne. One of the chairs faced the door and in it a man lay sprawled with his legs stretched out before him, his hands dangling limply over the arms and his head tilted backwards against the cushion. Sukey thought at first that he was asleep . . . but how could anyone have slept while she was fighting for her life just a few feet away?

Jim put a restraining hand on her arm. 'Stay there,' he commanded. He moved to the window and carefully drew one of the curtains aside. Sunlight flooded in and fell on the man in the chair. His eyes were staring vacantly at the ceiling and his mouth hung open; the blue discoloration of the skin and the bruises on his throat left no doubt as to how he had died. In his case there had been no one to rescue him from Harry Ashton's murderous grip.

Sukey had no difficulty in obeying Jim's instruction. The realization that she might so easily have met the same fate struck her like a punch in the stomach and she leaned on the doorframe to keep her balance. Jim came over and took her arm to steady her while manipulating buttons on his mobile phone with his free hand.

'You'd better go and sit in the car,' he said. 'You're in shock.'

'I'd rather stay here with you,' she begged him. 'Please.'

'Sorry, you'll have to leave. This is a crime scene and

members of the public aren't allowed.' His tone was jocular, but she knew what he meant. She had wheedled her way into coming with them on the premise that she was a private citizen who had been subjected to an assault. He wasn't going to let her get away with a change of role now. Another member of the SOCO team would examine the scene. She hoped it would be Mandy; at least, she could be relied on to pass on whatever information she gathered.

Jim was speaking into the phone, putting into action the procedure for dealing with a suspicious death and receiving confirmation that reinforcements to deal with Harry Ashton were already on their way. As he switched off, a sudden series of bumps and oaths from the next room sent him hurrying to Radcliffe's assistance, leaving Sukey momentarily alone with the dead man. For the first time she found the courage to take a closer look at the body. She knew better than to move about the room before the detectives had had time to examine the scene in detail, but even from the doorway and despite the discoloration of the features, she was reasonably sure that it was not Mark Brinton. Another unexpected caller who had triggered one of Harry Ashton's uncontrollable fits of rage? A vague thought came into her mind, but she couldn't pin it down. Her head was feeling muzzy; she shut her eyes and willed it to clear. After a minute or two she opened them again but the thought still eluded her. She continued her study of the man. He was wearing a jacket; there would no doubt be some identification in his pocket for the detectives to find.

Beneath the empty chair she could just make out the corner of what was possibly an attaché case and beside it the sunlight glinted on something which might have been metal or glass. She squatted down in the hope of seeing more and her head swam again; she almost lost her balance but managed to struggle upright by clinging to the door.

A few more minutes passed. Her legs began to buckle and she looked round for somewhere to sit, but the only chair available was in the murder room, which she knew she was not supposed to enter although for the moment she could not quite remember why. Then she heard the wail of a siren and the crunch of wheels on the gravel drive. The next minute a procession of uniformed figures raced past the door; shortly afterwards they returned, half dragging, half carrying a dementedly struggling Harry Ashton. He spotted Sukey and screamed an obscenity at her before they got him outside and into one of the waiting cars.

She tottered back into the kitchen and sank into the nearest chair. Jim had his back to the door and was talking on his mobile again but she could make neither head nor tail of his end of the conversation. She heard him say something about 'a suspicious death' and 'waiting for Dr Blake'. *What suspicious death? What does he want Doctor Blake for?* she wondered vaguely. As he ended the call he turned round and his eye fell on her. 'Are you all right?' he said.

'No,' she replied, hiccuped, and broke down in tears.

'Andy, see if you can find some brandy in one of those cupboards and then arrange for someone to take her back to the station. Tell the driver he's to get the FME to have a look at her and those bruises on her neck will have to be photographed. And we'll need to get a statement as soon as she feels up to it.' Castle rattled off the instructions in a crisp, impersonal voice, but she barely heard them. Her tears flowed more freely. Something strange was going on in her head; one minute she could think clearly, the next everything was a muddle. More than anything else in the world at that moment she wanted Jim to give her a reassuring hug and a few words of comfort. She felt desolate and alone.

The next hour was a blur. Unable to find brandy, Radcliffe suggested black coffee, which she accepted gratefully. Despite the warmth of the day she was shivering, but no one thought to find a rug to put round her. After she had drunk the coffee she was driven back to headquarters by a young woman constable whom she recognized but could not put a name to. She was escorted to an interview room to await the forensic medical examiner, a woman with a hearty manner who came bustling in after what seemed an eternity, asked her to stand up, walk round the table and then sit down again, made her pick up various objects and move them around before subjecting her to a series of questions, some of which she repeated at irregular intervals.

'I'm sure I answered that a few moments ago,' Sukey protested on being asked for the second time what day of the week it was.

'Well remembered!' The doctor beamed. 'No evidence of hypoxia.'

'What on earth's that?'

'Lack of oxygen to the brain. It can cause a decrease in motor co-ordination, memory loss and inattentiveness.'

'That was me a couple of hours ago,' Sukey said with feeling.

'Shock can do funny things to the system. Be thankful the pressure didn't last long enough to do serious damage.'

'It felt like forever at the time.'

The doctor gave a sympathetic chuckle. 'I can imagine. Just a couple more checks.' She felt Sukey's pulse and took her blood pressure. 'Pretty good, all things considered,' she said approvingly. 'It seems you got off lightly, young woman. Let's have a look at the external damage.' She peered at the marks on Sukey's throat and prodded them gently. Sukey winced. 'Sorry! That's going to be a bit sore for a day or two; otherwise you're in pretty good shape. Have you had any lunch? No? I'll get someone to fetch you a sandwich while you're waiting for the photographer, and then I suggest you go home and have a lie down. Take these first, they'll help you to relax.' She put a couple of white tablets into a plastic envelope and handed them over.

Sukey was only too thankful to follow the doctor's advice. When she reached home she scribbled a note for Fergus and left it on the kitchen table for him to find when he came in from work at five o'clock. She went up to her bedroom, kicked off her shoes, stripped to her underwear, swallowed the tablets with a drink of water and crawled under her duvet. Within minutes she was sound asleep.

She was awakened by Fergus gently shaking her shoulder. 'What time is it?' she mumbled. 'Did I miss the alarm?'

'It's seven o'clock in the evening,' he said. 'You've been asleep for hours; I couldn't make much sense out of your note and I was beginning to get worried, so I called Jim to find out what had happened.'

'Oh Lord!' She put a hand to her throat as memory returned with a rush. 'What did Jim say? Has Harry Ashton made a statement? Has the dead man been identified?'

'What dead man?'

'Didn't Jim tell you? We went to Ashton's cottage and he attacked me and then we found a dead man in another room.'

'He didn't tell me anything. He asked how you were; I said you were asleep and he said you'd tell me all about it when you woke up and then he rang off.'

'OK, I'll tell you everything when I've had a cup of tea. I'll get dressed and come down.' She struggled into a sitting position and for the first time Fergus saw the marks on her throat.

'Mum!' he exclaimed in alarm. 'How did you get those bruises?'

'Ashton took a dislike to me and tried to throttle me, but Jim and Andy got him off before he could do any serious damage. Just put the kettle on, there's a love, and I'll tell you all. I'm all right, honestly,' she went on, touched by the concern in his face. 'The FME gave me a thorough check-up and she said I was OK.'

Sukey had just finished her account of the drama at The Old Barn when the phone rang. She grabbed it, hoping it was Jim, but Elspeth was on the line demanding to know if there was any further news about Sabrina.

'None that I know of,' said Sukey. 'I promise to let you know as soon as I hear anything. Did you manage to see Dr Gardner, by the way?'

'No. It's so annoying. I rang the surgery again this morning but all they would say was that he's away and they don't know when he'll be back.'

The vague thought that had eluded Sukey as she contemplated the scene in the sitting room of The Old Barn suddenly crystallized into a question. 'Elspeth,' she said, 'do you happen to know Dr Gardner's first name?'

'Why do you ask?'

'Never mind that for the moment. Do you know it?'

There was a short silence before Elspeth said, 'I'm not sure, but I've a feeling . . . yes, I remember now, it's on the plate on the door of the surgery with the names of all the partners. He's Dr Mark Gardner.'

Twenty-Nine

'This has got to be one of the saddest cases I've ever dealt with,' said Jim. 'Young Harry Ashton never had the slightest chance of anything approaching a normal life. Nor, come to that, did poor Sabrina. Thanks, love,' he added as Sukey handed him a glass and a can of beer. He pulled off the ring, poured the drink and took a long draught before putting down the glass and saying fervently, 'Boy, did I need that!'

Two days had passed since the drama at The Old Barn. It was the first opportunity they had had to exchange more than a few words. Sukey's chief concern, once she had recovered from the shock of discovering the blunder she had made, was that there should be no further harassment of Mark Brinton and his wife. 'I feel really guilty at having put them through all that grief,' she told Fergus on receiving confirmation, in the form of a brief message from Jim, that the dead man was indeed Harry Ashton's uncle, Dr Mark Gardner. 'It was bad enough for them to have a complete stranger come barging in and poking into their private life, without having a visit from the police. When two detectives suddenly appeared on her doorstep poor Jennifer must have thought I'd betrayed them.'

Fergus had done his best to reassure her. 'It was a natural mistake, Mum,' he insisted. 'Anyone could have made it. It was just an unfortunate coincidence that the two doctors had the same first name.'

'I suppose so,' she agreed with a sigh. 'It's a fairly common name, though; I shouldn't have been so ready to jump to

214

conclusions. I just hope there's been no lasting damage to the family.'

'Oh, they'll sort it out between them,' said Fergus with the airy confidence of youth. 'Anyway,' he went on, 'all that stuff about Annie Bee might never have come out if Dr Brinton hadn't lied about the last time he saw Sabrina.'

'Gus is right,' Jim agreed when the conversation was reported to him as they relaxed with their drinks in Sukey's sitting room. 'Sabrina was on the right track when she claimed her father had been murdered, although for the wrong reasons. She knew nothing about Harry Ashton until her fatal visit to The Old Barn. With hindsight, we should have taken her more seriously, but the evidence for accidental death seemed so clear.'

'Dr Blake had his doubts,' Sukey could not resist pointing out.

'At first, yes, but once he heard evidence of Soames' medical condition he withdrew them straight away. As it turned out, most of that was false.'

'Whatever do you mean?' said Sukey.

'Jim, why don't you tell us the whole story from the beginning?' Fergus demanded impatiently.

'I'll do my best, but we're still piecing it together and there are gaps to be filled,' said Jim. 'Gardner left a letter that goes some way to explaining what happened, but the story goes back many years. His widow is still in shock and under sedation; we have to wait until she's calm enough to make a detailed statement before we have the complete picture. There's a child too; she's being cared for by a relative.'

'It's a dreadful tragedy all round,' said Sukey sombrely.

'What was in the letter?' asked Fergus.

'It says Harry was badly traumatized in childhood, first by a violent, alcoholic father who had terrorized him and his mother before smashing himself up in a motoring accident, then by the death of his mother when he was only ten and finally, just as he was beginning to settle down in what everyone thought was a safe haven, by the attentions of Arthur

Soames. The degrading and humiliating treatment Soames inflicted on him had haunted him for years; to have him suddenly come back into his life must have been devastating. Gardner claims he would have gone to almost any lengths to spare him the ordeal of a police inquiry and the attendant publicity.'

'What made Gardner write this letter?' asked Sukey. 'He couldn't have known Harry was planning to kill him.'

'Harry wasn't planning to kill him, it was the other way round; he was planning to kill Harry and then himself.'

'Good heavens!' she gasped, open-mouthed. 'Why?'

'Harry was already a killer twice over and was becoming a danger to anyone he saw as a threat, either real or imaginary. And Gardner himself was an accessory to the killings.'

'Twice? Are you saying Harry killed first Soames and then Sabrina, and Gardner helped him cover up both times?'

'You've got it. And you turning up at the cottage represented a further threat. Gardner says in the letter that when you almost blundered into his car he recognized you as someone he saw talking to one of the officers who attended the inquest on Soames and he was certain you'd report Harry's attack to the police.'

'That's right,' said Sukey. 'I remember, I had a job that morning near where the inquest was being held; I spotted Andy Radcliffe getting out of his car and stopped to have a word with him. Dr Gardner must have arrived about the same time.'

'I guess so,' Jim agreed. 'He knew then that the game was up and rather than have Harry face the ordeal of a trial he was planning to trick him into accepting that he needed medication, give him a lethal injection and then do the same for himself. We found a hypodermic charged with morphine in the room and there was another one in his bag containing a similar lethal dose. He claimed it was the only option left to him.'

'What a ghastly situation to be in.' Sukey's skin prickled as she pictured Gardner approaching Harry with gentle, reassuring words, no doubt trying to persuade him that he needed something to calm him down and here was something to make him feel better. Exactly what happened after that would never be known for certain. Perhaps Harry had become suspicious and refused to co-operate, knocked the syringe from Gardner's hand and then, in one of his uncontrollable fits of rage, seized him by the throat and throttled him. Overcome by emotion, she leaned against Jim, seated beside her on the couch. He put an arm round her shoulders and held her close.

'What I don't understand,' she said when she was calmer, 'is why, if he believed Harry was a danger to others, he didn't arrange for him to have treatment long ago? He was a doctor; he knew how the system operates.'

'He had no reason to,' said Jim. 'Harry had never shown signs of being a danger to anyone; on the contrary, he was withdrawn and went to great lengths to avoid contact with strangers. What sent him over the top was seeing a photo of Arthur Soames in the local paper.'

'I suppose he'd been waiting all this time for a chance to get at Soames?' Fergus suggested.

'I doubt it, although of course we'll never know what went on in his mind. On the face of it, it was an unlucky accident; being a keen gardener he took an interest in the competitions the local council used to run every year, although he was too inhibited to take part in them himself. This year he was reading the reports in the local paper and what did he see staring out at him but the face of the man who had literally blighted his life. Locations of the winning gardens were given, together with photographs of their proud owners. Harry went storming round to Soames' house to confront him.'

'And shoved him down the stairs to his death!' exclaimed Fergus excitedly. 'So Sabrina was right after all.'

'According to the letter, he swore it was an accident. When he got to the house the old man tried to shut the door in his face. I don't suppose for a moment the old man recognized him as one of his schoolboy victims; he probably thought he was trying to sell something. Anyway, Harry shoved his way in and Soames fled into the kitchen, turned round to face him by the open door into the garden, lost his balance and fell backwards down the stairs. Whether Gardner believed Harry's version of what happened isn't clear, but what is clear is that he covered up for him.'

'I think I can guess what happened next,' said Sukey, remembering the sighting of Gardner's car near Soames' house on the day in question. 'Harry panicked and phoned his uncle, who came rushing round, saw that Soames was dead and hustled Harry away before the body was discovered.'

'He did more than that,' said Jim. 'Doctors carry a prescription pad around when visiting patients and he scribbled one out for Soames, back-dated it and put it on the mantelpiece in the kitchen where he knew it would be found. Later, he went to Soames' file in his computer, falsified his record to show a visit that never took place and a condition he didn't suffer from, and told the coroner that the dead man asked him to call because he'd been suffering from dizzy spells. He'd written out a prescription but Soames had obviously failed to take the medication.'

'So he lied through his teeth at the inquest?'

'Oh yes, he admits that.'

'He was taking a fearful risk,' said Fergus.

'Yes, but it was a calculated risk. He was Soames' GP, so he could claim to know his medical history, confident that no one would challenge him.'

'And when the verdict was accidental death and the case apparently closed, they thought they'd got away with it,' said Jim. 'Until Sabrina turned up, that is.'

'Does the letter say what happened to her?'

'Oh yes. It doesn't go into a lot of detail, only that Harry lost his temper and throttled her, with Gardner trying vainly to get him off her. We can certainly believe that,' Jim went on, running his fingers lightly over Sukey's neck. She shuddered at the memory. 'Those marks are fading nicely,' he added gently.

'I gather from the TV news that you think her body's buried somewhere in the garden,' said Fergus. 'Have you found it yet?'

'Not yet. The letter was pretty vague about the exact location, but we'll find it all right.'

'Maybe the samples I took from Sabrina's car will provide a clue,' Sukey suggested.

'Yes, we've called in a soil expert to examine them. Incidentally, you were quite right about Sabrina's car, Sook. Gardner drove it to the address on her driving licence and Harry followed in his car to take him back. We found the key in the cottage. DCI Lord was very impressed with your detective work, by the way.'

'Well, at least I got something right.' Sukey gave a deep sigh. 'I'm still worried about the Brintons, though. If the arrangement with Sabrina about Annie Bee's adoption is made known to the authorities it will cause so much distress for them all.'

'Why should it become known?' said Jim.

'You mean you're not going to report them?'

'It's hardly a police matter.'

'Oh, thank goodness for that.' She gave him a hug. 'Do you want another beer?'

'What a good idea.' He gave her his empty glass. 'What's for dinner?'